CABIN
FEVER

ALEX DAHL is a half-American, half-Norwegian author.
Born in Oslo, she studied Russian and German linguistics
with international studies, then went on to complete
an MA in creative writing at Bath Spa University and
an MSc in business management at Bath University. A
committed Francophile, Alex loves to travel, and has
so far lived in Moscow, Paris, Stuttgart, Sandefjord,
Switzerland, Bath and London. She is the author of
three other thrillers: *Playdate*, *The Heart Keeper*,
and *The Boy at the Door*, which was shortlisted
for the CWA Debut Dagger.

Also by Alex Dahl

The Boy at the Door
The Heart Keeper
Playdate

CABIN FEVER

Alex Dahl

HEAD ZEUS

An Aries Book

First published in the UK in 2021 by Head of Zeus Ltd,
This paperback edition first published in the UK in 2022 by Head of Zeus Ltd,
part of Bloomsbury Publishing Plc

9 7 5 3 1 2 4 6 8

A catalogue record for this book is available from
the British Library.

ISBN (PB): 9781789544053
ISBN (E): 9781789544060

Typeset by Divaddict Publishing Solutions Ltd

Printed and bound in Great Britain by
CPI Group (UK) Ltd, Croydon CRO 4YY

Head of Zeus Ltd
First Floor East
5–8 Hardwick Street
London ECIR 4RG

WWW.HEADOFZEUS.COM

To Fevziye, my favorite Leo, in memory

'Only the wounded healer can truly heal.'

– Irvin D. Yalom

Prologue

You're in the woods. You're alone. You've never known aloneness like this before, but now that you do, it will remain beside you like an unshakable shadow for the rest of your life. So much will be lost in the far recesses of your mind; no life can ever be retained in all of its moments, but you will remember this – the bitter, sickly taste of blood in your mouth, the thousand shades of green enveloping you, the taste, and color, of death. The deafening rumble of your heart echoing through your blood. The sharp-edged leaves knifing your arms and face as you crash through the foliage. Your fear – this vast and uncontrollable fear, as black and deep as a Norwegian forest lake. It will surge through you forever, prompted by big and small triggers entirely unrelated to these moments, and you'll learn to live with it; you'll have to. Sometimes it will roar at you, other times it will whisper. Every breath you take will bear its faint aftertaste. Every forest you walk through will merge with this one. Every sharp sound will take you back here in a split second. And every part of you will be reshaped, contorted into new configurations: like a city rebuilt from ruins.

To save you, your mind will invent escape routes. Your brilliant mind will take your broken heart away from these moments in the only way it knows how – by running.

You run, faster than you've ever run before, and even now, you know you'll be running like this for the rest of your life. You'll run because you don't know that the only way you could ever be free is to stop.

Part I

SUPERNOVA

I

Kristina, October

She's my two o'clock on Fridays, the second last before the weekend. Perhaps this makes me naturally more relaxed and good-humored, but Leah Iverson has always been a client I look forward to seeing. She's reflective and interesting, with a natural ability to tap into my deepest empathy, and genuinely invested in the therapeutic process. In other words, she isn't hard work. That's not to say we haven't done hard work together, at times very hard work. Leah first came to see me almost three years ago, in the aftermath of the publication of her first book, *Nobody*. The book was loosely based on her marriage in the popular Scandinavian trend of autofiction inspired by Karl-Ove Knausgaard, and it was translated into over twenty languages, and so she found herself an unlikely literary celebrity.

At first, she had taken it in her stride, reveling in the unexpected career change from journalist to published author. She traveled the world and spoke of her inspiring healing journey from emotional and physical abuse at various events. But as time went by, Leah began to struggle with the life changes this had brought, and her elevation to 'famous-author' status. Her book remained at number one, and was optioned for a TV-series adaptation. The gossip press preyed on her, speculating over which parts of the book were true, and which parts were fictionalized. Leah made enough money to buy a nice apartment in an upmarket part of town, and a cabin in the mountains of Telemark, too. In spite of all this success, Leah was a nervous, fragile shell of a woman back then, someone who winced when our eyes met or if I asked her a question she didn't know how to answer. Her sentences would begin with, 'I'm sorry,' or, 'I know this is stupid,' or, 'This is so ridiculous, but...'. She didn't trust herself back then, but she came to trust me, and eventually, herself.

As we began to build our therapeutic relationship, a wide array of underlying problems emerged, squirming in the room between us like worms coiling out of the earth. Leah cut herself, and had been doing it since her early teens. She once pulled up the sleeves of her jumper to reveal row upon row of neat incisions, some fresh and pink, many old and white. She had a highly complicated relationship with food, alternating between binging and starving herself, sometimes for weeks on end and until she'd black out. She suffered from debilitating panic attacks and terrifying compulsive thoughts, sometimes suicidal. She was always quick to reassure me that her suicidal thoughts were without intent, and I would point out that they were just thoughts. At the beginning, Leah spent many sessions just staring emptily into the space between us, and I would let her be, without any prompts at all. Occasionally she'd look up, her startled hazel eyes meeting mine before scanning the room, as though she momentarily had no idea where she was.

Over time, I watched as Leah grew stronger. In the therapy room she made great progress, too. It's always incredible when a client comes to therapy at the right time, with the right therapist, and that is what I believe happened for us. Layers of conditioning and trauma and deeply buried pain and untruths peel away, revealing a vulnerable but very strong person underneath – it's powerful to watch and become part of. Though she has significantly battled with writing a follow-up to *Nobody* over the past year, she hasn't regressed to the chaotic, destructive state of when she first came to therapy. She's a very grateful client, one who often makes a point of saying that it's all because of me that things are getting better, but I like to say that I only hold the mirror – she's the one that looks in it.

I boil the water for our tea and rearrange the tea bags fanning out in the dish on the low table. I make sure there are two of each flavor and that they are laid out by color. It's interesting how some clients will choose a different tea each time, whereas some will always have the same one. Leah doesn't always choose one at all, arriving with a takeaway coffee from Kaffebrenneriet across the road. Other times, she chooses a green tea with lemon.

It's five past two, and still no Leah. Unusual – she is extremely punctual, and I actually can't recall a time when she wasn't sitting in the waiting room when I opened the door at two on the dot. I check again, though I would have heard the door open, and the room is still empty. Outside, heavy rain is falling, and slick orange leaves stick to the windowpanes. October always makes me feel both withdrawn and a little wistful, though I've never known why. Perhaps it has to do with the beauty of the decay, how intoxicating it is to observe all the death around us.

This year is worse than ever, so much has changed, so much loss.

All I want for this weekend is to shut myself away in the house with Eirik, lying across from him on the sofas, reading and sipping a rich, dark Malbec, occasionally looking up to meet his eyes and smiling. This weekend is going to be far removed from that gentle domestic dream, and I feel tired in advance just at the thought of it. Tonight I will be supporting my husband at a gala dinner at the prime minister's residence. I feel a nervous ache in my stomach at the thought, but then, who wouldn't? Then, tomorrow, we are visiting my sister and her young family in Drøbak for the rest of the weekend, which is lovely but hardly a relaxing time.

Ten past two, and still no Leah. I bring out my phone to call her – something unexpected must have happened – but just then, I hear the door to the waiting room open. I take a deep breath and entirely clear my mind so that Leah has my full, uncluttered attention for the forty minutes that are left of the session.

But it isn't Leah, not the Leah I've seen every Friday for over nearly three years. This is someone else entirely, a ghost of the woman I know. She's trembling all over and soaked wet. Her right eye is a medley of violet and red and inky blue, swelled shut.

'Jesus, Leah,' I begin, but fall silent at the look in her eyes.

'Can we just begin,' she whispers.

'Okay,' I say, and usher her into the room. My heart is pounding hard and my palms are slick with nervous sweat, as if I'm the client, not the therapist. I've lit a discreet votive candle on the windowsill like I always do, and there are fresh flowers on the table, autumnal amber roses, and I make a point of taking each of them in briefly to center myself. Leah settles into the chair opposite me and fidgets strangely with her jacket sleeves, as though she can't control herself and is at the mercy of a motor running inside her that she can't shut down. Her fingers loop through and around a little hole she's made on the sleeve, making it bigger and bigger. As it recedes, her sweater underneath becomes visible and I see that it is speckled with blood.

'What's happened, Leah?' I ask softly, in spite of my usual habit of letting the client begin the session at their own point of urgency.

'I…' The words seem to catch in her throat.

'Someone has hurt you. Do you think you can tell me about what happened?' I watch as tears drop from her eyes onto her hands, still working away at unraveling the jacket sleeve. 'Leah?'

No answer.

'Have you gone to the police?'

'No.'

I nod, and let the 'no' hang for a while on the tense air between us. 'It's not like they'd do anything much,' she continues in a whisper.

'Maybe it would be good to speak with them anyway,' I say, but she shakes her head curtly. 'Leah, did Anton do this to you?' The abusive and vindictive ex-husband seems like a natural assumption.

Blank stare.

'There is something I have to tell you,' Leah says, her eyes returning to the busy performance of her hands tearing at the jacket sleeve. I remain silent, fully concentrated, ready to receive her words and to help her hold the intense emotions she must be feeling. For a long while, she doesn't speak. She closes her uninjured left eye and I can't help but stare at her now that I know she can't see me. I allow the intense empathy I feel for Leah to wash over me. I hope she can feel that, in these moments, I am all hers, and that I stand beside her witnessing her distress and her pain.

'You know I told you about my cabin? The one I bought in the mountains? Or, the forest really. With mountains nearby.'

'Yes.'

'I want to go there. I just want to go there and collect myself; it's the only place I've really felt at peace. Ever. You know how we've spoken so much about my need for newness all the time? And the need to escape. It's been like an itch, always. As a child, I always wanted to be someone else. It's the same now. I just want to be away. Away. Faster, better, more. Away. I live my life wanting to be somewhere other than where I am. Except for at the cabin. It's like that place is me, but me as a physical place, does that make sense?' I nod. 'It's like it's not only mine, but *me*.'

'That sounds like a very good place to be.'

'Yeah.' She doesn't embellish. I glance at the time, only twenty minutes left.

'You mentioned earlier that there was something you needed to tell me.'

Leah nods. She avoids my gaze, lets her one seeing eye

travel around the room until it comes to rest on the flowers. Then she closes it and tears rush from beneath her thick dark lashes, dropping off her chin and onto her wrung, red hands. I wait.

'I…' she begins, her voice scratchy and raw, like she's been screaming at the top of her lungs. I feel deeply unsettled in her presence, she is so unlike herself, even the way she was at the very beginning. She stands up.

'I'm sorry,' she says, her face twisted and grotesque.

'We have some time left,' I say, but she's already crossing the room and reaching for the door.

'I…' she begins again. 'It's too late,' she whispers.

'What's too late? Leah, talk to me. Tell me what's on your mind.'

'No, it's too late.'

'Why is it too late?'

'Can… Can you come to my cabin?'

I sigh, we've had these kinds of conversations before. 'Leah, you know that the therapy room is our meeting place.'

'Please.'

'I can't come to your cabin. You know this.'

Leah wrenches the door open and turns to look at me. 'I need you to…' she starts, her eyes shining with fresh tears, then she lowers her voice to barely a whisper. 'This is about the truth.'

'Stay a little longer, Leah, please. I have some extra time this afternoon. It's okay. Talk to me.'

She shakes her head forcefully and fumbles around in her jacket pocket with her right hand. She hands me a crumpled envelope with something solid inside.

'Please come.'

'Leah—'

'I'm sorry... I'm so sorry...'

'Wait, sorry for what? Leah, wait.'

But Leah is already running down the stairs, her footsteps echoing up the stairwell. I rush to the window and watch as she bursts onto the street and crosses the road to the royal palace park, where she becomes blurred and distorted in the crashing rain.

2

Kristina

As soon as I get home, I go to the kitchen and pour myself a large glass of Californian red. I walk through each of our large rooms steeped in autumnal darkness even though it is only four o'clock, and enter my walk-in wardrobe, placing the wineglass on a shelf. My reflection is mirrored back at me from several angles, sliver after sliver of Kristina. I look tired and pale. I take a big glug of the wine and run my fingertips across a long row of little black dresses, which are perfectly hung and grouped by fabric. Silk, then chiffon, then satin, cotton, jersey, merino wool, cashmere. Tonight will be formal and I need something special. It's the Conservative Party's annual autumn gala, held at the prime minister's private residence. My husband is second in command of the party and many eyes will be on us this evening. I move toward the jewel-colored dresses, teal maybe, or a deep emerald; those colors tend to offset my dark hair. I select a beautiful ocean-blue silk Bottega Veneta dress and step out of my work clothes. I look at myself for a moment in the full-length mirror and take another big sip of the pinot noir. Woman, thirties, thin and a little drawn-looking, drinking wine in her underwear in a closet – that's me.

I feel unsettled, like something is happening at the back of my mind that I can't quite grasp; it's the feeling of trying to recover a forgotten dream. My thoughts return to this afternoon's session with Leah Iverson. There was something alarming in her level of intensity – in all the time she's been coming to see me, I have never seen her in a state like that before. I know I'll need to return to the session, write up some notes and consider whether to intervene further, but right now, I need to focus on the evening ahead.

I step into the dress and watch myself transform from weary and anonymous-looking to something close to glamorous. Definitely this dress. I choose a cashmere Louis Vuitton scarf to drape across my bare shoulders and a little violet clutch bag with a clasp set with turquoise stones that pick up the color of the dress. From the wall I unhook my trusty skyscraper nude Louboutins and wince at the thought of wearing them all night; my feet are more accustomed to Uggs and sneakers these days. I put the shoes on and go through to the bathroom to do my make-up.

'Black is better,' says a voice from the doorway. I jump, smearing mascara to the side of my right eye. My husband is standing there, smiling bemusedly at me, beads of rainwater studding his jacket, some dripping from his hair onto the tiles.

'Don't you like this?' I ask, turning to face him. He looks me up and down.

'You look beautiful. Ravishing in fact. But on this occasion, definitely black. It's a very formal event.'

'Okay,' I say, and return to the mirror to remove the mascara blob. I feel a pang of disappointment. I wanted Eirik to be impressed with my choice, but my husband is even more of a perfectionist than I am, and this is his work event, so I am happy to choose another dress.

I take a sip of the wine while Eirik gets in the shower, and I watch the outline of his big body through bursts of rising steam, like a skyscraper behind fog. For a moment I consider joining him, slipping my arms around his wet torso from behind, holding him close. I decide against it; Eirik will be fully focused on the evening ahead and most likely needs a little time to himself to get in the right headspace and go over his speech again.

When he emerges from the shower, I've changed and am wearing a foolproof silk-and-taffeta gala dress I bought in Paris several years ago and have only worn once. I've coiled my hair into a high bun, securing a few stray strands to the side in place with discreet diamanté slides. Eirik takes me in, a slow smile spreading across his face.

'Wow,' he says. He wipes himself briskly down with the towel and then throws it into the corner of the bathroom. He sidles up against me where I'm standing at the sink and puts his arms around me from behind, our eyes meeting in the mirror. He pulls me very close and nuzzles my neck, and I can feel his erection nudging against my buttocks. With one hand, Eirik undoes my hair from its clip, sending it flowing around my shoulders, and with the other hand he hoists the dress up around my hips and then he's inside me, moving hard but slow, our eyes still locked on each other's in the mirror.

Though it would be less than a five-minute walk, a black Conservative Party car picks us up and drops us at the residence. Before we step outside onto the pavement, where several reporters and photographers await the arrival of politicians and various celebrities, Eirik gives me a reassuring smile. I lock my eyes on his confident, calm gaze, suddenly feeling nervous. This isn't my world, but if Eirik wins the elections, it will be. I might even live here someday, I think to myself, glancing up at the dramatically lit, imposing residence. It's still raining heavily, and a man swoops in with an umbrella and opens my door, ensuring not a single drop of rain touches me. Eirik and I pose for the photographers under an awning and I feel a deep thrill in my stomach at the surrealness of it; of waking up this morning, seeing clients all day, then coming here and being photographed for newspapers and gossip magazines because I'm married to one of Norway's most popular politicians.

The dinner is exquisite, filet mignon and lobster, and as the last course is cleared away, the speeches begin. I allow myself to drift about on my thoughts, taking in my surroundings and the other guests, making sure to laugh when I hear laughter, and clap when everyone else does. A blonde woman at a table close to the row of windows catches my eye. I feel a sudden jolt – she looks so much like Elisabeth in profile that I lean forward to get a better view. She is craning her neck to see the woman speaking, so I have only a limited view of her face. Her eyes crease as she smiles and her hands are clasped together, as if poised for the next round of applause. Her hair is glinting beautifully; tiny glass beads are woven into her updo, catching the light from the enormous chandeliers overhead. I imagine the woman getting up and walking across the room to me, beaming, her arms outstretched, and for the briefest of moments it's *her*, it really is her, Elisabeth, and none of the terrible things that have happened were real, it was just a dream. Just another bad dream.

I must be staring at her, mesmerized, and as if she realizes she's being watched, the woman turns in my direction. For a second, our eyes meet across the room. I realize that the woman is Mette-Marit, the crown princess, and that she looks nothing like Elisabeth after all. I clear my throat and let my eyes drop to the table in front of me. The palms of my hands are slick, my heart hammering. Will I forever be seeing the ghost of Elisabeth in the faces of strangers? My thoughts dart briefly to Leah Iverson, and I realize that the way she behaved this afternoon in our session also reminded me of Elisabeth. The disjointed sentences, the bruises, the desperation she emanated. I wonder where Leah is right now; I really hope she is safe and taking care of herself tonight.

The woman who was speaking, the minister of education, has stopped and returned to her seat. From every corner, waiters swoop in and refill wine glasses, conscious of the brief lull in proceedings before the next speech. Eirik squeezes my knee lightly.

'I'm on,' he says, winking at me before standing up, the room erupting into an enthusiastic round of applause. He walks to the top of the room and stands still, waiting for the applause to die down, smiling and nodding. There is nothing about his composure that suggests he is even mildly nervous to stand here in a room full of the upper echelons of Norway's society, including the crown prince and princess, about to give a speech. I am mesmerized watching him speak; he comes across as a man entirely in his element – confident, knowledgeable, with a dash of humor thrown in. It's strange to think that this is the same man who sleeps next to me every night, whose most intimate moments are shared with me. I think about the sex earlier, how it felt more like the thrilling sex between strangers than the usual, less adventurous sex we normally have, carefully planned around ovulation cycles and likeliness of conception. For a moment, I allow myself to imagine that tonight of all nights was the time it actually worked, and that in this very moment that much-wanted child is beginning inside me: a single cell breaking into two. I make myself stop this train of thought because it hurts too much. Every month, no matter how hopeful I've felt, no matter how hard I have tried to believe that it will happen for us eventually, the dreaded blood arrives. My heart beats faster. I take a big glug of champagne and return my attention to Eirik's speech. I hear him speak my name and get the sudden sensation of several hundred pairs of eyes on me.

'My wife, Dr Kristina Moss,' he says. 'None of this would have been possible without her.' People smile and clap and a flash goes off somewhere, and it occurs to me, perhaps for the first time, that Eirik needs me as much as I need him.

3

Kristina

I wake to a repetitive muffled sound. Eirik is gone from bed and I sit up, blinking several times, but it feels as though my eyes have been stuck together. My pulse is fast and a vivid headache chases through my skull. I remember last night, all the drinks, the hours of sitting through moderately interesting speeches about political reform, progress, prosperity. For a moment I see the crown princess in my mind, how beautiful she looked with her radiant smile and subtly glinting updo. The neon light from a phone screen moves around from over in the corner, sending roaming shapes across the room.

'Eirik?' I whisper.

'Hey,' he says, shining the light toward me. 'Sorry. Sorry, I didn't mean to wake you.'

'What's happening? What time is it?'

'It's 5.15. I'm going to have to fly to Bergen, unfortunately. A car's waiting outside to take me to the airport.'

'Wait, what? It's Saturday.'

'I know.'

'We're going to spend the night at my sister's, remember?'

'I know. I'm sorry. Look, this is strictly confidential, but there's a situation at the west coast party office. One of the guys I directly oversee has been accused of gross misconduct.'

I feel tears of disappointment pricking my eyes, though I know I'm being dramatic. Eirik's decision to go from international corporate law into politics was a joint decision and I knew full well that it would be demanding on our marriage. Or did I, really? There are so many things in life we can only truly understand once we're actually living and feeling them.

'Okay,' I say.

'I am sorry, Kristina.' Eirik comes over to my side of the bed and squats down beside me. 'Pass on my love to Camilla and the kids. I'll be back tomorrow afternoon. I love you.' He presses his lips to my forehead, and I catch a whiff of his familiar cologne, the same he's used since his student days, when we met: Fahrenheit by Christian Dior, and for some reason this brings more tears to my eyes. He rushes from the room and I imagine him stepping into a shiny party car pulled up outside the building, his mind razor sharp and trained on the day ahead. He has an ability to completely compartmentalize his career from the rest of his life and never lets anything impact his work. I think it is because he lost his mother in childhood and became accustomed to closing off parts of himself and his feelings for protection. For several minutes after he's gone, his scent clings to the air in our bedroom and I close my eyes, though I know I won't get any more sleep.

* * *

We walk down to the soggy, deserted beach, stopping for the kids to jump in every single puddle. I make myself smile at them and say all the right things when they rush over to where I'm standing with Camilla under a giant oak tree to show us some trinket or another, but inside it feels like I could fall to pieces just looking at my niece and nephew. What hurts so much is taking in their impossible sweetness; it's like being taunted by everything I don't have.

I zone out from the long story Camilla is telling me about the audacity of her awful colleague and try to allow those feelings – they may feel like a numb, impenetrable kind of nothingness, but that is never the case. I remind myself that if I was one of my own clients, I would feel so much empathy for the woman standing on this beach watching those beautiful children play.

Also, I suppose I'm still a little upset that Eirik didn't come with me, though it's nice for Camilla and me to have this rare time together, just the two of us and the kids. Her husband, Mikkel, decided to go on an overnight fishing trip when I explained Eirik couldn't make it, giving Camilla and me some 'sister time'.

'Look!' screams Vilja, holding up a chewed stick triumphantly.

'Wow,' I say.

'Look at this,' shouts Birk, shoving his little sister aside, who responds by throwing the chewed stick hard at the back of his head. Camilla rolls her eyes at me, then intercepts, speaking calmly and diplomatically until the argument dies down and they run back down toward the sand, laughing and shouting. My sister – the perfect mother. She really is. She took to motherhood like a duck to water, like she was born to take care of little people, unlike me. I feel a surge of familiar jealousy toward my older sister, though these days I recognize it instantly and am able to consciously choose to not rise to it. We are fourteen months apart, and as a child, it was hard to be in the shadow of someone always that little bit faster, cleverer, more accomplished. I often felt like a lesser version of her, and it wasn't until I was older that I realized I probably got treated as such. As a teenager, I made a real point out of distancing myself from Camilla, dying my hair blonde and barely acknowledging her at school. As adults, we are extremely close – I'd say Camilla is the person I'm closest to besides Eirik.

Still, our relationship occasionally feels difficult for me – ever since Eirik and I started trying for a baby two years ago. I suppose I took it for granted that I would just get pregnant as soon as I wanted to, like my sister. That I still haven't, in spite of everything, feels like a profound betrayal by my body and these are things I work intently on in my own therapy. I'm not sure I'll ever be able to make my peace with it if we remain unsuccessful, especially if the underlying reason turns out to be the aftermath of trauma. The irony of dedicating my life to healing other people's trauma, while being held back by my own. I swallow hard and turn to my sister.

'Did I tell you that we're taking a break from IVF?'

'No.'

I nod. Our eyes meet; hers are full of kindness. She looks how I hope I look when my clients share something important with me.

'Yeah. Well. My body was literally crumbling from over-stimulation. It's a relief to have a break from all the injections.'

'I can imagine. I'm sorry, Kristina. It will happen.'

'Yeah.' I look at Birk and Vilja chasing each other down the beach, their wellies leaving soggy footprints that moments later get erased by the surging, cold waves.

'It will.'

'Yeah. You know, it sounds a little mad, but I sometimes feel this irrational hope that it could still happen naturally. That if we could just remove ourselves from all the stress, from the invasive procedures, the injections and the carefully timed sex that doesn't feel sexy at all, then it might just happen—'

'And it might.'

I nod and think about last night again, how different and exciting it felt. 'Yeah, it might.' One cell that becomes two that becomes a thousand that becomes a million; it could be happening inside me right now. But I don't dare to believe anymore, and consciously shut down these thoughts – nothing hurts more than false hope.

I move my thoughts away from my own problems and stare out at the raging, gray sea, but feel a flicker of the anxiety I felt after Leah Iverson's session on Friday return. I wonder what she is doing at this moment, whether she is doing better. I think about the envelope she handed me, and its strange contents. I stood watching as she ran across the street after the session, still clutching the little package she'd handed me. Her shape became distorted in the fierce downpour, like a spectre, then it disappeared, merging with the trees and bushes in the park. I opened my hand, then the envelope in it. Inside was a set of old-fashioned keys, like the ones to my grandmother's farmhouse in Valdres. There was also a local area map, with handwritten instructions scribbled on it. A location was marked with an 'x' in the middle of what seemed to be a vast forest. 'Bekkebu', Leah had written above it – the name of her cabin, I recalled. Near a lake called Heivannet, she'd made a second marking – a 'p' for 'park here'. At the top of the map, she'd written 'Please please please come.'

It's not the first time a client has asked me to meet outside the therapy room – it can be very difficult for people to grasp the boundaries between therapist and client, when therapy is necessarily built on emotional intimacy. I've had clients who constantly ask me personal questions, and who have spent significant amounts of time attempting to convince me that we would make great friends in real life. Leah, too, has on a few occasions expressed curiosity about who I am in my personal life. Still, it is definitely out of character for Leah Iverson to behave like this, imploring me to meet with her at a remote cabin – she seemed almost possessed and not at all like herself. I make a mental note to get in touch with her GP tomorrow morning, and to email Leah to suggest she come in for an extra session this week.

'Why don't you stay until tomorrow?' asks Camilla, bringing me back to the blustery beach and my little niece and nephew laughing into the wind, their white-blonde heads thrown back, their hands extended as though they are trying to embrace the whole world.

'I would, but I have a client at eight thirty,' I say. This isn't exactly true – my first is at eleven, but I'd like a couple of hours in my peaceful, bright office before seeing anyone, catching up on emails and case notes like I always do on a Monday morning. Besides, I am exhausted after a full weekend with Camilla, Vilja and Birk and I want to enjoy a long evening at home with Eirik, cooking together and snuggling by the fireplace.

I leave Camilla's at four and start the drive back to Oslo, but get caught up in the painfully slow Sunday-afternoon traffic of weekenders returning to the city from their cabins. At one point it completely stops moving and I put the car in neutral, securing the handbrake. I sit, cocooned, listening to the slam of the rain, which is falling heavily again for the ninth day in a row. I turn the wipers off to better hear the rain and, without them, the world instantly becomes a gray blur. I still feel disconcertingly empty, like I have all weekend. I'm not sure if it's due to how emotional I sometimes get being around my niece and nephew, or a lingering sense of worry for Leah Iverson. I am usually good at switching off from my clients at weekends – I have to be. Or it is because this is the first time I've returned to Oslo on this same road without stopping in to see Elisabeth. And I never will again. Villa Vinternatt is down there, set snug in a leafy forest between the motorway and the sea, less than three minutes' drive away from where the traffic has ground to a standstill. And she isn't there. Of course – that must be why I feel unsettled and a little melancholic.

Still no movement on the road, so I fish my phone from my handbag and glance at the screen. There are two missed calls from a number I don't recognize. And there is a message from Eirik, sent fifteen minutes ago, probably right after I texted him saying I was on my way home.

I thought you'd be home much later. You said Sunday night? I'm with Lars, we thought we'd catch a movie at six.

I feel a stab of annoyance. We hardly ever see each other – why is he making plans with his friend on a Sunday night? And if he really thought I'd be home later, why didn't he cancel with Lars when he received my message saying I was on my way home? I'm not a demanding wife. At least I don't think I am. I just want to feel prioritized by Eirik, and the truth is, much of the time, I don't. Especially lately.

The traffic has started moving again, leaving a wide gap between my car and the one in front, so I put the phone away and nudge the gas. The drive, which usually takes forty minutes, takes over two hours, and by the time I shut the door to the apartment behind me, breathing in its warm, familiar scent, it's six thirty. It's actually rather nice that Eirik is out; I've got used to having the apartment mostly to myself. I throw my weekend bag and handbag onto the sofa and decide to run a bath. I'll pour myself a large glass of red and soak for as long as I want, reading my book or maybe an interiors magazine. I turn on the tap and stand for a while in the bathroom, looking myself in the eye. If I were one of my clients, how would I describe the woman in front of me?

Kristina Moss, thirty-six years old. Married, no kids. A little tired-looking, with harsh blue circles beneath my eyes tonight, thanks to the late night on Friday and last night spent tossing and turning, snatching just a few hours of sleep in the early hours before Birk and Vilja rushed into the room at six like beautiful little hurricanes. My lips are full, my eyes a very dark brown, my chestnut-brown hair is pulled back and fastened in a messy topknot. A long, thin scar runs down my forehead. Strong nose and arched eyebrows from my father. Dimples and straight teeth from my mother, my favorite two things about my face.

A sound separates itself from the flowing water and I stand still, listening. It is a metallic sound, like two components of machinery clashing together, but then I realize it's my new ringtone and the sound is exacerbated against the marble surface of the lounge table where I've left the phone. I reach it before it stops ringing, noticing that it's a different number from the previous missed calls I haven't yet returned.

'Hello?'

There is no response, though I can hear someone is there, breathing into the phone.

'Hello?' Still nothing. I stay on the line for a while, listening to the faint, raspy breathing. This kind of thing doesn't frighten or unsettle me; it has happened quite a few times, and when I've looked up the caller ID on 1881.no it is almost always some client or another, struggling late at night or on a weekend, who couldn't resist calling to just hear the sound of my voice. It comes with the territory, and I never bring the calls up in the subsequent session. They actually make me feel especially empathetic toward a client, and besides, I know the feeling myself, of just needing to hear your therapist's voice when everything feels impossible and pitch black. Tonight, I wonder if it could be Leah Iverson calling. I stay on the line, sitting on the side of the bathtub and watching bubbles pop on the water's surface, for four minutes and thirty-nine seconds, until the line goes dead.

4

Leah, two weeks before

In the small hours, when the sky is still dense with darkness, Leah is jolted from fretful dreams by the sound of a door slamming shut somewhere in the building. There's a doctor on the second floor – he comes and goes at odd hours; it might be him. Or it might be the young girls sharing an apartment on the ground floor – they often come home when others start to wake. There's a cello player across the landing from Leah's own flat, a quiet and skinny man in his forties. She doubts it was him; the only sounds she ever hears from that apartment are mournful rising and falling concertos.

Or… Or it could be Anton. She feels the little hairs on her forearm prickle and stand up at the thought of Anton coming up the stairs and makes herself take several long, deep breaths. *He doesn't know where you live, Leah.* She imagines Kristina's calm, soothing voice speaking the words directly into her ear.

She turns over in bed, wishes she wasn't alone, though

she usually is. She flicks the radio switch and the buzz of voices fills the bedroom. Two men, discussing the situation in the Crimea. She turns the faux-ancient dial on her brand-new radio until soft music fills the room. Cello, in fact – Bach. She closes her eyes but knows she won't sleep again, not tonight.

She'll be exhausted by lunchtime, and feels her stomach tighten with dread at all the long hours in front of the computer awaiting her, trying to find the words she needs to write. They don't come anymore, and she almost can't remember the days when writing was something joyful, when the words seemed to scatter from her fingertips. She'll return to bed in the late afternoon, reading, checking her phone, listening to music, crying, the loneliness and yearning as insistent as bacteria burrowing into her bones. But then sleep does come, and Leah is lulled by dreams. The vision of bacteria inside her body somehow seeps into her dream, a strange world where she's carried through narrow maroon canals as if on a boat, before being expelled into cool air through a purple-edged wound.

5

Kristina

All the jokes about Mondays fall flat on me – I've always liked Mondays, a fresh start every week. In my line of work, I sometimes feel worn down and jaded by the time Friday rolls around and it takes the weekend to process and clear my head. But I love what I do, and by Monday morning, I can't wait to get back to my office. I rent a pleasant, airy space at the pedestrian end of Hegdehaugsveien, in what used to be a large turn-of-the-century apartment, together with two other therapists and an osteopath. We call ourselves Homansbyen Terapisenter and share a kitchen and bathroom. We've become friendly over the years, sometimes heading to Lorry's, the pub on the corner, for a drink after work on Thursdays, and quite frequently passing new clients on to one another when someone isn't quite a match.

On Monday mornings I'm here alone, sometimes for several hours – my colleagues have a policy of not booking clients early on Mondays. So do I, but I still come in early because I love this time to catch up with myself and prepare for the week ahead. It's important to me to always be organized; it prevents so much chaos. Eirik makes fun of me for it sometimes, saying it's almost creepy how one could open any drawer in our house at any time and it would always be immaculately ordered. *Where do you keep the loose ends, the mess, the stuff you want to keep hidden?* he'll ask, laughing. I don't; I go through the mess, and then I get rid of it. I aspire to achieve a mind and a life as transparent as my brightly lit, meticulously ordered closet with neat, instantly recognizable thoughts and feelings sorted like clothes in open shelves.

I get up but almost immediately sit back down – the feeling of restlessness since the weekend hasn't quite left me. I make myself focus on the notes on the screen in front of me. I need to jot down a few notes about today's clients, as well as get in touch with a couple of GPs with regards to clients' medication – I like to stay informed and updated in the cases where someone might be taking mood-altering medication in addition to psychotherapy.

I look up Leah's phone number in my client list, and compare it to the unknown numbers that called me last night. The last one was hers. Where was she when she called? What was she doing in those long minutes she had me on the line? I imagine her in bed, sobbing in the dark, her beautiful face twisted in a grimace of pain, the bruises on her face starting to fade from indigo to pale violet and sickly yellow.

I open my calendar, which is busier than usual, with two new clients starting and a few extra sessions requested by established clients, but I do have a couple of free slots, one this afternoon and one on Wednesday. I hope Leah will take one of them. I redial her number, but it goes straight to voicemail without ringing. I try again, with the same result. It's still early, only just gone 8 a.m. I don't imagine she gets up early, as an author working from home; I don't assume she would have anywhere to be this early. I'll email instead, and she can get in touch when it suits her.

To: liverson@vimeo.no

Subject: Sessions

Hi Leah,

I wanted to check in with you after Friday; you've been on my mind. How are you doing? I know you called me last night; do try again, if you like. I also wanted to let you know that I have a couple of free slots available this week, if you'd like some extra support. I can easily add an extra session or two to your therapy scheme with your GP, so you won't be billed – let me know.

All best,

Kristina

I press 'send' and get up from my desk. I take my delicious Kusmi tea, which I don't offer to clients, from the cupboard and flick the switch on the kettle. While I wait for the water to boil, I draw the scent of the blend deep into my lungs and watch people milling around on the street two floors down. There's a long line at Kaffebrenneriet, snaking all the way outside onto the pavement. A jam-packed blue tram inches past, sandwiched by slow-moving cars heading toward Solli Plass. A blonde woman emerges from the café and dashes across the road. She's wearing wide-leg trousers and impressively high heels, clutching a tall coffee, shielding her bouncy hair from the rain with a document folder.

I hear a ping from my computer, and instantly my thoughts return to Leah – I hope it's her, responding straight away. I realize how worried I am for her by the way I feel a dull ache in my stomach at the thought of her. There was something about the look in her eyes. The way she begged.

The email isn't from Leah but from a woman called Tess who is looking for a therapist to help her 'navigate the worst divorce ever'. I make a mental note to respond to her later, saying I have plenty of experience with divorce, and schedule her in for next week. I open a new email draft and write to Leah's GP, a competent and kindly man called Dr Albert who refers many clients to me and my colleagues for psychotherapy.

I believe there is reason for concern for Leah Iverson's well-being, I write. *She has made repeat mentions of self-harm and suicidal ideation, and while I haven't considered her high-risk previously due to her encouraging response to psychotherapy, I feel concerned that may have changed.*

I have emailed Leah this morning to offer extra support, and I will suggest that she also makes an appointment to see you with a view to discussing more intensive support, and/or further intervention.

***

The day passes in a blur, with back-to-back clients, and it isn't until 3 p.m. that I get a chance to check my email again. No response from Leah. The free slot I have is at the end of the day – at 4.30, and I decide to stay until then in case Leah gets in touch and wants to come by. My stomach growls and I realize I haven't had lunch. There's nothing but some dried crackers in my cupboard and I'm not in the mood for prepping something in the communal kitchen; someone will inevitably appear for a chat. I am feeling introspective and restless today, and just want to be in my own space. I message Eirik and ask about dinner plans, and though he reads my WhatsApp straight away, the minutes tick by with no response. I am used to this, but suddenly it makes me angry.

I walk downstairs and out into the misty rain – it's the kind that doesn't seem to dissolve into individual droplets, but that envelops you in a moist sheen. I cross the road to Kaffebrenneriet, which is entirely empty now, and place my order, a tall white Americano and a chicken-and-pesto baguette. My phone vibrates in my pocket and I glance at the message.

What time will you be here? Making butterflied chicken, your favorite! Will Eirik be joining us?

My mother. My heart sinks. I fish my calendar out of my handbag and realize that I had, in fact, written 'Dinner with Mum' on October 26th – today. She gets lonely when my father travels, and he is away this week in Iceland with the geology society he is a founding member of. I vaguely recall speaking to her on the phone last week and making dinner plans, but I completely forgot and don't feel up for it – my mother can talk anyone's head off and I'm simply not in the mood. I think about messaging Eirik again but he's clearly forgotten too so I decide to just go on my own.

The next hour drags past and I'm irritable and unfocused, so I feel relieved when Leah doesn't show up, hoping she'll take the free slot on Wednesday morning instead. At 4.50 on the dot, I leave the office and walk fast alongside the heavily congested road by the royal park to the train station on the other side. Again, I see Leah in my mind, the way she rushed from the session on Friday and outside into the heavy rain. There was something ghostly about how she was swallowed up by the gloomy fog, like she had never existed at all, and I keep my eyes locked to the drenched pavement.

6

Kristina

I open the door without knocking and stand for a long moment in the hallway, drawing in the familiar scent of my childhood home. I run my hand lightly across my father's battered golf bag and smile at a childhood picture of Camilla and me on the wall. I take my drenched parka off and hang it on the wall hook, letting it drip onto the tiles. I remember sitting on this same floor as a child, struggling to get out of my bulky winter boots, loving the warmth from the underfloor heating after coming back inside from playing in the snow for hours. The house smelled exactly the same then – of laundry, food always prepared from scratch, the distinct, chalky smell of the rock samples in my father's office, the orange roses my mother favors: home.

I avoid my gaze in the mirror, the drowned cat look was never a good one, and I need to summon all my energy to get through the evening with my mother when what I want is to just withdraw to the bathtub with a large glass of wine and my own thoughts.

'What are you doing standing there, honey? Oh, gosh, you are absolutely soaked!' My mother has appeared in the doorway without me noticing and pulls me into a close hug. I'm surprised by how good it feels to be held by her and I stay in her embrace for a little longer than I normally would, noticing that she feels slighter and smaller than I think of her. It's a special sorrow, that moment when you realize that your parents have grown old.

'Hey, Mum,' I say.

'Oh, Kristina, you look so…'

'Terrible?'

'No, of course not. Tired and wet. Never terrible, you beautiful, silly girl.' She ushers me into the open-plan living area that she insisted upon a couple of years ago, knocking through the small, cozy rooms of my childhood and creating a 'more modern home'. She presses a glass of white wine into my hand and I take a big, grateful sip and sit down in my usual place at the table.

'It's so good to have you here. I haven't seen you in so long! How long is it?' says my mother, placing two heaped plates on the table, chunks of chicken swimming in watery red-onion gravy.

'It's just a couple of weeks, Mum,' I say, but grant her a smile. It's not her fault that I'm worn out. 'How have you been?'

'Busy. It seems like the petition has a good chance of winning, though if there's one thing I've learned, it's not to take anything for granted. After we were featured in the newspaper, I was invited to speak about the situation on the radio. That raised awareness, as you can imagine.'

'Yes.'

My mother has spent the last year relentlessly campaigning against the council's plan to place a new stretch of the E18 motorway exactly through where my childhood home stands.

'Of course, I now have to do much of the work on my own. After what happened with Elisabeth, Idun just can't face doing what needs to be done, so I'm doing it all. To be honest, she can barely get out of bed in the morning.' I nod, but a visceral dread spreads out in the pit of my stomach and I focus on chewing my food slowly, so I can't be expected to respond. I knew my mother would want to talk about Elisabeth. It's only natural, considering, but I'm still reeling from her loss and find it difficult to manage my emotions when her name is dropped into the conversation without warning. 'I don't think she'll ever get over it,' continues my mother. 'Such a terrible waste. In spite of everything, she didn't see it coming.'

I nod again and look outside to the garden where Elisabeth and I used to play as children. I decide to bring my feelings of guilt and grief over Elisabeth to my own therapy tomorrow, like I already have, over and over, since August.

Elisabeth's family have always lived next to my own, in a house the mirror image of my family's. Our gardens border each other, separated only by a low hedge, which became trampled and mangled over the years as Camilla and I constantly scrambled across it to get to Elisabeth. Because we were friends from before I can remember, I have no recollection of any firsts – the first time we met, the first time we laughed together, our first sleepover. She was just always there. Elisabeth was an only child, which makes her death an even crueler tragedy for her mother and father. As a child, she was jealous of me having an older sister. She used to say that she was the third sister and, well into our teens, she'd introduce me to people as her sister.

Elisabeth was intense, creative, moody, fiercely intelligent. She'd come up with the games we'd play and all the kids in the neighborhood generally followed her lead. I remember her as always having an audience, whether it was just me or many other kids too. It was always *The Elisabeth Show*. We loved her. She'd become famous and celebrated when we grew up; this was accepted among us kids as fact. But she didn't. She died in what should have been her prime, in the most tragic of circumstances.

'I need to get home,' I say, pushing my half-eaten plate of butterflied chicken aside. The dull ache in my stomach from thinking about Elisabeth is spreading outwards and I just want to go home and get an early night. Eirik is working late, I have the apartment to myself.

'But… But you only arrived an hour ago. Why don't you take the eight o'clock train? That will give us a little more time to catch up—'

'I'm sorry, Mum. Really. The food was delicious. I'm just a little tired. It must be the weather. It's so awful; it's like it settles in your bones. And work is stressful at the moment.'

'What about Idun? Aren't you going to pop next door to see her? She'll be expecting you.'

I swallow hard. I can't face Elisabeth's mother, not today. I shake my head, and stand up, avoiding my mother's disapproving gaze.

I decline the offer of a ride to the station, and walk fast through the rain, which is falling sideways now, dragging across the street in bitter columns on a brisk wind. It beats into my face, pummeling it raw. I take the shortcut through the woods, using my special mindfulness technique of focusing purely on the sensation of my physical being in its environment to feel safe. The wet thud of my Nikes on the path scattered with brown pine needles. The sound of rain hitting the crowns of trees and dribbling down their stems. My fingertips turning rigid and red with the cold. The way distant woodsmoke from the suburban neighborhoods surrounding this little patch of woods drifts across on the moist air and settles in my nostrils. The woods give way to a huge parking lot and a gray, huddled building rising from the concrete: the train station; I made it.

On the train, I check my phone. Nothing from Eirik other than he's working late. These days he only rarely arrives home before I go to sleep, and most mornings he's out the door before I wake. And I'm a night owl who gets up early. There's a message from my colleague, Alice, asking if we can share a room at the integrative therapeutic practice conference we're both attending in Tromsø next month. And there is an email from Dr Albert.

From: Walbert@medicus.no

Subject: RE Leah Iverson

Dear Dr Moss,

Thank you for getting in touch with me with regard to Leah Iverson. I, too, am concerned for her well-being, and especially considering her current circumstances. I saw her last week for a routine check-up and she did not appear well. I will get in touch with the borough's psychiatric team as I think Leah may benefit from more support, especially over the coming few months. Could you let me know of any developments after your session/s with Leah later this week? Also, just to confirm – are you aware of Leah's pregnancy (13+3)?

Best wishes,

Dr Wilhelm Albert

7

Leah, two weeks before

It's just gone 4 a.m. and she's still up. It's her favorite time, when almost everyone else is asleep. It's a confirmation of aloneness, a validation – she really is alone then, rather than just feeling alone, like the rest of the time. The words won't come. It is a special kind of pain, waiting for words to form and emerge, perhaps it can be compared to waiting for a baby: it won't come until it's ready.

She stands up and looks over at her bed. Her mind is razor sharp and buzzing. Her body, too, feels like it is throbbing with life and restless energy. She turns to the window and looks out at a dry, crystalline night, shivering slightly with cold she can see but not feel. A thin sheen of ice has formed on the cars parked along the street, making them sparkle in the moonlight. The trees have shed the last of their leaves and stand stripped and resigned to the coming winter. They're more beautiful like this, she thinks, when you can see their underpinnings. Like a woman undressed, supple skin and soft curves glowing in low light. She steps out of her cozy home tracksuit bottoms, and unzips its matching top. She undoes her bra and removes her underwear too.

In bed she relaxes into her own touch, kneading and pushing and rubbing. Her thoughts go from soft to hard; from the gentle curves of a woman to the need to be held by someone bigger than herself, to the exhilarating feel of strong hands closing around her neck, squeezing hard then easing up and stroking her, then squeezing again. Her body responds and she feels herself inch closer, then closer still. She angles the sharp spike on her bracelet against the taut skin of her throat and lets it dig into her flesh. It makes her gasp with pain, and it gives her another surge, closer.

8

Kristina

It's a beautiful morning, the first in a while. It's bitterly cold with ice crystals shimmering on the hoods of cars and the trunks of trees, but the sky is a vivid blue, and a brilliant sun bathes Oslo in a golden autumnal glow.

I leave the house in a daze, the sleepless night lingering like a membrane between me and the cold morning air. For hours and hours, I lay tossing and turning, my mind spinning and my heart aching. I pretended to be sleeping when Eirik came home around ten thirty, but he must have known I was awake because he held me tight in spoons, nuzzling my neck and stroking my arms and stomach lightly. I wanted to cry, but managed to stop myself by focusing on even, deep breathing.

I wish calling my clients and canceling today's sessions was an option – the thought of sitting across from someone, listening intensely, fills me with restlessness. But first, supervision – it will be good to talk to Vera about what's going on.

On the corner of Parkveien, I stop and buy a coffee at Kaffebrenneriet and, stirring the brown sugar granules through my Americano, it occurs to me how absurd it is that I know the most intimate details of my clients' lives, but I have no idea how they take their coffee. I consciously construct an image of Leah in my mind, ordering a coffee at this very same café, which she may well do in real life – she doesn't live far away. I imagine her quick smile for the barista, a moment of deliberation over a pain au chocolat, and her distinctive, quick way of moving as she leaves the café, clutching a paper cup. Almond-milk macchiato, I decide. Leah is someone who makes conscious choices about everything she eats and drinks, and it has more to do with a desire for control than healthy life choices, though she proclaims that is the primary reason. She is most likely even more conscious of her dietary choices at present, considering her circumstances.

It's Tuesday and I still haven't heard from Leah. I am going to have to explain to her in our session on Friday that as our relationship is entirely based on mutual trust, and because our work simply cannot bring change unless that trust is there, we do need to be committed to answering emails, and especially after an episode such as at our last session.

I look around the busy café and make for the door with my coffee, but still an image of Leah lingers on my mind; only now, she is visibly pregnant. She's sitting at one of the tables in the corner, looking out onto the busy street, smiling serenely, drawing the gentle floral scent of a jasmine green tea into her nostrils, resting a hand on a tiny but unmistakable bump. How could I have missed it?

Each time my mind goes to the pregnancy it recoils. I just don't understand why Leah would hide such a thing from me. Or how it is even possible that I have missed the changes that must have been happening in her for a while now – has her skin been particularly radiant and glowing, has a soft swell started to appear on her belly? I run these questions over and over in my mind, but she has been the same all along, I'm sure of it. Did I simply not want to see it? Did I sense it on some level, but subconsciously refuse to acknowledge it since she never mentioned it?

I take a moment to determine whether it still affects me so deeply to learn of another's pregnancy. And – yes. Yes, it does. It hurts like hell; it hits me with the sudden, shocking force of a finger smashed in a doorway – every time. I fill my empty stomach with the hot, bitter coffee and start walking again, chasing away the image of Leah pregnant. The wind is picking up again, tearing at my hair and making my eyes sting.

Kristina, are you aware of Leah's pregnancy?

I open my mouth to speak, but nothing emerges, just a sad little squawk. Vera leans forward, empathy and warmth in her eyes, her mouth set in a commiserating little line.

'You look sad this morning, Kristina.'

'Mmmm.' We sit in silence for a long while – I watch several minutes drain from the digital clock above the door. Vera never prompts me, just sits there like a soothing presence. I often channel her calm, comfortable approach to silence when it comes to my own clients, something which didn't come easy to me early on in my career. I had to fight the urge to fill any prolonged silence with a question or just a sound to indicate I was still listening and soaking up whatever the client brought to the session. Now, I think I have become more like Vera, interested in the silences and able to let them unfold and speak for themselves.

'It's one of my clients,' I say, at last. 'Leah Iverson. You know, the Swedish novelist.'

'I remember.'

'She was very agitated in our session on Friday. She literally ran off before the end of the session, and begged me to meet her outside the therapy room. I explained why that isn't possible, of course. Then she called me late on Sunday evening, but she said nothing. I figured she needed to know I was there so I stayed on the line until it went dead. On Monday I tried to return her call, but it went straight to voicemail. I then emailed her offering extra sessions this week, but she hasn't responded. I felt worried over the weekend. It was as if I couldn't stop thinking about her; it was so out of character for her to behave like that. She's usually quite composed, though in the last year she has increasingly been showing emotions in our sessions, like she is able to connect with them more. I emailed her GP yesterday, saying I felt concerned and that we may need to consider getting Leah some extra support. She's been a self-harmer for years, though nothing very serious. As you know, she's spoken of suicide quite a bit, though more in terms of compulsive thoughts than actual intent.'

'Did she speak of suicide or self-harm on Friday?'

'No. She did say she needed to tell me something, several times. But then she didn't. She asked me to come to her cabin and even gave me a key to it. She seemed very out of it, not at all like herself. Also, her face was bruised but she refused to say what had happened.'

'Yes, it sounds like she was experiencing something very distressing. What did the GP say?'

Again I open my mouth but no sound will come. Tears gather in my eyes, then roll down my face.

'He said he agrees about providing extra support for Leah. And he asked if I was aware of the fact that she's pregnant.'

'I see. And were you?'

'No. She hasn't told me.'

'That must be difficult to understand.'

'Well, I know that she isn't obliged to tell me anything at all and that it's not right of me to expect that of her. It's just, this came out of left field and I suppose it triggers my own experiences.'

'Yes.'

'I've worked with other pregnant women and have a couple of new mothers at the moment, and I'd be lying if I said that it isn't challenging at times, considering the fact that Eirik and I so far haven't managed to get pregnant.' And not for a lack of trying – seven cycles of IVF with nothing to show for it. 'But I think when it comes to Leah, it feels especially unfair and difficult because I know she wouldn't want to be pregnant and is pretty likely to have an abortion. She doesn't have a partner, or a lifestyle suitable for a child. What would she be able to offer it? She's working through some very complex issues which present in ways that would be directly harmful to a child...' I trail off, and wipe at tears, looking out the window at the brilliant blue sky. I can't bear Vera's immense empathy in this moment.

'But Kristina, she hasn't yet spoken to you about her pregnancy. People do change, and perhaps Leah is making changes to her life that would benefit a potential child. It occurs to me that in this case, you don't know what is going on, and perhaps it feels like a rejection that she hasn't chosen to share this with you.'

'Yes.'

'And on a personal level, her presumably unplanned pregnancy feels unfair to you due to your own painful struggle to conceive.'

I nod, not even trying to stop the fresh rush of tears.

'Do you think you will be able to support her through her pregnancy, no matter how it ends?'

'Well, yes. I mean, of course. I'm just shocked, I guess. And grieving.'

'Which are both very natural human emotions.'

'It's just been a bit much recently. I saw my mother last night and she wanted to speak about Elisabeth, and I just need some space from what happened. But it's like she wants to instruct me in how to behave, and how to grieve, acting all disapproving when I won't do what she expects.'

'What do you think she expects?'

'I think she wants me to make big displays of how I'm feeling. To support Elisabeth's mother more, when I can barely handle my own feelings. My mother wants me to share my grief with her – you know, sobbing together and looking through childhood photographs.'

'But that's not what you need?'

'No, it isn't. I need to make my peace with it all. To forgive myself for not saving her.'

'It wasn't your job to save Elisabeth, Kristina.'

I nod, but my throat is constricted by a painful lump. I allow myself a few long moments to breathe through these feelings and feel grateful for Vera's soothing presence.

'I just keep wondering if it could have been different.'

'It sounds as though a lot is on your mind at the moment, both in your personal life and with your clients.'

'Yes.'

'Do you feel confident that you have the tools to process it?'

'I think so. I'm conscious of maintaining my boundaries with my mother. I'm allowing all the stages of grief over Elisabeth and trying to not become stuck in thought patterns. But I see her everywhere, you know? The other night… I was looking at this woman at a party, and it was as though her face briefly became Elisabeth's and it just hit me so hard. And Leah… I think Leah reminds me of her. Last week, there was something so raw and desperate about her, and something about the intensity of her need. I lived with Elisabeth's need for so long. And then, discovering Leah's pregnancy, it just really threw me and triggered my feelings about motherhood. I am going to work on not allowing my feelings to impact my support of Leah; it's crucial that no part of me would judge her for her choices.'

'That sounds very reasonable.' We sit in silence for a while, the softly lit, warm room like a cocoon, and I want it to be Vera who speaks first. 'Kristina, I've been meaning to ask,' she says eventually. 'How are you sleeping at the moment? Any more disturbing flashbacks?'

'No. Well. I've been sleeping quite well.' This is a white lie, but I don't want to get into the sleepless nights today, and besides, they're nothing new. 'I've been really busy. I have quite a few new clients and in the run-up to the elections, my husband needs a lot of support…'

'It doesn't sound like there is a lot of time for you.'

'Well. That might be a good thing. Considering the circumstances.'

'Perhaps you are avoiding thinking about or processing certain things by keeping very busy, and keeping your mind on the surface.'

'Vera. I allow myself to feel and to process.'

'Good.'

'Just. I suppose I have been confused recently. It does feel like I am having a hard time deciphering what exactly my feelings are about stuff. Sometimes I feel so angry I could smash something at the smallest provocation, like if my husband doesn't answer a text message fast enough. Other times I feel like crying, but for no reason.'

'No reason?'

'Well, you know – it seems triggered by the strangest little things. A beautiful, wilting flower. Or a disturbing dream. A song on the radio I'd forgotten, that takes me back to… to the past.'

'What kind of disturbing dreams, Kristina? I thought you said you'd been sleeping well?'

I feel irritated with myself for slipping up and bringing the conversation to my dreams because it will inevitably lead us down a path I don't want to take – not today. 'Mostly well. Occasionally not, I guess.'

'And do you think that coming to terms with what happened to Elisabeth might be bringing some of those old memories and wounds to the surface?'

'Yes. Of course,' I say softly, closing my eyes. I don't

want to go there now, I want a moment's reprieve from the thoughts that chase through my mind like a gathering storm.

'They are, of course, closely linked. I'm just wondering whether new things might appear as a result. Things that have felt intangible or lost.' I nod and look out the window. I'm buying time, trying again to dislodge the lump in my throat.

'I think I need to spend the last ten minutes discussing Natalia Martinussen. She's, uh, very overwhelmed by her family commitments and I want to develop more of a strategy in supporting her.' My voice noticeably trembles as I speak, but Vera doesn't bat an eyelid at my obvious diversion from my own personal circumstances back to my client. I muster all the control I can to discuss Natalia's course of therapy, blocking any other thoughts from entering my mind. After a few moments it becomes easier, and it feels good that I am able to control my thoughts and emotions.

But then, as I leave Vera's snug office at Holbergs Plass and walk the short distance to my own office, slowly, past the park, my control falters and I feel a wild surge of anxiety. Or grief. Or maybe it's a bad premonition, a sense of all the losses still to come, how can I know? I should feel better after supervision, but I don't. I feel unhinged, and unfit to see my first client in less than half an hour. I shut the door to my office and set the timer on my phone to five minutes. Five minutes to cry my eyes out.

9

Kristina

At home, I lean back against the front door as soon as I've shut it behind me. I still feel strangely liquid, like I might dissolve into more tears, or erupt in a rage. Up until this summer, my life was good; predictable, comfortable, stable. It hasn't been without its challenges; like everyone else I have my demons and things to deal with from my past, but in the last few years I have felt as though I am capable of navigating my life, even when it gets really tough. But now, it's as though one thing after another is coming loose from the structures I've built, tearing at the very foundations of my life. I was supposed to be a mother by now. Or pregnant at the very least. *We can't find any reason for it*, say the doctors of my inexplicable infertility. No reason. And yet, there is a reason, there always is; they just can't find it.

And then there's Elisabeth. The way she keeps appearing in my mind constantly, in the face of the crown princess or random women on the street, or even in my own blurred reflection in a shop window as I rush past through the seemingly endless autumn rain. There is an element of obsessive compulsion to these appearances, like my mind is running on a loop and whatever it is I'm actually looking at, it morphs into Elisabeth. I may consider discreetly seeking out some cognitive behavioral therapy from a trusted colleague to address it. But CBT isn't going to change the fact that I will never see Elisabeth again, that I failed her, and I can't bear it.

I walk aimlessly through the dark, hushed apartment. I can't remember where Eirik is or what his excuse was for missing dinner today. I stare at the closed door of the larger of the guest bedrooms, the room in which Elisabeth took her very last breath.

I move my gaze to the second spare bedroom, the one with the lovely outlook into the interior courtyard of our building, with its barbecue spots and sweet little playground. The room we intended for our child. I push the door open and stand for a long while in the sparse, cool space and watch the wind tear at the tarpaulin covering the summer garden furniture three floors below. Raindrops rush down the windowpane and I follow a couple with my fingertips, making myself breathe deeply. *It's just a hard day, Kristina*, I tell myself. This was something my first therapist taught me, back when I had mostly hard days. It doesn't mean that tomorrow, or the next day, or the one after will be hard. *It's just one hard day.*

I shut the door behind me and wander aimlessly into the kitchen. It's five thirty and I suppose I could pour a glass of wine, but it's only Tuesday and I feel a little guilty if I drink during the week, especially if I'm by myself. I consider a coffee but my sleep is broken enough as it is. I settle for a glass of water but pour it out after a couple of sips. I go through to the living room and switch on all the little lamps on each of the three windowsills, casting the big room in a lovely golden glow. I sit on the sofa and pick up an interiors magazine from the pile I haven't gotten to yet. *Elle Interiors*, from April. I'm about to start reading when I realize that I am absentmindedly staring at one of Elisabeth's paintings hung in the next room behind the dining table, visible from where I'm sitting. I look around, and there are another two smaller pieces in this room. And in the spare room, the last room Elisabeth ever saw, there's another. I get up. They have to go. How can I move forward if I'm constantly reminded of the past?

I swiftly unhook the two smaller ones from the wall in this room and leave them face-down on the floor. Then I go through to the next room and run a finger lightly across the largest canvas, which is almost the entire length of the dining table. To think that Elisabeth guided the brush along exactly this same spot just a few months ago is impossible to believe – in a way it's as though she hasn't been alive for many years. It feels as though I lost her that night so many years ago, the darkest of nights, the same night parts of myself were lost, too. With time, those lost and wounded parts began to take on disturbing shadows in the depths of my mind. Though patches of my memory were erased, I could still feel, and the shadows of that night would come back with the force of earthquakes, and with as little warning, shaking me to the core. What had once been one – one girl, one life, one mind – splintered into various broken narratives and personas and coping mechanisms, and it took years to begin to reintegrate those pieces back into a kind of whole. It was intense therapy, followed by my own psychology studies and finally, a doctorate in trauma psychotherapy that brought me to a relative peace with the past. Like Jung said, *I am not what happened to me, I am what I choose to become.*

Just look at me, I think to myself. *How far I've come.* I allow my thoughts to revisit the young woman I was, when I myself first came to therapy. After all these years, the image still packs an emotional punch. I went to therapy against my will at the insistence of my parents. My attitude at the time was that it was a formality before a certain death. A waiting room for the determinedly suicidal. I was skinny and traumatized, my mind and emotions dulled with drugs from my stay at Vinderen psychiatric hospital. I'd spent two months in a residential mental health care program, where the doctors were more interested in medicating away my symptoms than attempting to understand their origins. One day I was unceremoniously released to my bewildered, anxious parents, with the promise that I 'no longer posed a risk to myself'.

But I did. Of course I did. I didn't have a single tool to deal with the images in my head, or the terrifying blank patches, and I've yet to see the pill that can erase the past.

At their wits' end, my parents sent me to a psychotherapist, a woman named Ingvild. I still remember the exact moment I opened the door to her office, which was in the basement of a villa in a residential, leafy street in Bekkestua, watching my mother drive off. I was twenty years old and ready to die. Inside stood Ingvild, a small, slim woman with soft blonde curls, whose presence seemed huge and radiant in the little room in spite of her slight stature. I don't remember what she said, nor what I said in that first session and in the many that followed. But I felt seen, and as though even the very darkest parts of me could be brought out into the light without judgment. Ingvild met me with unwavering empathy and an unconditional presence I had never known before. It was her constancy that became her legacy, and one I always aim to channel into my relationships with my own clients.

Ingvild liked to work with colors in her therapeutic approach and sometimes asked me to describe or draw the colors of my feelings and memories. Back then, when it felt as though I had neither feelings nor memories, only a terrifying void inside, I did manage to ascribe colors to the storms in my mind, and they were invariably the waxy dark greens of forests, and the vivid rich hues of blood, both fresh and dried. I used to pray for a milky white nothingness, the pure, unbroken color of death, silence and release.

I'd tell her I wanted to die and unlike my parents, who'd burst into tears or shame me for being broken, making it all about themselves and their own fears and their expectations of me, Ingvild would listen, unafraid. She'd speak about the lack of language for pain this intense, and how people often say they want to die when what they mean is that they can't live with such torment. I'd insist that it was death I wanted. I couldn't bear to be around Elisabeth, either – I knew that the haunted look in her eyes was mirrored in my own. Ingvild would ask me what the alternative to death might look like, and I said that returning to my old life just wasn't possible. *I wonder whether there could be a middle ground*, she'd say, *not death, and not your old life. A new normal. A life worth living, now.*

I look around my home and realize that I have really made a life worth living, now. I have a home, a stable marriage, purpose. But I don't have Elisabeth and I can't shake off the self-hatred I feel for what I did and didn't do for her. Her life is a closed chapter and she will never find a life worth living, now. The only solace she found was in hard drugs and in her art, and in me, and she was equally devoted to all three, though none of them could save her.

I unhook the huge painting from its mooring on the wall but underestimate its heaviness and it comes crashing to the floor, one sharp corner landing on my bare foot. I scream, so loud I'm sure the neighbors could hear it. The cry of pain just becomes crying and as if I have no control over myself, I grab a bronze candelabra from the table and smash it full force into the painting, effortlessly ripping the canvas. Elisabeth's hypnotic swirls of emerald green and burgundy reds burst open and are swallowed up by great, jagged rips. When there is nothing left of it except the edges that are stapled to the wooden framework, I gather up the strips and chunks of limp canvas that once held the imagery of Elisabeth's inner world and place them into the glass-walled fireplace. I place a couple of logs on top, one wrapped in newspaper, then set it alight. I stand in the middle of the room for a long while, listening to the crackle and hiss of the flames, breathing in the chemical smell of burning paint, practicing a deep, slow breathing pattern to calm my nerves.

When the canvas has entirely been engulfed by the flames, I walk slowly back through the big room to the kitchen, mindful of my bruised foot, the flames still dancing on my retina. I pour a glass of wine from a carton in the fridge and drink it straight down standing at the window, looking across the rooftops at the black bones of trees in the royal park. I hear Eirik's key in the lock. I realize I don't know what time it is or even whether I have had dinner. It feels as though I've just woken up from a nightmare – those stunned, spent moments of blinking in the dark, grateful to emerge into a world more peaceful than the one you just left behind. I move quickly now, and step into my husband's arms as he walks through the door and he lets out a little sound of surprise at this onslaught of affection, but he holds me tight and smooths down my hair at the back of my skull firmly and soothingly, the way you'd stroke a beloved, sleepy dog.

'What's going on?' asks Eirik, finally breaking our embrace and kicking his shoes off. I take his camel jacket and hang it in the cupboard, brushing off a few stray droplets of rain. My husband's face is creased and pale in the low light of the hallway, and he rubs at his eyes and massages his temples.

'I burned Elisabeth's painting,' I say. 'The one in the dining room.'

Eirik stares at me. 'What? Why?'

'I couldn't bear to look at it for another moment.'

'But... I thought you loved that painting?'

'No.'

'Perhaps it would have been a good idea to donate it to her mother? Or to Villa Vinternatt?'

'It was its very existence I couldn't bear. I wanted it gone. It fucked with my head.'

Eirik looks at me carefully, his eyebrows knitting together over the bridge of his nose. 'Kristina. This sounds a little odd.'

'I know. I just thought you should know. There's some, uh, debris in the dining room. I'll clear it up.'

'Look. I know things are still quite raw. And that work is stressful. You've got quite a few new clients at the moment, right? But right now, up until the end of November, we just have to keep it together. I *need* you to keep it together. This is the most important time of our lives. We can't let anything get in the way of this. Think about how hard we've worked, how much we've both sacrificed to get here. Less than a month to go. You have to let go, Kristina. Let it go. You did everything you could possibly have done, you—'

'No. I... I see her everywhere, it's like she's haunting me, she's even in my own goddamn reflection in the mirror, and it's all my fault—'

'Don't you ever say that. It wasn't your fault. None of it was your fault.' Eirik takes both of my hands in his and kisses the top of each tightly clenched fist. He pulls me close to him and raises my chin with his fingertips so I'm forced to look him in the eyes.

'This is not the time for allowing irrational behavior or bad thoughts. I can't afford you falling to pieces now, Kristina. This is the time for focus and graft and control. Okay?'

I nod, but I know more about bad thoughts and the shadowy recesses of the mind than my husband ever will. I nod again, more firmly, and take a deep breath through my nostrils. This is a time for control. *I am not what happened to me, but what I choose to become.*

10

Leah, two weeks before

It's the doorbell that wakes her. It's been one of those rare nights when she just fell asleep, without tears, without rumination, without fear. Her hand instinctively goes to the rounded bump on her lower stomach, as if to reassure herself this pregnancy wasn't just a dream.

She sits up in bed, drawing the cool air of the bedroom deeply into her lungs. It is completely dark and she can't even make out the outline of the door leading to the living room. Outside, the wind rattles down the street, carrying little bits of trash and tearing the last leaves from the trees. She checks her phone, but there are no new messages. She messaged him earlier in the evening, begging. *Please come*, she said. *Please, please, please. I need you.* He didn't respond, as usual. But he's here now, downstairs, on the street, ringing her doorbell.

The doorbell rings again, filling the hushed apartment with its shrill sound, and Leah moves swiftly from the bed, through the living room, to the door.

II

Kristina, three days later

It's Friday, and I'm feeling much better than earlier in the week. I've mentally reclaimed the driver's seat and will not allow myself to become overwhelmed or terrorized by irrational thoughts. I've committed to taking care of myself this week and feel refreshed. I haven't drunk anything since Tuesday, I've caught up on all my client notes, and Eirik and I have managed a couple of simple but cozy dinners together. All the stress around Elisabeth was triggered by the strange episode with Leah Iverson, but now I'm more aware of it, I'm able to place them into the compartments where they belong in my mind. Elisabeth: tragic, but gone. Eirik is absolutely right, I have to let it go now. And I did what I could. Then there is Leah – a client for whom I hold much hope, and I need to remain committed and focused on supporting her, not letting her behavior or circumstances trigger my own personal reactions.

Arriving at the office, I'm looking forward to the day ahead. I only have three clients today as one called in sick. A fairly new client named Marisa, who struggles with debilitating anxiety and apologizes constantly for absolutely everything, at eleven thirty. Then Leah at two, followed by Siri Engevik, who feels trapped in a bad marriage, but is very obviously herself a wounded woman with a difficult character.

It isn't difficult to access feelings of empathy for Marisa and I listen intently as she painstakingly recounts how she feels like her family take her for granted and don't care about her frazzled nerves. *They don't even ask why my hands are bleeding from the constant handwashing, or why I count under my breath or why I sometimes burst into tears when I'm cleaning.*

When she leaves, I pop down to the coffee shop for a sandwich and a freshly squeezed orange juice, like I sometimes do on a Friday as I have a big gap between Marisa and Leah. When I think about the fact that in just over an hour, Leah will be sitting across from me again, I feel the flutter of trepidation in my gut. Was last week just a dramatic lapse in her emotional well-being, or will she turn up even more unhinged today? I know I will look for signs of pregnancy in her, but I've steeled myself now, and done my work – I know that Leah being pregnant doesn't mean I won't also get pregnant. I just needed to reason with myself. I wonder whether she will tell me or simply never mention it and get rid of the baby. I swallow hard at the thought of Leah's baby, snug and tiny inside the shell of her womb, becoming.

Back in the office I relight the votive candles on the windowsill, still liquid from Marisa's session, and replenish the tea supply. I place each tea bag equidistant from the next on the tray, organized by color. It's incredible how soothing these tiny details can be, and performing them makes me feel like I'm realigning my internal order. Leah usually chooses green tea with lemon, and leaves the teabag in the mug until she's finished, the swollen bag nudging at the tip of her nose for the last few sips. She drinks slowly, unlike some clients who gulp it down and then fuss about with the kettle on the table between us, trying to make another while keeping our conversation going over the screech of the gathering steam.

I make a concerted effort to be very still and very deliberate with my clients. Predictability and transparency is what I try to convey. They will always find the same teas, arranged in precisely the same way. They will always see me drinking plain water, nothing else. I also try to wear minor variations of the same outfits and keep my hair in the same style, swept back in a high ponytail with lightly curled ends. Pretty but professional. I'm the mirror, not the person looking into it, which is where focus needs to lie.

I scroll on my phone for a while, counting down to two o'clock. Instagram offers nothing new, only the usual wistful autumnal posts of children playing in leaves and choosing pumpkins to carve, and typical Norwegian gleeful couple selfies amid stark, rain-lashed mountains. *VG* and *Dagbladet*'s headlines are the usual underwhelming small, peaceful nation ones: *Man Fled Bear in Trøndelag, Real Estate Up 5 % in Oslo, The Five Things You MUST Do to Prepare Your Cabin for Winter.*

I go to the bathroom and reapply my mascara and undereye concealer, and return to the office to pour some fresh water into my glass before Leah arrives. Except she doesn't. The clock strikes 2 p.m., then five past, ten past... I remember last week and how she arrived late, but the minutes tick by and still she doesn't arrive. At two fifteen

I call her, but her phone goes straight to voicemail. I try again with the same result. I also send her a text message asking her to please get in touch. Could it be that Leah has ghosted me? It has happened before, that a client has suddenly terminated a course of ongoing psychotherapy for whatever reason, and not bothered to tell me until weeks later, perhaps feeling guilty or awkward about explaining why. I wouldn't have thought it of Leah – she has always been vocal about the profound effect therapy has had on her life. That said, she has been showing more resistance in recent months and has more aggressively pursued my personal opinion and advice than previously. It could be that she has chosen to go elsewhere if she hasn't felt that she is getting what she needs from my methods. *I need to know what your personal feelings are about this*, I recall her saying to me relatively recently, referring to some situation with whomever she was dating, and I deflected by saying that I found it interesting that she places more weight on my opinion than on how she actually feels about the situation. Could she have grown frustrated with my methods and decided to just stop our sessions? But last week, she insisted she needed to speak to me about something outside this space even though she knows that isn't possible.

I go through all my email folders to make sure I can't possibly have missed a message from her, but there's nothing. I check on 1881.no that her phone number or address haven't changed, but they remain the same. I make a mental note to get back in touch with Dr Albert to see whether he has heard from her. I spend fifteen minutes talking to my colleague, Alice, in the communal kitchen, who is also between clients.

'Sounds like ghosting,' she says, frowning into her milky tea.

'I just don't think she would do that,' I say.

'I never did, either. But then it's often the ones you expect more from who do.'

'Hmmm. Should I call her next of kin or something?'

'No. Kristina, it's not part of your job description. You're the receptacle, not the detective.'

'I know, but—'

'No buts. Okay, back to work, it's almost three. Drinks later?'

'Possibly.'

'It happens again and again,' says Siri Engevik, a middle-aged woman with a deep frown, looking at me from behind thick turquoise glasses. 'He promises he'll change, but he never does. He doesn't even particularly bother to hide the evidence anymore. The other day, a woman called several times when we were having another one of those godawful, silent dinners in an old-fashioned steak restaurant. You know the kind. Unheated plates. Rodeo-style interiors. Laminated menus. Why won't he take me to sushi? I want to go to one of those fancy Asian places in Tjuvholmen. I bet that's the kind of place where you go. With your husband.' She gives me a little wink to let me know she knows very well who my husband is, a tiny triumph.

'Siri, you were saying that a woman rang repeatedly?'

'Yes, his phone was on the table. It kept lighting up and vibrating. Knut glanced at it and I could see the name

"Amanda" flashing across the table. I asked who Amanda is and he just shrugged and kept chewing. I swear, the way he eats drives me crazy. It's like he shovels the food into his big wet mouth and sends it around in circles in there. I wanted to walk out. I really did.'

I glance at the time. Twenty past three. Siri Engevik has been coming for around a year and is quite a demanding client; she becomes easily frustrated with the necessary limitations of the therapeutic relationship and can become agitated if I cut her off to say our time's up, or if I decline to answer a personal question. She frequently finishes her musings with *Don't you think?* and though I point out that what I think isn't necessarily the point, she'll keep pushing and say – *But what do you think? What's your opinion? You must have an opinion.*

'Why didn't you?' I ask, gently.

'Why didn't I what?'

'Walk out. You said you wanted to walk out. And that you feel disrespected by your husband.'

'Well, yes. How would you feel if your husband sat at the dinner table taking calls from another woman, some old bitch called Amanda. Tell me, Dr Moss, how would that make you feel?'

'Siri. Let's focus on how it makes *you* feel. I sense a lot of anger here.'

'Well, wouldn't *you* be angry?'

'I think anger would be a very natural response to the situation you're describing.'

'It's pathetic, though. Getting so angry over little things.'

'Little things?'

'The way he chews. Amanda. His silence. He never asks

me a single question. It's because he doesn't care about the answers. He doesn't care about me. He…' Siri begins to cry softly and I discreetly push the box of tissues closer to her. She doesn't take one, but wipes at her tears with the sleeve of her chunky-knit purple mohair sweater.

'Those things don't sound like little things to me.'

Siri stares at me, then nods, sending more tears streaming down her face. I feel her pain acutely in this moment, and can't help but think how much pain there is in most relationships, layer upon layer of it, even in those relations that on the surface seem harmonious and healthy. A slightly insensitive comment. A rebuff in bed. The silences between partners when there's nothing more to say. Little lies that become big lies.

'So what do you think I should be feeling right now?'

'Only you can answer that.'

'But I don't know. It can't be normal to never know how you're feeling?'

'Not knowing what you feel is a feeling, too, isn't it?'

'Hmm.' She stares out the window for a while and I follow her gaze, watching the brief, gray day fade into a deep, blue afternoon. 'Do you think it's ever okay to stay in a marriage when you're both unhappy?'

'I think every marriage is different and that only the two people in it can know what is right for them.'

'I think I need you to advise me here, Dr Moss. I want to know what the recommended course of action is for this sort of thing.'

'Siri. You know that isn't my role. And I don't think there is a recommended course of action.'

'We've been to couples' therapy before, and that therapist

was quite clear about what the various options were. But you... You won't ever say.'

'My role is to be here for you and to help you understand how you feel, not tell you what to do.'

'We have a house together. A house full of things. A grown-up son. A cabin. An apartment in Antibes. I can't just walk away, I'm trapped—'

'Siri. We are going to have to continue next week.'

'What?' Siri stares at me with a blank expression, as though I were behind a one-way mirror and she only now realized that I'm here.

'Our time is up, I'm afraid.'

She takes me in with an expression of mild disdain, then nods absentmindedly. 'Oh. Right.' She stands up abruptly, gathering her rose-patterned billowing scarf and padded purple velour jacket and pauses at the door for a moment as though there was one more thing she needed to say. I do sometimes wonder what she gets out of these sessions, she seems so in opposition to the therapy structure and the way I work. I make a mental note to ask her about this next time; maybe we should consider referring her on to a colleague with whom she has more personal chemistry. My Fridays are going to be wide open at this rate, if Leah has ghosted me and Siri were to see someone else.

I stand up and walk over to the window. The gloomy morning has given way to a beautiful afternoon with indigo skies streaked by pink gauzy clouds, and I wish I could sit by the sea, looking out over its calm surface, releasing all the nervous energy I feel pulsating beneath my skin. I have the strange sensation that if I were to slice my skin open, tension would flow out of me in thick, black bursts, like tar.

I think about what Siri said, about feeling trapped in a life you don't want, no matter how privileged you might be. I can't imagine a situation in which Eirik and I stayed married merely because we owned property and possessions together, a life in which we'd eat in silence, where we'd stopped caring about each other, or where he'd be courting other women, not even bothering to hide it. I feel a sharp bolt of anger and fear at the thought, followed by gratitude for the things in my life that are good.

I go back to my desk and check my phone and emails. Nothing from Leah, no explanation. It's the start of another weekend, and she'll be on my mind until I know what is going on with her. I go into my contacts list and select 'Leah Iverson', and click on 'next of kin'. Listed is her mother, Linda Iverson, with a Swedish number.

Hi Linda,

I was wondering whether you are in touch with Leah. She's missed a session with me which is unusual for her. I'm concerned for her well-being and wanted to make sure she is okay.

Best wishes, Dr Kristina Moss.

I've barely put the phone back down on my desk when it vibrates. It's Leah's mother.

She's fine. I've spoken to her. Thanks, L.

I sit down and open my client notes. I select Leah's file

and enter 'no show' under today's date. I scroll back up through my own notes from the last few weeks to make sure I haven't overlooked anything of importance, but there's nothing. I still can't quite believe she didn't come today. I feel a pang of sadness at the thought of how unfinished our course of therapy feels. I really believed I could help Leah, and that our bond was strong and transformational, similar to my own bond with Ingvild, when I first came to therapy and found that it had the power to change lives.

Leah is one of those clients I always look forward to seeing, and it's because she's eager to grow, she really wants to learn about herself. She believes in trying to become whole. *Like you,* she'll say. It seems to me like she believed in this possible wholeness all along, that she trusts in therapy, unlike some clients, who resist every step of the way. They question everything, applying their own limited understanding of amateur psychology based on having read one self-help book to everything I say. *Oh, so you are referring to reparenting*, they might randomly ask. *Or, yeah, this is definitely an ego response to underlying rejection issues.* Frankly, it's annoying.

Leah's different. She listens as much as she speaks. She feels the spaces between us and seems to understand the unconditional trust I've tried to build there.

I shut the computer down and make sure everything in the office is in its right place. I feel a need to get out of here so strong it's physical, so I blow out the candle on the windowsill, put my winter jacket on, then shut the door behind me.

12

Kristina

I go the same way as I always do on a Friday afternoon, but today my steps feel leaden, and I know deep down I'm going to turn around before I even get halfway up Bogstadveien, which is busy with schoolkids and those taking an early weekend milling in and out of the shops. Still, I proceed to Rosenborggata, where I turn right. I walk all the way up to the white, immaculately kept turn-of-the-century apartment building and slide my finger down the familiar row of buzzers until it settles on the right one. It wouldn't be so bad to go up. I would be met with nothing but kindness. But it's the kindness I can't bear. Something occurs to me, and I check my phone. No new messages. I open Google maps and enter Leah's address, found and memorized from my client list before I left the office. It's just seven minutes' walk away, across Theresesgate and toward Adamstuen. I glance up at the building in front of me one more time. *Not today,* I say to myself, refusing thoughts of how in this moment the tea will be brewing, the home-made cakes will be meticulously laid out on a tray; they'll be waiting for the buzzer to sound. I walk away.

I head back down Bogstadveien and past my office, and after less than ten minutes, I find myself standing in front of Leah Iverson's apartment building on Benneches Gate. Leah lives in a beautiful yellow-and-white art nouveau apartment building, and I stand for a moment on the pavement looking up at the windows, trying to guess which ones are hers. She's never really spoken to me about her apartment – whenever she speaks about home, she speaks of the apartment where she grew up with her mother, or more recently, her beloved country cabin. She always lights up when she speaks of the peace she feels there, far away from other people and the stresses of city life. I look at the names on the doorbells and find her name at the top. *L.K. Iverson* it reads, and I rest my finger on it for a moment. Without thinking, I press the buzzer down for a long moment and imagine it ringing shrilly in Leah's apartment. Will she be angry with me for coming here? Experience tells me she's more likely to be moved; clients tend to crave feeling important and cared for by the therapist.

Leah has often asked me whether I really care about her, or if I only pretend because I get paid. A lot of clients ask me similar questions and it is one of the more difficult things to address when it comes to therapy – how can they truly trust that I care about their well-being and mental health when we both know I am also there because I am paid? But I care, deeply, about all of my clients. It was something I occasionally worried about during my training, whether I would encounter clients for whom it was impossible to feel empathy and connection. To this day, it's never happened – every single person I have met throughout my years in therapeutic practice has turned out to be fundamentally worthy of empathy.

I press the doorbell again and imagine Leah rising from the sofa and padding across dark hardwood floors to the door on bare feet. I have a feeling she isn't here. But what if she is, only she's hurt herself? Despite Linda's reassuring text, I can't shake off the feeling that something serious is going on with Leah. I feel my stomach sink at the random thought of Leah in her home, thinking about ending her own life, perhaps several days ago. How lonely would those last hours have been; how desperate would she have felt? Still, I don't believe she would take her own life. I press the buzzer again, for longer this time.

Come on, Leah. I care about you. It's why I'm here.

This is about the truth. Those were some of her last words to me. What could she have meant by this? Over the years Leah sat opposite me every Friday afternoon, I became privy to many of her truths. As we began to explore her inner world and she developed the awareness to make increasing sense of it, we discussed conditioning and how the things we are told about ourselves aren't necessarily true.

During her marriage to Anton, Leah was conditioned to believe she was worthless and disgusting, that nobody else would ever want her and that she deserved to be punished. It took us years to begin to untangle these beliefs, in part because it became clear that she'd held them even before her marriage, perhaps results of bullying as a young child and her father's departure. Could this be the misconceived 'truth' she was referring to? Or could it be her pregnancy? Or was she referring to some other truth? I've wondered, sometimes, whether the truth itself had felt central to Leah's suffering, that by writing about it so brutally honestly in *Nobody*, she was left feeling exposed and vulnerable.

'Hello?' says a man's voice, making me jump. I'd been lost in thoughts, momentarily forgetting I'd pressed Leah's buzzer.

'Uh, hello,' I say. 'Who is this?' I feel suddenly deeply embarrassed, turning up on Leah's doorstep when she is probably just cooped up with a new boyfriend, the father of her child. But... Friday. She was hurt. Someone hurt her. There is a long pause.

'Who's asking?'

'My name is Kristina Moss. I'm...'

There is a long pause, and when the man speaks again, his voice is cool.

'I know who you are.' The buzzer sounds and I glance down the street as though someone might appear who could tell me what to do, but there is nobody around, so I push open the door and step inside.

13

Leah, two weeks before

I'm not supposed to be here, he says.

No, says Leah. *And yet. Here you are.*

I can't stay away from you.

Good.

What is this going to cost us? He whispers, tracing light shapes with his fingertips down her bare chest, across her stomach, its swelling barely noticeable, then further down, and draws her even closer, pressing her face into his broad, warm chest. She looks up, makes him meet her eyes.

It's okay, her eyes say.

I miss this so much, he says.

I've missed this my whole life, she thinks. She's tired, but doesn't want to sleep, she wants to be held, to lie here all night just being held, feeling him fill the apartment, the spaces inside her, the night itself. She hadn't seen this coming, this deep and easy feeling of coming home.

14

Kristina

I step into a vast foyer lit by a huge industrial-style wrought-iron lamp. I hear a door unlock higher up in the building and take the stairs slowly, trying to make sense of my racing thoughts. Am I about to come face to face with Leah? Who is the man, and why did he instantly recognize my name? I assume she has met someone fairly recently, and for some reason, didn't want to discuss the relationship with me. But wouldn't Leah have told me? She tells me everything. Or so I thought.

It seems surreal that I am here, climbing the stairs to Leah's apartment. Her apartment is all the way at the top, and the door has been left ajar. To the side of the door is a small bronze doorbell reading 'Iverson', and I imagine her choosing it in a little shop, writing her name down on a scrap of paper, to be engraved.

'Hello?' I say, stepping into a narrow hallway. A man emerges from a room to the right. He looks young, almost like a high school student, and is dressed in navy sweatpants and a hooded sweater with a giant red Ralph Lauren Polo logo. He's a good-looking guy, with dark-blonde hair and light-blue, striking eyes. He looks tired and his clothes are crumpled, as though he was sleeping on a sofa and has just woken up.

'Hi,' he says, stepping forward to shake my hand. His grip is firm, and his hand is cool and dry. 'Anton.'

I can't help a sharp intake of breath at the shock of coming face to face with Anton here, in Leah's apartment. Her ex-husband is an abusive man and Leah had to take out several restraining orders against him. I fight the urge to flee from the apartment, but I need to see Leah and make sure she's okay.

'Hi,' I say. 'I'm Kristina Moss.'

'I know. She talks about you. A lot.'

'She talks about you a lot, too,' I say, my voice trembling with anger, but also fear. I have to tread carefully here. Anton slowly raises an eyebrow and scrutinizes me as though committing me to memory. His jaw clenches.

'Is Leah here?' I ask.

'No, she's not.'

'Do you know where she is?'

Anton releases a sharp little breath, as if to suggest that my presence here asking questions is completely incredulous. 'Why should I tell you?'

'Look, Leah and I have worked together for several years. I have been under the impression that it's been helpful for her, and I want to make sure that she's okay. She didn't turn up for a scheduled session with me this afternoon, and it's left me concerned for her well-being.'

'She's fine.'

'Have you spoken to her?'

'I saw her a couple of days ago.'

'Wait, how?'

'She's at her cabin working on her next book and I went there to see her.'

'I'm sorry, I don't... I find it hard to believe that she's at her cabin and working and that she would have invited you there.'

'She didn't invite me. I went there to check on her as I felt concerned too. She didn't respond to my messages or calls and I felt like I had to see her to...' Anton trails off and I stare at him hard, refusing to break his gaze. I don't believe him.

'I've been trying to call and email her and I feel that it is out of character for her not to respond.'

'There is no reception up there. It's really remote.'

'What was her state of mind when you saw her?'

'She was fine. Focused on the book.'

'Fine?'

'Yeah.'

'I find it hard to believe she was fine. She was extremely distressed when I saw her last Friday. She was also hurt. I'm assuming you might have played a part in that?'

Anton drops his gaze to the ground in the way of the guilty. 'No.'

'May I ask what you're doing here?'

'What *I'm* doing here?'

'Yes.'

'Firstly, I'm not sure how I see that is any of your business. Secondly, I'm in a relationship with Leah.'

A little incredulous laugh escapes me – the sheer nerve

of this man, speaking as though Leah still wanted him. *I would have died if I hadn't escaped from him*, she's said, many times. But what if she's died because she did escape? I swallow hard. He's hurt her, I know it. She must have met someone new and gotten pregnant, and Anton must have found out and tracked her down. I stare at him, more furious than frightened now, and try to determine whether this man could be capable of hurting a pregnant woman.

'I don't believe you.'

'Look, Dr Moss,' he says in a mocking tone, 'I know what a quack you are. Your so-called therapy has done exactly fucking nothing for Leah. The thing that has helped Leah get to a better place in the last few months has been returning to me. To allow herself to be loved fully.'

I'm stunned by his claim. Could it be true that she's gone back to him? It would explain why she hasn't mentioned the pregnancy if she has rekindled something with Anton, after years of sharing her experiences of a very turbulent past with this man. After writing a bestseller about the abuse he subjected her to. How could she have gone back? I feel irrationally angry.

'I don't believe you. Where is she?' I try to look past him and into the apartment, but he's a big guy and he's blocking the doorway.

'I've got to say you've got some nerve, Dr Moss, coming here and accusing me of lying when you clearly don't know a thing.'

'I know what she told me. I know that she was afraid of you. She used to lie awake at night, worrying about you discovering where she lives. And you're standing here saying you are back together and that she is at her cabin, but not responding to calls or emails. How am I supposed to believe that when I know that she had to get a restraining order against you?'

'A restraining order against me?' Anton laughs, and looks genuinely surprised. 'Wait, Leah even lies to her therapist?'

15

Leah, two weeks before

For once, the loneliness she fears and writes about and lives by and even courts, dissipates. He's here. He came back again. Every time, he says this is the last time, it has to be. He holds her, for hours. She curls into him, like a mollusk into its shell.

We need to talk, he says.

I need you to hold me, she says, so he does.

We need to talk, he says, again, later.

No, she says, *not yet*. She places his hand on her left breast so he can hear the thud of her heart and turns around to look into his eyes. He can't resist her like that, he has said that himself many times. She takes his other hand and guides it down, down, and he moans softly when his fingers touch upon her wetness. She's quick to press her lips to his and prize his mouth open with the playful tip of her tongue. He sighs but doesn't, or can't, resist her. He sighs deeper as she gets on top and lowers herself down onto him, rocking back and forth, her tongue probing his mouth, his hands buried in the thick tangle of her hair. She stops, pulls back, looks into his eyes. His mouth is still open as though he hasn't realized the kiss has ended, and she leans back in, closes it with her own.

She gets on all fours, he's behind her, one hand clutching her hip for balance, the other in her hair again, he likes that, and he's gathered it into a thick, glossy rope.

Pull it, she says, and he does. *Harder*, she says. So he does. *I want you to hurt me.* So he does.

I want you to love me, she thinks. But he doesn't.

When she wakes, she's alone. There are bruises on the insides of her thighs, on her arms, along her collarbone, on her wrists, where he pinned her down. A tuft of dark hair he tugged from her scalp is left on the pillow. Her trachea hurts where he squeezed it, and though he didn't actually want to do it, he did it when she insisted.

She gets out of bed and steps under the hissing jet of a hot shower. She turns her face into the rushing water, and rubs the night off her skin with gentle soapy fingers, taking care where it is raised and blue. She allows tears to flow and doesn't get back out until they stop.

She stands a long while in front of the mirror, noticing how the baby has grown since she last did this. She touches her lower belly, gently cradling the tiny, taut bump. The thought of someone hurting the person inside like she herself has been hurt, makes her heart race and her mind run blank with dread.

I love you, she thinks to herself, but has to avert her eyes at the intensity of her own gaze. She knows it's time, now, to do something about the situation.

16

Kristina

'Look. I'm sorry if we got off on the wrong foot. I would appreciate it if perhaps we could talk some more,' I suggest, gauging Anton's reaction – I have to get to the bottom of what's going on here and to do that I need to diffuse the atmosphere between us. I need to make him trust me. He seems agitated below the surface, nervous energy running through him like a frothy river about to break its banks. I don't believe a word he says. 'It seems like there has been a big misunderstanding.'

'Clearly.'

'Why do you think Leah would have told me that she was afraid of you if it weren't true?'

'We have had a difficult relationship in the past. But we love each other. I love her and would do anything for her, I'd fight for her, I'd...' He breaks off and rubs hard at his eyes and I wonder – *would you kill her?*

'I know you've hurt her in the past.'

'You clearly know nothing at all.'

'I'm Leah's therapist, as you know.'

'Yes, well, she clearly lied to you. Like she's lied to everybody. Her life, and her career, all of it, is based on a lie.'

'So, you're saying you never hurt her and she didn't have a restraining order against you?'

'Yes.'

He appears genuine, and despite instinctively not believing him, I can't disregard the possibility that Leah really has gone back to him; abuse victims so often do, over and over, reenacting the only pattern they know. It would explain why Leah was so distressed last Friday and why she was so insistent on wanting to tell me something. I need to change strategy and get Anton to trust me with the truth; it seems like Leah hasn't.

'You seem nervous,' I say, keeping my voice as even and calm as I can manage, trying to convey sympathy, watching his reactions carefully. 'Or upset, perhaps? Do you think you could talk me through what's happened?'

He thinks about it for a moment, then nods reluctantly and indicates a door leading off the hallway with a visibly trembling hand.

'I'll make coffee.'

I follow him through into a small, but beautifully furnished, living room. There are framed posters from Leah's travels – Zanzibar, Havana, Cadiz, Marseille – hung above a shelf on which three curious little trees are lined up. Japanese bonsai trees, I realize. There is a tidy, open-plan kitchen in the corner, with ancient-looking wooden support beams painted gray partially separating the space from the living room. I would have guessed Leah enjoyed cooking, though she's never actually mentioned it, but this is definitely the kitchen of someone who mostly eats out.

There's a beautiful little gilded writing desk by the window and I conjure her up in my mind, sitting there sipping green tea with lemon, humming to herself, writing a little, pausing to look out at the comings and goings in the street below.

I sit on the sofa while Anton makes coffee. He seems familiar with the layout of Leah's apartment and effortlessly locates the coffee pods and the sugar in the cupboards, placing them on a little lacquered tray. He pours milk into a jug and I wonder whether Leah bought it, or if Anton did. Has he hurt her and is he posing as the concerned boyfriend, staying at her apartment and pretending to wait for the woman he claims to love to come home? It wouldn't be the first time a violent, jealous man has done something like that. I feel a dull ache in the pit of my stomach. It's that breathless sensation that follows a punch, before the pain fully sets in.

'When did you last see Leah?' I ask as Anton sits down across from me.

'I told you. A few days ago. Uh, Saturday.'

'When did you see her before then?'

'On Friday morning last week.'

'You were with her on Friday morning?'

'Yes. I stayed over and in the morning we had breakfast, then went for a walk. I left around ten thirty.'

'Right.'

'Look, I took a picture of us.' Anton pulls his phone out from his jeans pocket and scrolls down until he finds what he is looking for. He turns the screen to show me. It's a selfie of himself and Leah posing in front of a fountain I recognize as the one in St Hanshaugen park, drained for the winter season. They are both smiling and Leah is looking slightly off into the distance, as though she didn't know exactly where to look into the phone camera.

'Show me when it was taken,' I say. Anton stares hard at me, visibly annoyed, then seems to decide it's a better idea to continue the conversation. He clicks on the photo settings to show me that the photo was indeed taken last Friday, at 9.20 a.m. Leah's entire face is visible, and without doubt, completely unscathed. Just hours later, she'd turn up for our session, terrified and incoherent, the right side of her face beaten to a pulp. My hand hurts and I realize I've dug my fingernails hard into my palms. I am barely able to contain myself, because I have the terrible suspicion I could be sitting here, sipping coffee with Leah's killer. Then something else occurs to me – what if something happened between them and he attacked her, and she came to my session, disorientated and afraid, trying to tell me she was about to go to her cabin to get away from him? She would still be there, too afraid to return to Oslo, pregnant and vulnerable, trapped with her own thoughts. Leah has told me many times that it's the only place she feels safe. Only, he's gone there, and I find it hard to believe that he just went to check on her. But she could still be there, hiding from him. Waiting for me.

'What happened after this picture was taken? Anton, did you have an argument?'

He stares at me hard and again, I feel a flush of fear spread out in my stomach, there is something unnerving about his ice-blue gaze. He surprises me by nodding.

'Yes,' he whispers. 'That's why I went to the cabin. I couldn't reach her and I wanted to apologize. Which I did. I even called you. Twice, on the Sunday, days before I went there, because I didn't know where she'd gone or why she wasn't responding and I figured you'd know. I thought she told you absolutely everything.' Anton's face creases in a slight grimace, as though it is difficult to think about those days when he was unable to get hold of Leah.

'That was you? On Sunday afternoon?' I recall the two missed calls as I drove home from Camilla's – I looked the number up in the phone registry, but it was unlisted. Hours later Leah called, but said nothing – the last I've heard from her.

'Yes.'

'What was the argument about?'

'Old stuff.'

'Old stuff?'

'I'm sure you know she wrote a fucking book about me. She sold what we had together as though it were a product. Then she fucked off, saying she needed therapy to deal with all the terrible things I did to her? I didn't do terrible things to her, we did terrible things to each other at times. But none of that came out in her so-called autofiction book. Everyone just gobbled it up as truth. How do you think it felt to be cast in that light? Watching her go buy this fancy apartment, a Range Rover and a cabin, too, while I had to move back in with my parents? I even lost my fucking job. I was a radio host and my channel dropped me, saying they couldn't employ a wife-beater. How are you supposed to defend yourself against someone who is apparently being a brave survivor by telling the truth, when actually, it's all lies?

And then she came back, earlier this year, full of promises and regret, saying she still needs me, and that therapy had made her see that so much of what had happened between us went both ways. I believed her. I took her back because I love her, but still, all the while, she was lying to me. I know it. She was fucking someone else.'

'Who? What do you mean? Anton, look at me.' He won't look at me. His knuckles grow pale around the coffee mug and I picture it smashing in his hand, its shards sinking into the soft white skin of his palm, spraying me with his blood. I swallow hard. 'Who, Anton?'

'I don't know. I just know there's someone else.'

'What makes you think that?'

'I found messages from him on her phone. Someone else's cufflink behind the towel rail in the bathroom. Once, I happened to walk past and there was a man in the apartment. I could see his shadow outlined against the wall, from the street.'

'Happened to walk past.'

'Yes.' He won't meet my eyes and I feel a flash of pity for him after all. I remind myself that nobody is all bad, people can't be cast in black and white.

'Anton. That sounds very painful. It's not surprising that you're deeply hurt by this. Anton. Look at me. I need you to tell me the truth. Why would she lie about all of this?'

'She told me recently that it was to punish me. For leaving her. And that she was sorry. She feels trapped by that narrative, now. She says it's stifling and awful to have to maintain that what she wrote in *Nobody* was the truth.'

'Anton. Let me ask you this and please be honest with

me. Have you hurt Leah?' Sometimes a careful but direct question is the best approach.

'No.'

'Never?' He shakes his head curtly and clamps his lips together in a tight line, as though he might say something he doesn't want to if he opens his mouth even a little bit.

I need to extricate myself and get home and call the police. Something is very wrong here and I just can't tell what to believe. I place the coffee cup back down on the table, and focus on keeping my expression open and non-threatening. I glance around the room again, committing it to memory. I feel Anton's eyes on me and clear my throat.

'Never.'

'Okay,' I say. 'Thank you for taking the time to talk to me, and to explain your version of events. I clearly haven't had the full story. The client–therapist relationship is a very unique one. Would you please ask Leah to get in touch with me as soon as she gets home?' Anton nods. 'Did she say anything about when she'd come home?'

'She said she needed to finish something and that she'd most likely come back this weekend.'

'Okay.' I'm about to walk out the door when something occurs to me. 'Oh, hey, Anton, do you happen to know what Leah's new book is about?'

'Uh. New book?'

'The one she's working on?'

'Right. No.'

'Has she not mentioned it to you?'

'Only very briefly.'

'Okay. Thank you. Well, I'll be expecting her call.' I don't believe for a second that Leah, a celebrated author who has struggled for over a year with the process of writing her second book, wouldn't have extensively discussed this with her so-called boyfriend.

Anton nods, and fidgets with the strap of his watch, which has come loose from its leather hoop. I stare at his nimble, strong fingers and wonder if they closed around Leah Iverson's neck.

When I've left the building, I cross the street and can't resist the urge to turn back around and look at the row of windows on the fourth floor belonging to Leah's apartment, but when I do, I catch a glimpse of Anton standing there in the middle window, looking straight at me.

17

Kristina

At home, I close the door to the apartment softly, then lean against it. All the lights are off and the hallway is gloomy, deep shadows stretching across the oak floorboards. I slip my boots off, trying to steady my breathing and calm my racing heart after the brisk, cold walk home.

I walk through to the living room and sit down on the sofa – I need a few moments to center myself and sort my thoughts after the disturbing meeting with Anton. I fix my gaze on the huge canvas hung across from me on the matte charcoal wall – Eirik's favorite. It's a medley of blues and grays and looks like something my nephew might have produced at nursery, and yet, it cost more than my BMW. At least it isn't Elisabeth's – the others are all off the walls now and in the cupboard of the spare bedroom. Eirik says this one represents the storms of the mind and that the tiny slash of white toward the bottom left of the picture apparently represents hope. Sometimes I enjoy the picture and lose myself in the chaotic, hypnotic blur of its swirling brushstrokes, but I feel fundamentally annoyed at the suggestion that this image has an underlying objective meaning that should be apparent to its observer.

I follow a long, dark line running from the center of the painting toward the far-right corner and though I keep my head entirely still, I can't hold the tears back now, and I don't fight them either. I was afraid in Leah's apartment, with Anton. I have an irrational sensation of being watched, and feel the compulsion to rush through the apartment, peering into cupboards and under beds, though I know I'm alone, like I usually am. Still, the fine hairs on my arms stand up at the thought of being watched by someone I can't see, someone I couldn't expose.

If my clients could see me now, what would they think? Anxious and high-strung, unsure of what to do or what to think – nothing like the calm, soothing presence they depend on. I check my emails, but there is nothing new. I try to Google Anton, but as I don't know his last name I get nowhere. I dial the number of the Majorstuen police station. After a series of automated questions, I'm put through to an operator.

'Crime department, Silvia Espensen speaking.'

'Hi, this is Dr Kristina Moss. I'm a doctor of psychology and a practicing psychotherapist at Homansbyen Terapisenter calling about one of my clients who I believe may have come to harm.'

'Can I take a name?'

'Leah Iverson.' I spell her name out, unusual in Norway, the –on ending making her obviously Swedish.

'Why do you think something may have happened to her?'

'Well, she has missed a session with me, which is very out of character. And she was highly distressed the previous week. She has a history of mental health challenges and an abusive ex-husband.'

'Can I take the name of the ex-husband?'

'Anton.'

'Anton?'

'I don't have his last name, unfortunately. But I've met him. I went to her apartment, and he was there, alone, though she has told me repeatedly she wants nothing to do with him and was even afraid of him finding out where she lives. He says she's at her cabin in Telemark and that he saw her there himself a couple of days ago. I don't believe him. I believe he may have hurt her.'

'What makes you think that?'

'Well, she is not responding to calls or emails. When she came to see me last Friday, her face was badly bruised. She refused to say who had done it, but who is it likely to be, besides the violent ex? Even if he hasn't hurt her, he may have compromised her mental health to such an extent that her life is in danger. She is a vulnerable person with a history of suicidal ideation. Still, I just don't believe this man, or that Leah's just voluntarily disappeared for over a week. I think he's lying and that she's hurt or in real danger.'

'Do you have her address?'

'Yes, and please hurry; you might catch him. I mean, surely there must be reason to apprehend him if he's at her house and she has a restraining order against him—'

'Look. Dr…'

'Moss.'

'Dr Moss, unless the next of kin or her employer has

reported her missing, there isn't very much we can do. We might be able to send a patrol around to the address...'

'Yes, I think you need to get this Anton guy in for questioning. But you need to urgently send someone to her cabin. It's in the mountains somewhere in Telemark – I think it's near Seljord; she's given me the exact coordinates. That's where you need to look for her.'

There's a long silence on the other end.

'I'm sure you can appreciate that we can't send a police car up to some mountain in Telemark to look for someone who may not have been reported missing, but like I said, I'll look into whether we'd be able to send someone around to Iverson's registered address—'

'Hold on, I've got them here, the coordinates for the cabin. It's, uh, fifteen minutes to drive from Seljord in the direction of Notodden, and then—'

'Dr Moss, is this your contact number you're calling from?'

'Yes?'

'I'll make sure someone looks into this and gives you a call back if we have any further questions. Do you know who Iverson's next of kin is?'

'It's her mother. Her name is Linda Iverson and she lives in Årjäng, I think.'

'Thank you for calling, Dr Moss.'

'Wait. Wait just a moment, please. Look, I've already been in touch with her mother, who said she's spoken to her, but that doesn't mean Leah is safe, or well. That she didn't sound worried doesn't mean much at all in this case. I know Leah and I genuinely believe she may be in danger. Listen, Leah is a very vulnerable person. Especially now. She's fourteen weeks pregnant. I believe she could be at risk of violence, or even suicide or serious self-harm. Please. You need to make this a priority and find her, now.'

Another long pause on the other end, and a slow release of breath. 'I'll make a note of this, Dr Moss. And I'll make sure someone looks into it.'

'Thank you.'

I don't know what I expected, but I suppose I thought the police would leap into action and immediately start looking for an unaccounted-for pregnant woman with a provably violent ex. After all, how many calls like that do they get on any given Friday afternoon in this sleepy country? I'm going to have to assume that the policewoman will look Leah up and find the previous reports she made against Anton, prompting them to take real action.

I go through to the kitchen and stand at the sink and look across the rooftops toward the silvery top branches of the trees in the distance. They are the king's trees I'm looking at – we're that close to the royal palace gardens. I wish there was something for me to clean, something dirty needing my attention, so I could spend time rubbing hard at an old piece of food stuck to a plate with the coarse end of the sponge, or rinse some delicate champagne flutes, but there is nothing. All the surfaces are smooth, the gold-veined black marble glinting in the spotlights. My husband always cleans up after himself if he's made a mess or fixed a snack, leaving the scent of disinfectant lingering on the air, even though he knows our cleaner comes twice weekly. Souvenirs of his year in the military, and growing up without a mother, he says.

I need you to— said Leah, interrupting herself, before walking out. But what did she need me to do? *Please please please come*, said her note, followed by the address to her cabin.

This is about the truth. I feel queasy just hearing her words in my head. Her hand was cold and dry when it brushed briefly against mine as she handed me the envelope. Her eyes were already elsewhere, as if she had left long ago and it was just the outline of her that remained there with me in that room.

Could it be that I'm overreacting? What if my mind is running wild and that what happened to Elisabeth is coloring my concern for Leah? Anton may well be telling the truth, and Leah could be at her cabin, just working away on her next book. Perhaps he never hurt her and just went there to apologize for an argument they had, like he said. Perhaps she isn't at any risk from herself, either – after all, suicide is very rare, especially among women, even those with occasional suicidal preoccupation.

I pour some of Eirik's expensive balsamic vinegar into the sink so that there is something to clean, some reason to turn the tap on, the sound of rushing water erasing the silence of the apartment. I look up at the king's trees again and focus in on a particularly impressive one, its branches black and gnarled against the gloomy sky, but now it's like I can see Leah hanging there, close to the trunk as though her body were an extension of it, her neck bent low and at an angle, her thin limbs like drooping branches trailing toward the ground. The palms of her hands are strangely white in the gloomy violet light of the afternoon, and streaked with blood and dirt as though she's fought someone off. The rope is taut and bright blue, reaching upwards into the dense canopy of the fir tree, swaying softly in the gathering wind. I turn away from the window and wipe my wet hands on my jeans, breathing slowly to still my heart.

'Kristina,' says a voice and I jump out of my skin, my heart shuddering in my chest. I spin around and Eirik is standing there, wearing black boxer shorts and a gray T-shirt I don't remember seeing before.

'What...' I start, but my voice breaks and trails off. It's just after five o'clock on a Friday – Eirik rarely comes home before seven, even on a Friday. 'Are you sick?' He does look pale – his face is drawn and deep-blue circles bruise the skin around his eyes.

'No,' he says, whispering into my hair. 'I wanted to come home early to spend some time with you. I feel like I haven't seen you in ages.' I still don't feel quite like myself. I'm aware that I'm trembling and Eirik takes another step forward before enveloping me in a close hug. I close my eyes and let myself be held by him. He smells like soap and wood smoke and fresh rain.

'Have you been out running?'

'Not since yesterday.'

I nod. I open my mouth to speak, to maybe to tell him about Leah, and Anton, but no words will come, only tears, and a flicker of alarm crosses Eirik's face. 'What's the matter, honey?'

'Tough few days at work,' I say, my eyes dropping from his pale face to the floor, and I try to stave off the images of Leah hanging, but it doesn't work – it is as though she has been etched onto my retinas, her limp body swinging back and forth in my mind like a grotesque pendulum. Eirik nods and waits for me to continue, but I don't.

'Come sit with me,' he says, leading me over to the sofa. I let myself relax against him. We fall into a long silence. Eirik gently strokes my hair, then cups my skull in his large, warm hand, kneading tension from my scalp. I love this soft version of my husband – out there, in the world, he comes across as so powerful and self-assured but here, at home with me, he is actually a very gentle man.

'I'm sorry for the other day,' I say.

'What day?'

'You know. The burned painting. It was quite the meltdown.'

'You're going through a hard time, my love. But there is no one in the world I would trust more to get through this time and emerge stronger.'

'It was triggered by some stuff going on at work.'

'What kind of stuff?'

'I...' I can't quite decide whether to tell Eirik about Leah and everything that's been happening; it feels difficult to divulge personal information about a client to anyone, even my husband. I never tell anyone anything about my clients, not even Eirik, no matter what. Besides, I've done everything I could, and my job is to listen, not investigate. It's a police matter now and I have to trust that they will question Anton, if only to find that he's telling the truth. I close my eyes and lean against Eirik's dense shape beside me. But still, all I can see is her, alone in the woods. Hanging.

'I'm worried about a client,' I say, finally, my voice low and trembling. I try to envision something other than the violent images in my head, so I look up at my husband and focus on his smooth skin, his strong jawline and his lovely, slightly puffy lips. I run a fingertip along his bottom lip and he looks at me seriously, waiting for me to continue. 'She's a writer. Quite a well-known one, actually. We've had a very productive relationship, or so I thought. But she's behaving completely out of character.'

'In which way?'

'She came to our session last week, extremely distressed. Someone had assaulted her but she wouldn't say who. She has a history of self-harm and some suicidal preoccupation, as well as an abusive ex-husband.'

'That sounds very worrying.' Eirik's eyes are still locked on mine and I love how he listens so intently, he's able to make people feel like the only person in the world when he turns his full attention to them.

'Yes. And then she missed her session with me yesterday. So I went to her house—'

'Wait. What? You went to her house?'

'Yes.'

'That sounds like an unusual thing for you to do.'

'It's an unusual situation. I have a bad feeling about it. Something has happened to her, something bad.'

'What happened at her house?'

'She wasn't there. Her ex-husband was. My client had a restraining order against the guy; there's a long history of emotional abuse and threatening behavior. So why would he be at her house? But he was nothing like what I would have expected. From what I've heard about the guy, I would've expected some kind of monster. You know, weird and shifty, behaving as though he were guilty of something. But he just seemed quite normal. But if he's telling the truth, that means she's been lying. A lot. He told me she's gone to her cabin, and that she's working on her new book.'

'And why wouldn't that be true?'

'I'm not sure I believe she's there, doing just great, working away on her book, after the state she was in last week.'

'So, you think he's done something to her.'

'Well, I know he's certainly capable of it, at least according to her. And he seemed quite bitter and volatile beneath the surface. He said he was upset about the way she'd written about him in her previous book; he talked about feeling compromised and misrepresented. Said he lost his job and had to go live with his parents as a result. She writes autofiction, you know, in the vein of Knausgaard and Vigdis Hjorth.' Eirik nods thoughtfully, still listening intently. I stroke his hand and uncurl his fist so that my hand fits inside his.

'Is this client Leah Iverson?'

'Yes. I mean, I really shouldn't ever name a client, but I guess it was obvious. So you know of her?' I feel worse now, having spoken of Leah to my husband – I should have known he would have heard of her.

'Well, yes. She's quite high profile, isn't she? Didn't she win a big prize?'

'Yeah. The Nordic Prize for Fiction, a very big deal, I gather.'

'I remember. She was on the cover of several newspapers.'

'Yes.'

'How long have you been seeing her?'

'Almost three years now.'

'Right. And her recent behavior is out of character?'

'Very.'

'Has she said anything that could indicate why?'

'Well, yes. She literally begged me to come to her cabin. I've explained why that isn't possible. She insisted. She said there's something important she has to tell me. I've tried to call and email her, but she hasn't responded. I mean, it's not like it's actually an option for me to go there and speak with her; that would be incredibly inappropriate.'

'Yes. Do you have any idea what it could be? Has she given you any indication at all?'

'No. Well. In the past few months, she has been more assertive with me in our sessions. She's asked quite a few personal questions, like what my thoughts are or how I would react in certain situations, that kind of thing. She seems quite preoccupied with me, which is actually very common – I see it in little things like dressing similarly to me or copying certain mannerisms. I'm confused because it's clear she has been hiding things from me, and I believed she shared everything going on in her life with me – she always gave that impression. The ex told me they'd rekindled their relationship, which is almost impossible to believe after the hell she went through with him.' I take another big glug from the red wine Eirik has poured for me, feeling the alcohol mercifully spreading out in my stomach, loosening my nerves. I focus on taking several deep breaths before continuing, I find it difficult to say what I'm going to say next. 'And then I found out from Leah's doctor that she's pregnant.'

'Oh. Wow.' Eirik looks enraptured, like I'm telling him an exciting story I've made up and he needs to know what happens next.

'But she never told me. And that, to me, feels quite sinister. I'm worried that the ex has hurt her.'

'I'm assuming he's the father?'

'He didn't mention it. Perhaps he doesn't even know. Or perhaps she's gotten pregnant by somebody else and he found out? I could imagine that would make him straight up dangerous.'

'Jesus.'

'Yes. Or he may have caused her to regress so much she might cause herself harm. I mean, you wouldn't believe the state she was in…'

'Poor girl. That's all really shocking. Do you actually think she might be suicidal?'

'I'm not sure. Yes, I think it could be possible, given the circumstances and this strange behavior. But maybe I'm so worried about suicide because of what happened with Elisabeth.'

'Well, she does sound quite desperate.'

'Yes. And I just don't know what to do. It's not my role to pursue this any further. I've done all the right things, I contacted her GP and her mother, and I called the police after I met her ex at her apartment. But after Elisabeth, it's like I just can't let it go. I can't stop thinking about her. I keep thinking that if I just went there like she asked me to, then I could save her—'

'You called the police?'

'Yes. I felt I had to.'

'And what did they say?'

'That they would try to send a car over to her apartment. I explained that she's not there and that they need to go to the cabin and it didn't sound like they would even consider that unless she's reported missing by her next of kin. So what do I do? I can't just do nothing. I can just tell that something bad has happened, or will happen...'

'Kristina. Listen to me. This does all sound very worrying. But you've done all the right things. I think you're letting Elisabeth influence how you are reacting to this. Not every troubled soul will do what she did. Most won't. And even if Leah Iverson did, it wouldn't be your fault. You've done everything you can.'

'I was so shocked to hear that she's pregnant. You can imagine how it made me feel. I completely broke down with Vera. You know, it's made me realize how I'm absolutely not ready to give up. I think we should call the clinic and make plans for a new round of treatment.'

Eirik is quiet and holds himself very still. I can tell he's thinking about how to word his response. 'You're right. It's been a few months now. But we need to wait until after the election.'

I feel suddenly, irrationally angry and turn away from him. Everything needs to wait until after the election.

'Come here, honey,' he says, pulling me closer. I let him hold me because there are tears in my eyes and I don't want him to see.

'I wish you could come with me tomorrow,' he says, after a long while.

'Come with you where?'

'I'm off to Bergen again tomorrow morning, remember? Six thirty flight, nightmare. The campaign? This one is really, really important. If I get the nomination there, I'm likely to win most of the west coast. And then I go on to Trondheim and Tromsø. Back on Thursday.'

'I don't remember hearing about this. I would have written it in my diary...' I untangle myself from Eirik's arms and go to get my diary from my handbag in the hallway. I've been looking forward to this weekend, to us finally having some uninterrupted time together. But there it is – *Eirik Bergen* it says, on Saturday 31st. I can't help the tears that pool in my eyes again, but immediately feel stupid. I feel unsettled and anxious about being here alone for so many days. What if Anton gets questioned by the police but released because of a lack of evidence and comes after me?

'Kristina, I told you about this,' says Eirik, pulling me back toward him. I nod and bury my face in the warm crook of his neck. 'You know it's not for nothing. I hate leaving you, but it's only for a few days. I'll be back before you even realize I'm gone.'

'Sorry. I just want one whole weekend together. It's October and I don't think we've had that this year at all, not once. In over ten months.'

'I know. It should calm down a little soon.'

'When? When you're prime minister?'

Eirik chuckles softly and kisses the inside of my palm.

'I don't want you to go.'

'Shhh. I'm here now. Besides, didn't you tell me you have a boozy brunch with some girlfriends tomorrow? That will keep you busy. And maybe you can go back to see Camilla and the kids.'

He's right, I've made brunch plans with my university friends, and just the thought of it makes me feel exhausted. I'll have to think of an excuse, but for now, I try to relax into his embrace, to enjoy the way his fingers trace shapes across my collarbone and the hollows of my throat, but my thoughts feel disjointed and dense, layered one on top of each other, like the many layers of paint in Elisabeth's artwork, made to look like a single color at first sight.

18

Elisabeth, June

Elisabeth gets up and stands a while at the window. It's a cool, overcast early-summer night, and though she can see no moon or stars, the sky is a pleasant light dove gray, even at midnight. Villa Vinternatt is quiet but it has the comforting hum of sleeping people gathered together. At the end of the vast sweep of garden, a pond. Then thick woods. Beyond the woods, the still and silvery Oslofjord, caught between two narrow headlands like a giant rock pool at low tide.

When she first came here, she couldn't sleep. She lay night after night on top of her bed, sweating and shaking, wracked with sobs, nausea and intense itching. They anticipated this with new arrivals and after dinner, one of the staff members gave her a fistful of pills to take, but she didn't take them; she kept them for a moment in the wet pocket of her cheek until she could spit them out. Nobody checked; Villa Vinternatt isn't that kind of place. She did take the methadone, but it took several weeks before she began to feel better, and several more before Elisabeth started to feel at home. But she still can't sleep.

This is a place to grow and to reconnect, they said when Elisabeth was first introduced to the idea of Villa Vinternatt. A rehabilitation center for artists with addiction issues, which offered progressive treatment for substance abuse, using a combination of methadone, intense group therapy and a chance to contribute to the arts, supposedly giving recovering addicts a sense of purpose and community. Some stay for a few months, some for years, all government funded. Many people want the opportunity to come somewhere like this, Kristina had said, and Elisabeth knew she was lucky. She hadn't had much luck in the years before coming to Villa Vinternatt.

For years, Elisabeth had sold herself for heroin. And if you have sold yourself, what, if anything, of yourself remains yours? She was there, in the little yellow room in the eaves, a woman without doubt. A tired and thin and pale one, but definitely a female human. There were brittle bones and broken veins and some patches of permanently bruised skin and a sweet, youthful face almost untouched by the horrors she'd lived. In her veins rushed blood, and she was often preoccupied with blood; it was in her therapy notes, and it was in her art – repeat mentions of blood, as if it was the source of everything that had happened. Hungry blood, bad blood, blood that needed something injected into its flow to give her body and mind what it craved: she had tried many analogies over the years to describe the notion that what drove her came from her very core, it ran through her veins. But was it always there?

For years, Elisabeth had felt dead inside, as if her internal landscape was a bleak and barren November afternoon. She was stunned by the trauma endured in her teens, and nothing helped; not the care of her family or her friends, or a long succession of various doctors and therapists. Then, in a group therapy session for PTSD sufferers, she met Andreas, who had kind brown eyes, trembling hands that moved her, and a blossoming heroin addiction. He helped, and the heroin helped, too. Those first few years with Andreas were one big high, and the darkness of her early twenties finally faded away in Elisabeth's mind and heart. Elisabeth and Andreas were the sexy kind of addicts, they used to joke; he was heir to a salmon farm fortune and could more than afford to fund them and access quality heroin. They lived in a beautiful apartment in central Oslo, and socialized and went to art school and loved each other deeply, but with time, every aspect of their lives became increasingly dominated by their love affair with the Big H. It began to show. People started to ask questions. Their families grew concerned, then suspicious, then horrified as the scope of their addiction became clear.

Though Elisabeth still doesn't consciously allows herself to return to the icy January morning five years ago when she woke up next to a dead man, the man she loved, those moments are always with her like a backdrop to her mind. Overnight, she was evicted from Andreas' apartment by his family. She had no job and had dropped out of art school several months before. She was thirty-four with nothing to show for it except a body full of broken and bruised veins. Her family tried to help, Kristina tried to help, the welfare office tried to help, but within weeks, Elisabeth was living in a hostel and working the streets, reeling with ever-increasing use to dull the grief. In those days, just *being* felt like falling through endless layers of hot burning air, and every night, lying on the hard hostel bed, coming down from a high, Elisabeth would be bombarded with gruesome images of giant needles plunging into frail veins, blood splattering to the ground, guns pointed in faces, the hairy backs of another faceless client, Andreas dead, his soft brown eyes open and staring straight at her. The only thing that helped, was the only thing that had ever helped – the intensely warm, euphoric lull of a clean, strong hit of smack.

It all feels like a long time ago now, almost two years. Tonight, Elisabeth feels calm and content. If someone were to place a bag of heroin on the table in front of her, Elisabeth wouldn't touch it. She'd be able to hold the memory of its potency in her mind, and still not be tempted. She has too much, now, even though if she were to compare herself to some people she knows, she has nothing at all. But she has a blossoming career as a painter, Kristina – the best friend who'd do anything for her, people she trusts and a sense of purpose. In the group therapy sessions that happen every day of the week except Tuesdays and Sundays, Elisabeth and her fellow residents at Villa Vinternatt explore their pasts, their current experiences, and their wishes for the future – that vague future in which they must leave Villa Vinternatt and reintegrate into society. Someday, she hopes to be ready. In her individual therapy, Elisabeth has begun to address how her family has been affected by her addiction, and ways to hopefully heal those wounds someday. Once a month, her parents visit. Kristina visits, too. And once a month, Elisabeth is released overnight and usually spends the night at Kristina and Eirik's, or her parents' in Bærum.

She looks out at the narrow Drøbak Sound and the wooded headland of Nesodden across the bay. She shivers in the cool breeze coming in through the open window, carrying the scent of Villa Vinternatt's rose garden. She watches the blonde hairs on her arm prickle and stand up, and in the twilight, the fading scars underneath are invisible.

Looking back at her love affair with heroin now, she knows it wasn't love at all, but a very human need for escape. And little wonder, Elisabeth had a lot to wish to escape from. She still does, it is heavy stuff she carries, and it is all the heavier for having to carry it alone. And yet, it has helped to be here and to express herself by returning to painting and being encouraged and supported to do so. Still, she is tired. Elisabeth often thinks of herself as a much older woman, someone who has lived a long life and doesn't yearn for more. Other times, she thinks of herself as an animal, a wild little thing who has exhausted itself just trying to stay alive, and who craves the long, dark months of hibernation, tucking herself away in a tiny cave, giving in to a dreamless, peaceful sleep. Elisabeth leaves the window wide open and returns to bed, tucking herself in tight with the light summer duvet. When the usual images insist themselves upon her and want to keep her up all night in terror, she holds on tight to the image of herself as a wild animal, exhausted but safe in its snug winter den, and it works, she's lulled into a heavy, dreamless sleep.

'Nightmare disorder,' the new therapist says, an attractive woman named Olivia with a faint American accent. Dr Olivia Hudson reads the diploma hung on the wall above her desk. Formal and impressive, thinks Elisabeth, and knows that must be exactly the intention. She studies the other woman's face carefully, trying to decide whether she instinctively likes her or not, if this is someone she could envision speaking to several times a week. Olivia sits opposite her on a blue sofa, casually dressed in jeans and a plain black T-shirt, her face clean of make-up except for a deep red shade of lipstick. Elisabeth is tired: though she fell into an initial, deep sleep, she woke up after less than three hours and the night was short and broken. She didn't want to come here today, running through her therapy notes from her previous shrink with the new one. *Getting to know each other*, Olivia had called it when she entered the room.

'What do you mean?' asks Elisabeth. 'I have bad dreams, so do a lot of addicts. I've read about it. Heroin changes the pathways of the brain and makes them more alive. Comes out at night.'

'Yes, but nightmare disorder, one form of parasomnia, is more than just having bad dreams; it's a disturbed sleeping pattern, being too afraid to fall asleep, to such an extent that it affects you during the day. How does it present itself for you? Are you restless during the night? Do you find that you've kicked the duvet off? Do you sweat? These can all be signs.'

Restless at night, Elisabeth laughs to herself – that would be a rather modest way of describing the full extent of her nocturnal demons.

'Honestly, I don't think there's anything much you can do or medicine you can give me for my nighttime terrors. Besides, I'm a big girl.' Elisabeth stares pointedly at the clock above the door: seven minutes left. She doesn't want to get into a deeper conversation about any of this; if she starts to talk about her dreams she can't be sure she could stop herself building the horrific images in her mind again. It can stay boxed up and maybe touched upon someday.

She leaves Olivia's office on the ground floor and walks down the empty corridors and up the sweeping staircase of Villa Vinternatt back to her room, passing a couple of unknown faces along the way. They look more like visitors than drug addicts, but you never know – Elisabeth knows the same has been said about her. Occasionally new people arrive. Most of them go back to shooting up in a matter of weeks, and Elisabeth can always tell who isn't going to last – she can practically smell the desperation for another hit oozing from their pores. She hasn't made any close friends here – friendships are in fact gently discouraged, as they exponentially increase the risk of setbacks. She is encouraged to think of the other residents at Villa Vinternatt as co-healers. There are a couple of people she prefers to others, but mostly Elisabeth keeps to herself, or speaks to her mother or Kristina on the phone during free time in the afternoon.

In her room stands a wooden easel positioned toward the window to give the best light onto the canvas. It's Italian-designed, a gift from her parents after twelve months clean. She looks out of the window now; the view is beautiful and she never tires of it. The rich green pines of Nordmarka forest in the distance with hundreds of trails for enthusiastic hikers, each path leading to somewhere new. The frothy gray sea, great big rolling waves chasing back and forth in the narrow sound.

She spots a sparrow sitting on the narrow ledge below

her window, cocking its head and chirping merrily, and wants to believe it is the same one she has seen many times before, and painted, too. The sparrow shakes off water droplets from its squat, fluffy body, after taking a bath in a drainpipe. Its movements are so precise and so fast, eyes darting everywhere to make sure it's safe. Another sparrow joins it and they both indulge in splashing about, dunking their beaks into the rainwater dammed in the drain blocked by twigs and leaves from the weekend's summer storms, when lightning and thunder tore at the skies. Elisabeth wishes she could be like the little birds, oblivious to the dangers of what really lies out there.

She takes out her palette and brushes which she keeps meticulously clean and rolled away safely in their canvas sleeves. There is something almost religious about untying the frayed green ribbon and slowly unrolling the fabric to expose the brushes, some so worn the varnish has whittled down to the wood. They're tatty, but they're hers, and they tell a thousand stories of her life when she used them back in art school, when Andreas was alive. She takes the palette knife and starts mixing the colors, always adding dark to light, like she was taught. Maybe that's her problem, she thinks; she always adds dark to light, in life and in her dreams.

Again, she thinks about telling Olivia everything, at least everything that happens in her dreams. She doesn't have to say that the dreams that torture her are real, visceral memories, scorched into the neuropathways of her brain. The irony, Elisabeth thought, when once, years ago, she learned that morphine, the medical derivative of opium, was named after Morpheus, the Greek God of sleep.

Elisabeth places the brush back into the canvas sleeve. Harder than intended, she puts the palette knife down in its holder on the easel, sending the sparrows scrambling into the air. She walks back down the stairs and along the corridors, all empty; it's just minutes until lunch time and most residents will already be waiting in the dining room for the unveiling of the buffet. She sees Olivia through the glass pane on the door, typing away on her computer at the desk. When she knocks on the door, Olivia looks up and smiles when she sees her.

'I'm sorry, you're probably busy. Umm. I could come back another time if that's better, or, like, if you're not the right person to talk to about this, just say, and—'

'Now is fine, Elisabeth. My afternoon is wide open today.'

'Oh. Umm, okay.'

'What's on your mind?'

'I thought maybe I should tell you about what happens in the night. The dreams I have. Or dream, really – it's almost always the same one.' She pauses, trying to find a way to describe what happens to her when Villa Vinternatt settles down for the night, purring with tired, sated humans. Her anxiety at dusk is visceral. Her skin starts to itch, the same way it used to when smack was leaving her body. Her senses bombard her with panic, and she has the sensation of drowning, gasping for air. She's endlessly tried to create a routine to relax, but nothing works; it's the same story, the same recurring nightmare, every single night.

'I'm running though a thick, overgrown jungle. I'm barefoot. Terrified. Wild animals are chasing me, they snap their jaws and tear pieces of flesh from my body, stripping me to the bone. I can feel warm blood running down my face and the metallic taste of it in her mouth. I fall down, I always do, and the animals encircle me, breathing heavily, inching closer; I can see the gnarly, bloodied teeth of wolves, the razor-sharp talons of a white-tailed eagle, and I can smell death in the air. I know that often people wake moments before something dramatic happens in a dream, like falling or being shot. I never do. For me, it is still only the beginning. The animals tear at what remains of my skin, ripping it from the muscle, my eyes are plucked from their sockets. I can feel my lifeless body being pulled in different directions until my remains sink deep into the forest floor, as if the branches and brambles will take whatever is left. When I wake up, I'm always exhausted, like someone has drained my body of blood, and my head spins with dizzying thoughts.'

'What kind of thoughts?' asks Olivia, softly.

'I don't know,' she says, and stands back up, making for the door, avoiding Dr Hudson's eyes. But she does know. These nights make her resent Kristina; it's not like she has night after night of this hell. She'll sleep peacefully, next to her perfect husband in her perfect home. It feels unfair.

19

Kristina

He's gone when I wake up, though it is still dark outside. Tomorrow November will be here, the darkest and dreariest month. Like several of my clients, Leah spoke of the coming winter a few times recently, and expressed anxiety about the dark months looming. Several months of near-constant darkness and cold take their toll on many people here in the north, myself included. It is hard to avoid the feeling of lethargy and melancholy that seems to seep into your very bones when it is dark when you go to work, dark when you come back home and often chucking it down with icy rain to top it off. I've had another one of those nights I often have, struggling to fall asleep, and then when I finally do, I have a terrible nightmare. I wake with a start, heart pounding, my face wet with tears, and no recollection of the dream, other than running away from something. After these episodes, I lie tossing and turning for hours, my mind ruminating over little details from the day, or a client's situation, or the past. By the time I fall asleep again, not even an hour remains until my alarm goes off.

Thankfully, today is Saturday so I've been able to sleep in and feel quite rested. I make the bed perfectly, then remain on top of it for a long while, staring absentmindedly into the walk-in wardrobe through the open door, at the rows and rows of Eirik's expensive shirts. Sometimes living with Eirik is like living with a ghost, one whose presence you can feel but never summon. I try to imagine him in my mind, the way he most likely is in this exact moment; intently focused on winning over a room, or an organization, or an important person sitting across from him.

He'll be smiling and laughing, well aware of his charm, subconsciously mirroring his audience, creating a bond of trust, gesticulating in that rather excessive way of his that makes him occasionally seem more Italian than Norwegian. He chooses his words carefully and isn't afraid of moments of silence, knowing how to use them. It makes him come across as authoritative, self-assured, measured. A leader. When Eirik and I met, fresh out of university, I was the only person who believed him when he said he'd be prime minister someday. Now everybody does. It seems to be only a matter of time.

It's not fake, the charismatic, trustworthy persona my husband projects. He is those things. He is also the sometimes tired, reclusive, spent man who needs calm and quiet at home, who likes to fall asleep with his head held snug between my breasts while I gently tickle the hair at the nape of his neck. And he is still the eager kid I fell in love with: an idealistic, unafraid small-town young man who lights up when he speaks of change and bettering the country. I think of how intently he listened to me last night, how close he held me, and smile to myself in the gloomy room.

I look around the room at the strangely blurred outlines of the furniture – I can't see much without my contact lenses. I switch on the radio and Soft Classics fills the room – perfect for early mornings and perfect for sex, though I certainly have more of the former than the latter these days. I close my eyes again, listening to Einaudi, running through the various options for today in my head. I don't particularly want to go to the brunch, but I have absolutely nothing else to do. My thoughts return to last weekend, to the rainy beach walk in Drøbak with Camilla and the kids – it's where I'd usually go on a weekend when Eirik is away or working. I could go today; it might be fun to tag along with the kids trick-or-treating, it's Halloween. But at the thought of the drive down to Drøbak and back, something tightens in my throat and I swallow hard to dislodge it. Up until August, I would always stop in at Villa Vinternatt on my way home and sit in the rose garden with Elisabeth. I'll never go there again, never again listen to the pleasant rise and fall of her soft voice, or see her fresh, sweet face.

I suppose I could hop on the train out to Sandvika and see my mother again, I felt bad for being abrupt with her earlier in the week. I'd have to pay my dues with Elisabeth's mother, but deep down I know I just can't. Not yet.

I pick up my phone to message the girls, saying I can't make it; the idea of sitting among them at Delicatessen, day-drinking and gossiping and discussing their toddlers' remarkable achievements fills me with instant dread. But maybe it won't be like that, maybe it will actually be fun – something to do that has nothing to do with Elisabeth or Leah or the fact that my marriage and my entire life is on hold until after the elections. Something that might take my mind off the anxiety and persistent dejection I've been feeling. It's been so long since I did something sociable, just for fun, not for Eirik's campaign or a work-related conference. I remember last night and how good it was to speak to Eirik about what's been going on, and I know he's absolutely right – I have to let go now.

I put the phone back down and get out of bed. I have plenty of time to run through my morning routine before meeting the girls at noon – contact lenses, shower, moisturizer, a light touch of make-up. I spend a while studying the pores of my skin close-up – my skin looks coarser than just a few months ago, maybe a result of both the stress of this year and the unusually cold October weather. Perhaps it's time to reconsider the Botox I've always dismissed – it was easier to turn down when my skin was still young and flawless. My thoughts are interrupted by the vibration of my phone on the bedside table. Someone is phoning from a private number.

'Hello?'

'Hi, is that Dr Moss?'

'Speaking.'

'Good morning. This is Hans-Olav Bjerre calling from Majorstuen police station. Can I confirm that you called in a tip yesterday about a potential missing person or domestic violence case to my colleague Officer Espensen?'

'Yes, that's right.'

'We've had a look into the information you provided.

There doesn't seem to be any reason for concern with regard to your client, Miss Iverson.'

'Have you found her?'

'We've been in contact with her mother, Linda Iverson, who confirms communicating with her daughter recently.'

'Yes, I know that.'

'It would seem she has gone away somewhere to finish a book or something. A cabin, it says in the write-up.'

'Yes. I asked your colleague to please send someone there. I believe Leah is in danger.'

'Such a request would need to come from her next of kin, and may be difficult to accommodate as there doesn't seem to be any reason to suspect she is in danger.'

'Did you send someone to her apartment? Her ex, against whom she had a restraining order, was there yesterday. You need to find out why.'

'We did. There was no one there.'

'Did you go in?'

'No. We rang the bell. No one was there.'

'How do you know he wasn't there and just didn't open?'

'Look. We would have needed a search warrant to enter the apartment.'

My mind darts to Anton at the middle window, half of his face cast in shadows, his pale-blue eyes cold and sharp on the street below. I shiver lightly. 'So what happens next?'

'Well, presumably what your client's mother says is correct and Ms Iverson will return to her home when she wishes to do so. Oh, and one more thing – it says that you mentioned to Espensen that your client had a restraining order against her ex-husband, Anton von Thaule.'

'Yes?'

'This is incorrect. It was von Thaule who took out a restraining order against Leah Iverson in 2015, after an assault. She tried to take one out against him, but it was discredited after the discovery of CCTV footage of the alleged incident.'

'What? Are you sure?'

'Absolutely.'

After hanging up, I go back to the bathroom and splash cold water on my face, the recently applied mascara dislodging from my lashes and running down my face in black streaks.

All the evidence suggests she's fine. I should relax now and return to my own life. All the space Leah Iverson has taken up in my mind in the past week needs to be freed up for the things that are actually relevant to my life – my work, my family, my remaining friendships, my marriage. But I'm not going to pretend I'm not a little disappointed in Leah, who, having clearly decided to take a temporary or permanent break from therapy, couldn't even be bothered to let me know. Intellectually I know that she is going through what is no doubt a turbulent time, but I am still human and feel affected by her actions. I make a mental note to take these feelings to my next supervision with Vera in two weeks' time. I am also surprised and disturbed that she has clearly extensively lied to me, both about her present and past relationship with Anton von Thaule.

Lying to therapists is surprisingly common, and in Leah's case, she was most likely ashamed of her own actions during her marriage break-up and reinvented herself as a victim. Then, her book must have exacerbated that false narrative and she got trapped in her own web of lies. This would explain why she was so disturbed and profoundly uncomfortable with her new status as author and well-known abuse victim. Or... Or she told the truth and he played her, perhaps taking out the restraining order to discredit her.

I lie back on the bed for a moment, my head spinning with disjointed, jostling thoughts. In spite of all my training, and all my own therapy work, I am unable to decipher my own feelings in this moment. Restlessness, I think. Underlying anxiety. A sense of unease – it's the feeling of staring at a puzzle and realizing that a piece is missing. But then again, I have had to get used to pieces missing. Since the age of nineteen, when I suffered severe trauma-induced dissociative amnesia, I have known what it feels like to have patches of your life simply erased. And though my own experience with memory loss is limited to one specific incident, I sometimes have the strange feeling in other contexts, of only seeing part of the picture.

Again, my thoughts return to Leah. I instantly grow tense and annoyed with myself for not being able to let it go now. Am I going to plague myself with ruminations about a troubled client for another week until she decides to turn up for our next session, or not?

Please come to my cabin, she said. Why would she beg me to come like that unless it really was important? Why did she lie to me about Anton? It's the lying I feel unsettled by – did Leah not feel enough trust and support in our therapeutic bond that she would be able to divulge the truth about her past to me? And why hasn't she answered any of my calls or emails if she really wanted to speak to me? I do recall her mentioning the exceptional remoteness of the cabin many times, and how she had no phone reception for miles. Still, she has clearly managed to get in touch with her mother.

20

Leah, two weeks before

A magnificent full moon bathes the October night in light. The curtains are open wide, letting a silvery shaft of light into the apartment. She's cross-legged on the floor in the living room, sitting in the moonbeam, like a forest animal resting for a while on a remote stretch of road. In front of her is a box of photographs, some scattered around on the floor. She picks one up, holds it up to the light. It's a photograph of herself as a young child, aged around four. By that age, Leah had already lost her father and was living with her mother, Linda, in a modest apartment in a nondescript suburb of Årjäng. She'd been a beautiful child, her light-brown eyes and dark hair giving her more definition than the classic Scandinavian look of white-blonde hair and ruddy cheeks of her little friends at nursery and in the neighborhood. But even back then, she'd felt different. Worth less. Unlovable.

She picks up a second photograph, this one of a slightly older child. It's Kristina, aged seven. The photo was taken in

Denmark and Kristina is standing on the rails of a wooden fence by the roadside, beaming at the camera. Leah knows this because on the back of the picture, someone has written 'Langeland, August 1993'. Next to Kristina stood her mother and her older sister, but Leah has cut them carefully out of the photograph. Behind Kristina is a rolling field, its late-summer sun-scorched grass having bled out with the passing of time into a faded ochre. A few goats stand in it, randomly captured for all time in the photograph. Leah places the two photos side by side on the floor. To a random observer, the two girls might have passed as the same person a couple of years apart. Kristina has darker-brown eyes than her, a slightly upturned snub nose, a gap between her front teeth and sun-streaked dark-brown hair tied up in a messy ponytail. The main difference between the two girls is the uncomplicated, mischievous joy in Kristina's smile, and the wan, careful expression on Leah's own face. Even back then, Kristina had been like a perfect version of herself.

Was that how it started? An initial sense of similarity between them, followed by a need to get close to it? The beginning is a long time ago now, a lot has happened.

She places both photographs back in the box among the many, many others. She considers trying to write, but decides against it; she can feel that it won't come to her tonight, either, and can't face all those long hours staring at the screen, waiting. She shivers lightly; it's turned suddenly and freakishly cold this past week, though it is still only mid-October. She rubs her upper arms, feeling goosebumps pricking beneath her fingertips. She rests both hands against the tight vault of her belly. In there, she imagines soft pink sludge is hardening and shaping into tiny bones, into a perfect little skull, into a beating heart. The baby will grow and grow until it fills all that empty, dark space inside her and then it will come out, and just by being, it will make her whole.

21

Kristina

I'm in the hallway stepping into my boots when the doorbell rings unexpectedly. I'm struck by a rush of fear, and immediately Anton and his cool blue eyes come to mind. No, it can't be. How would he even find me here? Like most therapists', my address is unlisted. I pick up the receiver and the video monitor flickers to life, revealing the person downstairs. It's a middle-aged woman wearing an oversized black raincoat, its hood obscuring her face. Still, I recognize her instantly – I've known this woman all my life.

'Hi, Idun,' I whisper into the receiver and she looks up, into the camera, and I'm taken aback by how thin she has grown – sharp cheekbones protrude over sunken cheeks, making Elisabeth's mother look bird-like and much older. Her eyes sit deep in her face, surrounded by dark circles. I press the buzzer, because what else can I do? I open the door to her wearing my jackets and boots and she realizes I was on my way out, her mouth tightening into an 'o'.

'I'm sorry. I should have called,' she says, shaking her head.

'You're going out somewhere. You look lovely, Kristina.' I feel guilty for the nice clothes and sophisticated make-up, and wish she'd caught me on any other weekend morning when I'd be in my usual old sweatpants and scruffy T-shirt. Now, I look like I'm going about my best life, just weeks after her only child died here in this apartment.

'Come in, Idun,' I say and decide to not offer an explanation for where I am headed. It's usually best to not over-explain. We hug briefly, and she feels bony and tense in my arms.

'I won't be long. I was just wondering if we could talk a few things through.'

'Of course.' I lead her through the apartment into the living room and only as she sits down on the sofa do I realize that she's facing directly toward the room where her daughter's big canvas used to hang on the wall behind the dining table. Eirik has replaced it temporarily with a Syeed Newham print on canvas and I watch Idun's eyes travel around the room and through the open double doors to the dining room. She's been here many times before for the Christmas drinks Eirik and I host every year, and I'm sure she's noticing the absence of Elisabeth's paintings.

'I was wondering,' she says, 'if you suspected anything in the weeks leading up to the eleventh of August.'

'What do you mean?'

'As a therapist. You must get clients in very dark places. Did you notice those kinds of tendencies with Elisabeth?'

'I see. As I wasn't the therapist treating Elisabeth, that is very difficult to answer. But yes, on a few occasions when we spoke in the summer, I did feel worried for her mental health. I wondered whether it was the start of a regression.'

'Were you aware of any episodes when she broke her sobriety?'

'No.'

'That's what I don't understand. She was so motivated. She spoke about the future. She'd made plans for a trip to Thailand with me in January. And then...'

'It happens quite often, unfortunately. If you want my professional opinion, I believe that many suicides, especially the ones that come as surprises, are impulsive acts in very critical low moments in a person's life, and not the result of longer-term planning.'

'I just can't believe she intended to...' Idun trails off, and her eyes shimmer with tears. She doesn't appear to notice, just blinks hard, sending them scattering onto her jeans.

'I don't think there was much doubt about her intentions. Sometimes, I've seen that it helps the family to know that the person actually did intend to die. Elisabeth wasn't trying to get high, she would have known a dose like that would be fatal. It might be even worse to think of a suicide as an accidental death after a desperate cry for help. In Elisabeth's case, there was little doubt that she, in those moments, truly intended to end her life. It does help me a little bit to think that she is at peace now.'

Idun nods and lets her eyes travel around the room again.

'I've taken some of Elisabeth's artwork down because I thought you might like to have it. It felt like the right thing to do.'

Idun nods, then reaches across and squeezes my hand. 'I'm so grateful for you, Kristina. Won't you come and see me soon? I know I'm not much fun these days, but it would mean a lot to me. Elisabeth was so lucky to have you. And it makes me happy to see you here in this beautiful home, living a meaningful life, still young and beautiful. Your whole life lies ahead of you. You have to live it for both of you now. For all three of you.' I have to look away. I feel a lump in my throat at the mention of Elisabeth, and Trine. It feels surreal that out of the three young girls who once did everything together and embarked on what was supposed to be the adventure of a lifetime, I'm the only one still alive. *You have to live for all three of you.*

'I'll come soon, Idun. I promise. I'm so sorry, but I need to leave in a moment, I'm supposed to be somewhere shortly.'

'Of course. Just one more thing.'

'Sure.'

'Could you show me where it happened?' My heart picks up its pace and I feel suddenly queasy at the thought of standing in that room with Elisabeth's mother.

'Of course,' I say softly, and stand up.

The spare bedroom is immaculately tidy and the bed is freshly made up – our housekeeper must have done it; I can barely bear to be in this room. There is a desk by the window and a big wardrobe used to store winter duvets and cozy throws. Idun takes a visibly deep breath and steps into the room. I follow behind her. She walks over to the bed and strokes the pillow, as though it might still hold the indentation of her daughter's head.

'Oh,' she whispers. I remain by the door, my knuckles tight around the door handle. Her shoulders begin to shudder as she cries, and I feel deeply uncomfortable in a way I never do at work when a client displays intense emotion. 'May I?' she gestures to the bed. I nod.

Idun clambers onto the high bed and lies down atop

the comforter, eyes wide open and staring at the ceiling. From where I'm standing she now uncannily resembles her daughter, the way I found her lying in the exact same place, her eyes also wide open and staring at the ceiling. I swallow hard; it feels as though I'm going to black out.

'I'll give you a minute,' I say, stepping back out into the hallway. I go through to the bathroom and from the highest shelf behind the mirror, I retrieve a tranquilizer from an ibuprofen box. I tuck it underneath my tongue, making sure it's covered with saliva, then swallow it dry. I lean back against the wall, wishing Idun out of my house with all my might, but my eyes fall on the black-and-white photograph on the opposite wall, taken the summer I was nineteen. I'm standing between my two best friends, grinning widely, Trine on my left, and Elisabeth beaming on my right. I force myself to stare at the photo for several long moments until our faces grow fuzzy and blurred.

'What did she look like when you found her?' asks Idun. I hadn't noticed that she'd emerged from the bedroom and is standing directly beside me.

'She looked peaceful,' I whisper, my voice trembling. It's a lie. But sometimes we have to lie.

22

Elisabeth, June

She wakes soaked in sweat. She sits up in bed, letting her eyes get used to the darkness, her head groggy with heavy sleep medication, before picking up her phone. It's only 1 a.m. and she's been asleep for less than an hour. She scrolls through Instagram and likes Kristina's most recent post, a picture of her and Eirik posing poolside in Thailand, sipping from the same drink, a carved-out watermelon cocktail. She stares into the darkness of her room and imagines Kristina in this moment, sleeping close together with Eirik in a languidly hot bungalow, beads of sweat studding her smooth, bronzed skin, her husband's arms flung possessively around her waist.

Elisabeth sometimes wonders whether she'll ever again sleep next to anyone. The idea of letting someone in, all the way in, like Andreas, feels impossible and wrong. She knows she hasn't processed his death yet, and though it's been over five years, she doesn't feel ready to fully take in the fact that he is gone, that he simply doesn't exist, that it could be possible to live in a world where she keeps breathing when he'll never take another breath. It was easier when she was out there, on the streets; at least she'd have a few hours every day when she was high, when everything just felt mellow and possible, even living without Andreas, even living with the carnage and fear of her past, which play in her mind on a never-ending hellish loop. Now, she has to stare reality in the eyes, sober.

Still, she knows she is lucky in many ways, and she especially feels that when she is immersed in her art. She feels overcome with beauty and hope and gratitude when she brings the elegant curve of a bird's wing to the canvas, or when she succeeds in capturing the spill of moonlight on the surface of the fjord in winter, like shattered crystals, or when she pinches a leaf from a branch in the garden and holds it up to the light, exposing its curiously perfect skeleton, later folding it into one of her thick coffee table books to dry.

There is a man here at Villa Vinternatt whose company she enjoys. He's much older than her, at least in his mid-fifties, and they sometimes paint together, positioning their easels side by side in front of the bay windows overlooking the sound. He'll pause his own work for long moments and watch her paint, handing her a color tube she hadn't yet realized she wanted and it's always exactly right. His name is Joel and in another life he was a concert pianist and hobby painter, whose life broke apart after his pregnant wife and his three-year-old son died in a car accident. He succumbed to alcohol addiction and eventually full-blown cocaine and heroin abuse, until he got clean after over a decade and got another chance at life at Villa Vinternatt.

Elisabeth gets up from the bed and sits at her desk in the dark, shivering slightly at the feel of the metal chair against her bare thighs. The huge house is quiet, yet comfortingly humming with the telltale signs of life – a tap running somewhere, footsteps in a corridor downstairs, the unmistakable feeling of a building filled with people.

She opens the selfie mode on the phone camera and studies herself. She still looks young, in spite of everything. She smiles at herself and takes a picture but when she looks at it she realizes she looks so sad it takes her breath away. She tries again, consciously bringing a smile not only to her lips but to her eyes. Better, but still visibly fake. She thinks about padding down the corridor and around the corner to room 21, where Joel lives. She could knock softly and he'd appear, disheveled but awake and he'd smile, happy to see her. They could sneak downstairs, through the big dining hall, onto the covered terrace overlooking the gardens and the fjord, and they could sit together on a bench, sharing a rollie Joel has smuggled into Villa Vinternatt, looking out on the trembling lights from buoys and reef markers on the water.

They could tell each other the stuff that is easier to tell a friend than a therapist or family member or doctor. She smiles at the thought; impossible, but still soothing. The residents aren't allowed to socialize at night. All the doors are locked. No tobacco is allowed on the premises and she doesn't even know if Joel would smoke, but it seems a fair assumption of someone who would shoot up heroin. There are cameras around the house, some no doubt angled straight onto the terrace. She doesn't have the vocabulary to speak to a kind-of friend about the stuff she might have needed to speak of. None of it is ever going to happen.

Elisabeth goes over to the easel by the window. She picks up the paintbrush and holds it suspended over an unfinished white patch of her painting in progress. It's one of her trademark paintings: reds and maroons and watery pinks swirled around and layered onto the canvas in splotches and streaks. This one is called Blood Storms. Some people, probably the ones who go through life mostly with quiet, kind thoughts in their minds, assume Elisabeth's motives are abstract floral references; an experiential interpretation of the virginal, soft inner petals of roses, or swathes of poppies bleeding into each other on a hillside. Others react viscerally to her explicit references to violence and blood and chaos; her favorite was the critic who called her work 'hypnotically grotesque'. To Elisabeth they aren't mutually exclusive interpretations; pain and bloodshed and that which haunts her can surely simultaneously take on a form of beauty?

But tonight she is tired of the evocative but draining imagery. She wants to bring a touch of lightness to the painting, something fun. She smiles at the thought of *fun*, what a luxury fun is. She retrieves a pressed leaf from inside a picture book about Judy Chicago and places it directly onto the canvas. She draws its outline lightly with a charcoal pencil, nudging its outer extremities into the carefully built layers of reds already there, smeared from one corner of the canvas toward the center. She smiles to herself and colors in the outline of the maple leaf in a bright yellow, just because the color makes her smile. The effect is strange, as if a child has walked into the room and taken liberties with her mother's painting in an unsupervised moment, bringing an unstudied, fresh energy to the piece, and maybe on some level that is exactly what has happened. She might kick herself tomorrow for having ruined the painting, one of those she's preparing for Villa Vinternatt's upcoming vernissage, but tonight it feels possible to laugh by herself in the moonlight, filling in the painting's blank spots with happy, bright shades of yellow.

23

Kristina

It takes me over an hour to calm down sufficiently to fully follow the conversation. I order garlic king prawns and chili mayonnaise chicken wings, busying myself with the food and the wine while my friends chatter, the volume steadily increasing with each unit of alcohol. After three glasses of cava, I feel more like myself again. Jenny regales us with one hilarious story after another of her adventures on Tinder – she's the only singleton in our group of friends, and it's pretty obvious that she's the one having the most fun. Carla moans about the relentless pressures of motherhood, and feels that being a stay-at-home mom to her fourteen-month-old twins is a lot harder than her previous high-flying job in management consulting. *I just want to sit on the toilet for five fucking minutes by myself*, she says, taking another greedy glug from her cava. Our eyes meet and I sense a quick apology in the way she looks at me – my friends all feel awkward discussing their children around me. They stopped asking about IVF and how it's all going a long time ago, and I'm glad they did.

'So how's that handsome man of yours?' asks Simone, our impossibly glamorous onetime French-exchange student who ended up staying in Oslo and married Arne, a friend of Eirik's.

'Away, as usual,' I say. 'After the elections, things will presumably calm down. We'll need to get a date in the diary and have you all over for dinner sometime soon. It's been ages.'

Everyone concurs, it has been ages. Over the past year, I've hardly seen my friends at all; Eirik's increasingly demanding career, as well as my own, combined with Elisabeth's tragic death and my own therapy work have all added up to a very busy day-to-day life. It feels unexpectedly good to sit here with my friends, drinking wine as the afternoon darkens into evening, listening to their loud, tipsy laughter, just letting myself grow fully relaxed and mellow, emptying my mind of all the stress and tension.

On my way home, I find myself giggling to myself – it's as though the seven-hour brunch replenished my energy reserves, though I'm sure I'll be sorry tomorrow. I try to call Eirik, I want to hear his deep, soothing voice and tell him I love him, but it goes straight to voicemail. He's probably at some boring dinner, listening to boring speeches by boring people. I giggle again and leave him a voice message on WhatsApp saying I wish he could be waiting for me at home, in bed.

At home, I walk from room to room, switching on all the little lamps, humming to myself under my breath. I used to like to sing, and I was pretty good at it – might it be a good idea to return to it, take some lessons, develop my voice? It would be something to do with the little spare time I have. I make a mental note to Google some options on Monday. I pour another glass of wine and sit down on the sofa. In this moment, nothing seems so bad. All the things that bothered me and made me fearful feel dulled by the warm, glowy feeling I have inside.

I wake with a start, my heart hammering, the remnants of a bad dream disappearing from my mind. I glance at the time, 5.50 a.m. All the lights are on and I'm still wearing my leather pants and silk blouse from the brunch. My mouth tastes terrible and I feel intensely dehydrated. I get up and stumble woozily toward the kitchen. For a moment, I wonder whether I might actually throw up, but feel better after a large glass of San Pellegrino. I realize that two chunky candles have been left burning on the windowsill, though I can't remember lighting them. They're both almost burned out, and one of them has started spitting wax and sending tall flames leaping out of the holder. If I hadn't noticed when I did, it might have set the curtains on fire.

I blow them out and go back to the sofa to lie down. I'm going to give myself ten minutes of scrolling through Instagram before I go back to bed; I want to make sure the nausea disappears completely while staying close to the bathroom. When I unlock my phone, a series of notifications pop up on the screen. A text message from Elisabeth's mother, sent last night, thanking me. *I hope you know that to Elisabeth, you were an angel*, she wrote. Another from my own mother, complaining about my father's inability to plan for their weekend away. And there is an email from Leah Iverson, sent at 10.31 p.m. with the word 'Supernova' in the subject line.

24

Leah, two weeks before

She has the idea one of the many nights when she's alone. The two of them, at Bekkebu. It would be the only way to paint a full picture. All that space, all the time they would have. She would understand. Or eventually, she would come to understand. Leah smiles to herself in the dark. She knows better than anyone that pain, while difficult, is the catalyst for growth. She's just the facilitator.

The doorbell rings. She feels afraid, then angry. She'd told him not to come this week. She wants to be alone, to think and to figure everything out. It rings again. She won't give him a key even though he keeps insisting on one. She glances around the apartment to make sure there's nothing lying around that will trigger suspicion or accusations or fury. She presses the buzzer and stands by the open door, listening to his steps getting closer, centering herself with deep, calm breathing. She places a hand on her lower stomach as if to check the bump, still only noticeable to herself, is still there. It is – a tiny and delicious secret she'd defend with her own life.

For a long while afterward, they lie awake. She feels confused and tense. The familiarity of him used to feel so good, it was worth all the pain, at least she thought so, but now it feels stifling.

I think we should make a baby, he whispers. She's speechless and turns her face away from him so he won't see the tears that appear in her eyes. How is she going to get out of this? He is never going to let her go. Unless...

Her thoughts return to Bekkebu. To the soft glow from the fireplace and the crackle of the flames. To the imagined scene of sitting across from Kristina Moss, telling her everything. She glances over at the man beside her and feels a sharp bolt of dread in her stomach. She realizes that everything that's happened and everything she has done could place her in danger. She needs a plan B. She closes her eyes and brings forth the images that never fail to fill her with awe – two stars colliding and bursting into mesmerizing luminous explosions, so bright they light up entire galaxies, if only for a moment in time.

25

Kristina, November 1st

I sit up fast, stabbing at the screen, waiting for the email to load. It was sent at 10.31 last night, and only a few sentences are written in the body of the email.

> Why haven't you come? I've been waiting and waiting for you. All I wanted was to tell you the truth. Something we have in common, you and I, is living a lie. And when you live in the shadow of one lie, you build more and more lies around that lie until nothing is true or real. If you'd come, we could have talked. I just wanted to tell you the truth. And I wanted to talk to you about Carúpano. But now – now it really is too late. Everything is lost. I wrote about you, and I wanted you to have it. I called it *Supernova* because that's the word that comes to mind when it comes to you and me, it's attached.

I look for the attachment, but there is nothing. I reload my email several times to see if it could have been sent after or filtered out of my inbox, but nothing. *Supernova*. I've heard the word before but can't discern its meaning off the top of my mind. I feel suddenly, entirely sober. I sit in the hushed silence of the apartment for a long time, hesitating over the email. The fact that she refers to an attachment and then doesn't attach it seems strange. What if Anton went back there and surprised her, furious after being questioned by the police and killed her? Or what if she's about to end her own life? *Now it really is too late. Everything is lost.* To me, these sound like the words of someone in an agitated state of mind, someone who has planned something.

That she mentioned Carúpano brings me an instant chill, a nervous tremble to my stomach, like the flicker of a tiny bird's wings. Could it be that she has been snooping around in my personal life, and thinks she's uncovered something she wishes to discuss with me. Leah clearly has no concept of how potentially damaging this could be. Or... could it be that she's written about me the way she wrote about Anton, isn't that what she's implying? I feel a wild surge of fury. How dare she?

I open Chrome on my browser and type 'Supernova'. After ten minutes of scrolling through websites from NASA to Wikipedia, I have learned that a supernova is the phenomenon of a star exploding spectacularly. The images of dying stars are beautiful and intriguing, their brightness sometimes reaching a billion times that of the sun. *A supernova is the biggest explosion humans have ever seen*, says NASA. *The original star is completely destroyed*, says Wikipedia. In obliteration, supernovae can outshine an entire galaxy, according to space.com. *A beautiful death*, I think to myself, picturing luminous, technicolor destruction drenching the dark corners of space with its light. I study the images, trying to still my racing heart and figure out why Leah referred to this phenomenon. Is this what she was getting at, comparing herself to a star whose death is both powerful and awe-inducing?

I called it *Supernova* because that's the word that comes to mind when it comes to you and me…

I consciously calm myself down slightly by reminding myself that the event she is referring to – Carúpano – is hardly a secret, there is nothing she could find out about me or my past that isn't a click away on the internet. And Elisabeth is dead.

But Leah is a novelist and a famous one at that – she is someone who is in a position to draw public attention to things that could ruin my life. I need to know what Leah is playing at; I can't sit around my house waiting for the phone to ring or something else to happen. *Have it your way, Leah*, I think to myself. I'm going to find her. And I'm going to shut her up.

26

Kristina

It's still early morning. If I leave now, I could feasibly be back home by late this evening. I grab a black leather weekend holdall from the closet and place a spare pair of contact lenses into it, as well as some underwear and a thick sweater. I'll be back tonight, but you never know what might happen and I like to come prepared. I get a torch from the kitchen drawer and throw in some chocolate chip cookies and a large bottle of San Pellegrino too. I grab the car keys from the key holder on the wall by the front door, then step outside into the foyer. I can't immediately recall when I last drove my car – living so centrally in Oslo, I never have to. All our groceries are delivered to the door, and both Eirik and I walk to work, and yet we keep both a BMW SUV and a Tesla.

As I lock the door, I have a sudden and violent conviction that I am doing it for the last time, that I will never again see these gray turn-of-the-century floor tiles, never again stand in this exact spot, resting my hand on the smooth wooden door handle, never again walk down these black stone steps, or open this door onto Incognito Gate, letting the blustery air rush into my face. I stop for a moment and look back up the sweeping communal staircase toward our apartment. What I am doing is clearly in breach of professional conduct and perhaps a little crazy, but I have the sensation that I don't quite know what I'm dealing with here. Could it also be dangerous?

27

Kristina

It's almost three hours to drive from central Oslo to Seljord, the nearest settlement to Leah's cabin, according to the coordinates on her note. Thankfully I've set off early, so I should get there before it gets dark. Hopefully, whatever I find, I can get this strange situation out of my head, arriving back home again before evening. It feels good, actually, to be on the road, driving fast and listening to the radio, doing something other than sitting across from a client or moving around in the hushed, oppressive silence of our apartment. Besides, if nothing else, someone needs to go and check on Leah since the police won't.

In the aftermath of difficult times in my life I have always been able to find some peace on the road, just letting all the hard stuff drop away from me, leaving it behind on the road dwindling away behind me. In my twenties I sometimes felt that going for a long drive alone was the only way to process, but in recent years I haven't turned to it in the same way. I guess I've been consumed by work and by my marriage. And it has finally been quieter inside my head. Until now.

I listen to the weather report: heavy snow this afternoon. Hopefully I'll have time to head back to the city before it sets in. I switch to a channel playing old hits and this makes me feel young again, like I might yet discover new things about myself or make decisions that would set my life onto a different path. This is of course true for everybody, but not many people live like that once the central pillars in life are in place; life partner, career, home. And yet. I could, technically speaking, retrain to do something else, just like I did once before, and live somewhere else, with another man. None of the things that feel fixed and set in stone truly are. This is something I try to convey to my clients in the therapy room, too – that, for better or worse, change is the one constant, and even if life feels unmanageable and impossibly dark in the present moment, it will change, if you can find a way to hang in there.

I pull into a picnic area by the roadside a few miles past Kongsberg. There is nobody here and the sky is an oppressive slate gray. Patches of dirty snow line the roadside. I feel profoundly troubled by Leah's words. I get out of the car to stretch my legs for a moment. Dark pines tower over the little parking lot, veils of mist twisting between their crowns, rising toward the low-hanging clouds. A bitter wind sweeps across the road, tearing at me. I can feel more snow in the air, and it occurs to me that I still have summer tires on the car.

What am I doing here, by the roadside in the depths of the woods, on my way to Leah's mountain cabin? Am I regressing into irrational behavior after having come so far?

Nobody knows that I am here, not even Eirik. I think it's because of Eirik that I've come here. Doing something out of character like driving halfway across Norway to check on Leah feels like a little rebellion against my husband's relentless recent travel schedule. Though I am fully aware of the demands of Eirik's political career, I sometimes can't help but feel this isn't what I signed up for. I worry about the toll on our marriage as his public profile grows, and that an ever-increasing distance will open up between us. There are times when I wake in the night and listen to Eirik's soft, even breathing in the dark, and it feels like being in bed with a stranger. But there are also the times that he pulls me close and looks me in the eyes and strokes me all over, and I feel close to him again.

I get back in the car, rubbing my icy hands together, but wait a moment to start the engine. I feel a deep trepidation in my gut that isn't entirely unpleasant. As disturbing and worrying as the developments of the past ten days have been, Leah's dramatic exit from the therapy room and apparent disappearance have dominated my thoughts, giving me something other than Elisabeth's suicide to think about. Like with Leah, I was the last person to see Elisabeth alive. Like Leah, Elisabeth trusted me with her innermost thoughts. Or so I believed.

I don't want to think about Elisabeth, not now; I want to just block her life and death from my thoughts and my heart, but I know better than anybody that it doesn't work like that. Elisabeth will always be on my mind. Elisabeth, whose talent for self-destruction overshadowed everything else – how wonderful she was, how intelligent, how good at her beautiful art she was, how very loved. But like most lifelong addicts, no matter how functional at times, she ultimately loved the needle more than anything else, including herself. And it killed her.

Tears again. Jesus, I'm not going to go there now. I have spoken about Elisabeth constantly in my own therapy sessions; about how it felt like she was a part of me – a shadow with a penchant for darkness. I am wracked with guilt over how her life ended. It came after a long period when she had showed so much promise and improvement. I wish, so deeply, that things could have been different. That she could have made better choices. I take a few deep breaths and center myself in the moment. This isn't about Elisabeth, or me; it's about Leah.

It's been nine days since I last saw her. She was afraid. And hurt. She lied to me about Anton. What else did she lie about? She didn't tell me she was pregnant, a kind of lie in itself. But why? And why did she say she wanted to speak to me about Carúpano? Every time I think about the way she casually threw that into her email I feel consumed by rage. And what will I find once I arrive at her cabin?

I start driving again, slower now – I feel a little tender, and the dual carriageway has narrowed into a small, windy district road as I head into the mountainous forests of Buskerud county. The forests become even denser after I pass into Telemark county, the sky briefly clearing and weakening into a gorgeous pink-streaked indigo as the sun lowers itself down towards the rounded, snow-capped mountains in the distance. Close to Seljord I stop in another lay-by and peer at the map on my phone. The forests crowd in on the car, like the road is a wound that the forest is trying to heal.

Leah's cabin seems to sit entirely on its own, high up against the crest of a hill overlooking Heivannet Lake. She wouldn't be within earshot nor easy walking distance of any other cabins, and I wonder whether she ever even meets anyone else up there.

I take several wrong turns before I manage to find the right forest track – they all look the same and they all inevitably end in a locked barrier. On my fourth attempt to find the right track, which is supposed to run alongside the lake, then rise to climb into the hills on its north shore, I'm successful. One of the two keys Leah gave me slots into the rusty padlock of the road barrier and the gate swings open. I drive through, then stop, leaving the engine idle while I return to lock the barrier behind me. Only the residents of a given area have the keys to the barriers on these remote forest roads, avoiding through-traffic and burglaries in scarcely populated areas. I feel a sudden irrational panic rise in me as I return to the car; for a moment I am dragged back in time to another forest, another car, another me. I slam the door hard and breathe calmly, focusing on the narrow road unfolding ahead, caught in the headlights. I urge the gas, my heart hammering wildly. *Stop, Kristina*, I tell myself. *The only thing to fear here is your own mind if you can't control it.*

The sky is changing again in the East – from frosty white to a dark charcoal. Thin wisps of fog drift between the trees, giving them an eerie, milky glow. Leah would have driven down this exact same track not long ago. Did she intensely commit all of this to memory like I am: the dripping spruces, the brown-black pines, the meek, steely skies, the black lake at the bottom of the valley, occasionally glimpsed through the dense crowd of trees?

The phone vibrates and a voice says: 'Your destination is on the left.'

There is nothing to the left except a wall of trees, but then I spot a wooden sign nailed to a trunk that reads 'Bekkebu' and next to it an even smaller track. I turn onto it and quickly realize I'm going to have to leave the car and continue on foot. Light snow begins to fall. There is a cleared, car-sized grassy area to the side of the track and a white Range Rover Evoque is parked there, tucked in neatly from the track, surrounded by mounds of hardened snow. I assume it is Leah's car, and as there are no visible tire tracks in the patches of snow surrounding it, it would seem it has sat here for days. It looks as though it has been placed here from above by the hand of a giant, like a Lego car.

I turn off the engine and the lights and sit for a long moment in the deep silence of the woods. I feel a nervous flutter in my stomach, but refuse to indulge this kind of irrational fear. Walking alone at night in central Oslo is much more dangerous than being out here in these remote, untouched forests, though it doesn't feel like that.

My phone vibrates in my hand.

Hey babe, all set up and ready to smash it, reads a WhatsApp from Eirik, accompanied by a selfie of my husband against the picturesque backdrop of Bergen harbor, a line of Høyre Conservative Party campaign flags snapping in the wind behind him. I smile at the goofy expression on his handsome face. It occurs to me that I haven't actually let Eirik know that I've come here on my own. I open the camera and take a selfie, angling the phone to catch the snow falling against a backdrop of thick forest outside.

Impulsive road trip, I write. *I've gone to Telemark to find Leah Iverson, long story. Turns out she wrote about me (!) so I've decided I need to speak with her and get her some intervention. Couldn't make it up. Good luck & call me later.*

I only have one bar of phone reception and have to press 'resend' three times before the message finally goes through. *You're not in Frogner anymore, that's for sure*, I think to myself and ready myself to step outside into the cold.

I grab a flashlight from the emergency pack Eirik insists I keep in the glove compartment and fasten the strap of my handbag across my chest. I shine the flashlight into Leah's car, but there's nothing unusual there – just a pair of iPhone headphones and a chewing gum wrapper on the passenger seat. I take a couple of steps back and am about to start walking when I let my eyes rest on the tires of the car. I can't help but release a shocked sound when I see that both tires on this side of the car are flat, clearly slashed. My pulse rising, I walk around the other side. These too, are flat.

I stare up the narrow, steep slope of the track. Again, I think about my sensation of danger as I left the apartment in Oslo. What am I going to find at the end of this track? I decide to leave the holdall in the car – I'm just going to do a quick sweep of the cabin. Hopefully Leah is there, safe and willing to have a real conversation about what's going on. We can talk in the car on the way back, no reason to remain in a remote cabin. No wonder she hasn't returned home if her car has been deliberately damaged and she has no phone reception. I get a sudden, terrifying picture in my head of Anton slashing her tires, angry with her for refusing to return to the city with him because she was still waiting for me. I have no intention of staying for longer than to convince Leah to come back to Oslo with me, but I simply have to get to the bottom of this. I glance at the crude map Leah drew for me, and walk for a good ten minutes, and my legs start to ache as the track's incline gets ever steeper. The snow is still falling in tiny flakes from a dull white sky, and as I turn and look back down the way I came, I see much darker, lower clouds encroaching, closer now. They're the kind that carry heavy, wet snowflakes capable of covering the landscape in a swift whiteout.

I reach the top of the hill and pause for a minute to catch my breath. The track flattens out and I emerge from a dense clutch of trees; I'm standing on the shoulder of the mountain. Far below me a jet-black lake spreads out in full view, its water held beneath a fragile lid of sparkling ice. I look around for signs of Leah's cabin, but can't see anything man-made at all. I notice a smudge of blue paint on a birch tree a few meters away, and realize it's a trail marker. I consult the map again, it seems I need to find a much smaller path winding further into the woods from the clearing. When I start walking again, I see a little hand-carved wooden sign strung from a tree that reads 'Bekkebu', with a pointed arrow in the direction I'm heading. I wonder if she made it herself; it seems like the kind of thing Leah might do.

How does she even bring groceries up here? I can't imagine wanting to stay in a cabin so remote you have to walk for twenty minutes from the parking spot up a steep, slippery track through the woods, but each to their own, I guess, and it is fairly common among Scandinavians to seek out this kind of very basic back-to-nature experience.

I stop for a minute and have to control another onslaught of sudden fierce fear of being here in the woods, so utterly alone, so far from my real life, but there is something rather exhilarating about it, too. I'm able to control my thoughts and dispel the anxiety. I feel proud of myself for being able to be somewhere like this, in the thick forest, alone, and not succumb to an irrational, blind panic.

I look at my phone, but as I suspected, I have lost reception. I'm about to keep walking when I glimpse a slash of wan white sky beyond the trees just ahead of where I'm standing. It must be another clearing, and I push my way through the trees and spot what looks like the low grass-topped roof of a cabin, noticeably straighter than the craggy clearing it edges on, nestled up against the woods, overlooking the lake and the valley. The snow, already falling thicker and faster, settles onto the roof and I imagine it's only hours until the cabin will merge with the surrounding terrain in a cloak of pristine white.

I walk toward it, slowing down as I approach because my heart is beating so hard. A light is on inside. I imagine Leah in there, sitting at an old wooden desk by the fireplace, typing quickly, her beautiful face glowing golden in the light from the snapping, lively flames. I approach the door and glance around for footsteps around the cabin, but the snow has already started to settle on the ground around the cabin, erasing whatever might have been there.

I knock on the door and listen, but can't make out anything other than the soft rustle of branches. I knock again. I could just turn back around and hurry to my car and call for help once I have reception. I have the sudden conviction that if I use the key Leah gave me I'll find her dead inside. Perhaps that's what she wanted, and why she tried to get me to come here in the first place. I don't want to find her dead. It's been less than three months since I walked into our spare bedroom and found Elisabeth on the bed, staring straight at me, unseeing, her sweet face already eerily different.

I knock for the third time, harder, then instinctively try the door handle. The door is unlocked and swings open inward.

28

Leah, one week before

She closes the door to the cabin behind her and draws its familiar scent deep into her lungs. No matter how the future plays out, at least she has this sweet, beloved place. She moves without fear through the silent, dark space and twists the knobs on the oil lamps lined up along the windowsill. She stares out at the impossible beauty of the valley, its trees shimmering in autumnal shades of gold, bronze and ochre in the last of the afternoon light. Already, the long, exhausting Friday-night drive from the capital is forgotten. She steps back from the window and her face is reflected back at her. Her expression is haunted and her left eye is still swollen shut. She runs a fingertip alongside the broken and bruised patch on her face, prodding gently for signs of broken bones.

In the kitchen she unpacks her one small bag of groceries. Minced meat, shredded cheese, cucumber, taco spices, corn tortillas – Leah has come to love the Norwegian obsession with Friday-night tacos. There is also a bottle of wine, some milk and a pizza for tomorrow. She pours herself a small glass of wine, they say just one doesn't hurt the baby, and sits on the sofa, just listening to the deep silence. She touches her hand to her belly and is filled with the most unbearable dread. She would give anything for this to be different. How is she supposed to forgive him for what happened in Oslo? But she knows she will, if only he'll come back.

In the meantime, there is nothing to do but wait; she has to believe that Kristina will come. *Please come*, she whispers into the air. *Please*.

She picks her favorite book off the shelf and sits down on the sofa. She opens *The Bell Jar*, flicking through it to where she last marked it by folding down the page.

> *What I want back is what I was*
> *Before the bed, before the knife,*
> *Before the brooch-pin and the salve*
> *Fixed me in this parenthesis;*
> *Horses fluent in the wind,*
> *A place, a time gone out of mind.*

It's this that finally brings tears to her eyes. Not the words, or the strike, or the devastating kindness on Kristina's face, nor the long, lonely drive on winding roads into the hills, then the mountains. It's Sylvia Plath who unleashes the storm of emotion Leah has held back, suppressed, and it's Sylvia who makes her lean into the pain, pushing herself deeper and deeper into it until she emerges into the still, black eye of the storm. From there she invites it all and observes its devastating rampage through her mind from the safe vantage point at its very core.

She gets up, suddenly filled with conviction about what to write. For so long, she's tried to force the words, though anyone who's ever tried to write knows words won't be forced.

As she starts to type, she fights the urge to both laugh and cry, consciously maintaining her focus on the screen. *I can't believe I didn't realize it before*, she begins, *that what I really wanted all along was to write to you. So that's what I'm going to do. A memoir, perhaps. No. A confession.*

And finally, the words flow, so fast that Leah can barely keep up, and by the time she takes a break, it's already past midnight and she is several thousand words in. It felt good, even though they were hard words to write. She still can't be sure whether this confession, or whatever it will be, is a work of love or a work of hatred; the two always seemed intrinsically linked, like we can only hate that which we also love and crave. She gets up and stands a while in front of the bathroom mirror, taking in her bruises; purple and blue and yellow, spreading across her face like supernovae shockwaves across the black velvet universe.

29

Kristina

'Leah?' I say, first gently and then louder. There is no answer. I'm in a dark entranceway and I fumble around for a light switch, but realize there isn't one. The cabin doesn't appear to have electricity – there are no visible wires or switches anywhere. I grab my torch, shining it around, trying to get my bearings. There are three doors leading from this tiny space. I try the first one. It's a large, empty bathroom, its timber walls painted a beautiful deep shade of aqua blue. A round gilded mirror hangs above a stone sink, and under the window stands an antique brass bathtub, big enough for two. I shine the beam from the torch into it as though Leah might be lying at the bottom.

I try the second door but it's a deep airing cupboard used to store linen and towels, as well as a thick down winter duvet. The third door leads into the cabin's main room and I quickly scan the space, but it's empty. Still, I call her name while shining the beam into all the nooks and crannies. I stand in the middle of the room for a long moment, deciding what to do. She's not here, that much is obvious. Maybe she's gone outside for some reason, a walk around the lake perhaps, though with heavy snow forecast I'd imagine she'd want to stay close to the cabin. Perhaps I'll wait for her for an hour or so; I can still make it back to the car before it's fully dark. There is also the possibility that she has been picked up by someone, and could be anywhere by now. Or, Anton really has hurt her and has had several days to cover up his crime.

I swallow hard and glance around the room for any sign of what could have happened to Leah. The cabin is made up of one large, open-plan room, with a built-in sleeping alcove in the far corner by the hearth. There is a cozy timbered kitchen nook held up by low, original beams painted a dusky gray. I take in Leah's space, the space she loves. *It's as if the cabin is a physical incarnation of my soul*, she once said, and with this in mind, it seems inevitable that this is Leah's space. Unfussy and sweet, unconventionally beautiful and a little cluttered, like its owner. There are books everywhere, crammed onto shelves, piled on the floor, stacked on windowsills and a couple splayed face-down on the coffee table.

There's a strange little stuffed animal sitting in a chair – it looks like a child's toy. I pick it up and quickly place it back in its seat – it feels wrong to snoop around and touch Leah's possessions. I walk into the kitchen and stand by the sink. The workbench is beneath a window, looking out at the empty valley, the lake and the white-capped mountains beyond. A chipped mug stands to the side of the sink and I pick it up. It bears a faded crest from Stanford University and I recall that Leah went there for a semester on an exchange program. It occurs to me that even as her therapist, there is so much I don't know about Leah and her life. In this moment she could be anywhere and with anyone, and there is a real chance I'll never see her again or learn what brought about her abrupt change in behavior.

Finding myself standing here, in her space, in the place she loves, looking at a quirky hand-made key holder and a framed poster for her first novel hung side by side on the wall, her walking boots carefully placed under a wooden bench, and a lingering scent of what I now realize is Leah's perfume, intensely familiar to me, I feel her absence acutely and just want to get to the bottom of this.

It's easy to understand why she loves coming here. *The cabin is my oasis*, she often says, and this makes perfect sense. And yet, it's quite a radical thing to do, for a lone woman to come somewhere like this on a regular basis. What, exactly, does she do here? I feel a strange jealousy of Leah's bravery, of her obvious connection to nature and commitment to this simple life – it's very far removed from the comfortable life I lead in central Oslo.

The cabin is miles away from the nearest dwelling, set in woods so thick I doubt one would be able to pick out the house from above. It has no modern amenities. What it does have is beautiful wood carvings, lovely rounded blonde timber walls that I imagine would take on a golden glow from the hearth when lit, and books everywhere, leaving the sweet, subtle scent of well-thumbed pages and firewood on the air.

I pick a random book off a heavily laden shelf – Dostoyevsky – and run my finger lightly across the cover.

I pick up another, Arundhati Roy's first, one of my own favorites, and feel pleased to see that it is well-thumbed and dog-eared. I let my eyes roam and everywhere they go, they find something beautiful and comforting. Books. Small, carefully curated paintings in the same warm hues as the timber walls themselves. A little black Chinese antique lacquered cupboard with fine crystal glasses lined up on its shelves. I lift one and hold it up to the weak light from the oil lamp I've lit, its intricate carvings glinting in rainbows. Leah clearly loves beautiful things.

And then it's like something in the air shifts, like she's here with me, having sidled up beside me, becoming clearer and clearer as I begin to sense her and now I can practically see her. She's sitting on the stone ledge next to the hearth, feet drawn up, beneath a collection of ancient copper pots and pans strung from a metal railing.

She's singing out loud, softly, rubbing her arms trying to get more warmth into her body. She's almost childlike in the way she's sitting, hugging herself, staring into the leaping flames, willing their heat to spread faster around the little room. Her beautiful face is red and glowing, like she's run here through heavy snow.

Sometimes in our sessions, she came across as almost childlike, too, displaying unusual mannerisms for an adult: picking at her jacket sleeve until it frayed, a constantly jerking foot, or an unusual choice of words. She dressed young, too, especially at the beginning, and I wouldn't have been surprised if she still wears items from her mid-teens, though she's over thirty. This is something I see quite often, and can be seen as a desire to hold onto youth and freedom, a subtle rejection of the demands of adult life. I see it particularly often in the very wounded, those clients who come to therapy with life-altering trauma. It's natural to seek out those feelings of security and protection we felt in childhood when we have had the experience of living entirely unprotected in the world and suffering deep wounds as a result.

A strange sound snaps me out of my reverie, and I hold myself entirely still, suddenly irrationally fearful. I hear it again, a long and exaggerated murmur, like an old animal exhaling slowly, sending air through obstructed passages. There is a series of splutters, like a throaty cough, then silence. Could an injured animal have gotten into the cabin, now dying in a dark corner? I feel the hair on my arms stand up and begin to shiver. I move slowly toward the kitchen nook, peering into corners, but see nothing unusual. I light another oil lamp and turn the torch back on to boost the light.

In the kitchen nook the noise starts up again and it turns out to be coming from a small refrigerator on the countertop, seemingly running off a generator placed on an open shelf near the floor.

I open the refrigerator and there is a bottle of white wine and a pint of milk, both open. There is a plate of cooked margherita pizza, but it has patches of mold on it. There are a couple of browning, shrunken limes and a wilting bunch of coriander. At the back, I find an unopened packet of minced meat, which expired two days ago. Another sound insists itself into the cocoon space of Leah's cabin. It is the wind chasing up the mountainsides from the lake in the valley, and it carries with it a smattering of snow, tiny perfect snowflakes kissing the diamond-gridded windows.

I close the refrigerator and stand for a while looking out into the main room; its hushed, peaceful atmosphere is intoxicating and instantly soothing, like standing inside a hug. And yet, there is something not right about this place and Leah's absence. Then I notice something I missed on my first sweep of the room. Next to the sofa is a small, low table on top of which sits a MacBook Air, exactly the size of the tabletop. I stare at it and have the disturbing feeling I often get when I try to reach back in time through my own life and come up against that blank wall of nothingness that shrouds significant chunks of my experiences. I know that something dark is there beneath the ominous white haze, like the charred bones of a burned-out house beneath deep snow, but I can't quite grasp it. Now, I feel as though I am looking straight at the missing piece of the puzzle, but still can't make out what the bigger picture is.

I move toward the laptop but feel a headache coming on, so I sit down on the sofa and press my fingers against my eyes, and I see Leah so clearly in my mind, as if she was stamped on my retinas like the blurred shadows that roam across my field of vision. That last session, her last day. Pleading with me, eyes wild. *Come to my cabin. Please, please, please.* I open the computer and it instantly lights up to the home screen, its backdrop a beautiful photograph of the valley below Bekkebu in summer, the hillsides draped in heather and the lake reflecting a bruised evening sky. The desktop is empty besides a document titled with a single word: 'Supernova'. I shiver lightly at the memory of her disturbing words.

This is about the truth.

I wrote about you.

I called it Supernova *because that's the word that comes to mind when it comes to you and me.*

And I want to talk to you about Carúpano.

30

Supernova

I can't believe I didn't realize it before, that what I really wanted all along was to write to you. So that's what I'm going to do. A memoir, perhaps. No. A confession.

Kristina, I'm waiting for you. I pray that you'll come. I'm alone and I'm afraid for the future and I want to use this time to put everything I want to say to you into some kind of coherent account. I want to tell you everything myself, I have it all planned out in my head – you'll come here and you'll sit across from me and we'll light the fire and I will start from the beginning and I won't stop talking until there is absolutely nothing unsaid between us. If you can't or won't come or if something outside of my control happens to me, you'll find what you need here. Either way, I need you to know the truth.

Let's imagine that the story of our relationship was a novel. Writing a novel is like constructing a body from severed chunks of flesh and then magically breathing it to life, sending themes coursing through its inner framework like blood through veins. Love, empathy, obsession, jealousy, fear, grief, memory, betrayal, redemption. Which would be the main themes in our story, Kristina? I think by the time I've said everything I want to say, we'll see that all of the above will jostle for space in a complex narrative in which past and present are as entwined as a body with its soul.

And which genre might such a novel fit into? My first instinct might have been that it was an unusual kind of love story, one that explores connection and vulnerability rather than romance and sex, but the boundaries between them became blurred a while ago and now they have come to seem increasingly indiscernible from one another. On second thought, just a few weeks ago, before I began to see the lines, the ones that link each occurrence in a person's life to the next and the next, I would have called it a nihilistic reverie of sorts; meaningless fragments of lives and experiences, souped together and brought to the boil. Now, I'd be inclined to call such a novel a psychological thriller. It would contain all of the components of the genre's best offerings – unreliable narrators, a missing woman, the dangers of love and desire, the past looming at the edges – more potent than ever, a dash of amnesia, murder. This is, of course, not a novel, though I'm finding it an interesting comparison. Like I said, it's a confession.

I'm calling it *Supernova* because it's the word I could never let go of. It's what I think of when I think of you. I can't let go of the images, either. Did you know that a supernova is a result of two stars colliding and they both end up dead? A big star and a little one, together in a celestial dance. The little white dwarf star steals material from the big one until it has too much, too much to carry and to hold, drawing both stars into a gigantic thermonuclear explosion so bright it can light up anything, anything at all. And afterward, a black hole, a rip in the lining of the heavens.

It's late at night and it feels as though I am the only person left in a cold and deserted world, but as you know, I have often felt like that in my life, and not only in the dead of a freezing October night. I have felt like that on hot afternoons in summer when the air is clammy and the stench of barbecue smoke drifts across the city, walking down streets and through parks aimlessly, surrounded by throngs of laughing people, unseen. I have felt like that in bed with lovers, feeling their touch travel across my skin, but actually being light-years away, shut away inside myself. I have felt like that in my family, as though nothing of me could have come from anything of them; at best I was like a ball of phlegm – expelled and forgotten about, certainly not loved or missed.

But I didn't feel like that with you. You changed everything and you don't need me to tell you what that kind of shift can mean to someone. It was seismic. And it was dangerous. It made me believe that I could be like you, and that I, too, could have everything. Those can be dangerous thoughts and in this moment, alone and waiting for you, I wish I could have learned to be content with what I *did* have: health, a home, people reading my words, you. But people always want more, don't they?

I am sitting here trying to imagine you reading these words, but can't imagine a world in which that would be possible, simply because I know what it would mean. It would mean that you never came. Or that I've been hurt. Or perhaps it would just mean that after writing everything

I want to say to you I'll come to the conclusion that I'd rather send it to you than speak these words out loud. Any way, I can't envision us ever sitting across from each other again, in that dear little room in Homansbyen that came to mean so much to me.

We need to go back to the beginning, though beginning in itself is a relative term – there are many story threads here and each one of them has a beginning – we'll get to each one of them in turn.

You were chosen for me, and I think of that with a measure of awe now. That a psychotherapist was assigned me and it just happened to be you; it seems almost impossible to grasp that the most important person in my life would be delivered to me by random allocation. *Fridays at two*, my GP said. *Dr Kristina Moss will see you. A very impressive psychotherapist. Fifty minutes.*

It was all paid for, all I needed to do was show up.

You know, you fully had me from the very first session. I became yours in a way I'd never been anybody's before, just by really being seen. Our sessions were my first meeting with being taken seriously and being fully listened to. You were the first person I ever met who offered me an unconditional relationship without judgment. My mother loves me, as we've discussed in depth, but her love was always conditional. She drilled into me that I was free to be whatever I wanted, but really, it was only true when I was little enough for her to still believe that I'd want to be like her. She celebrated my achievements, but only when she could take credit for them. She commiserated when I failed, too, but wouldn't want any credit for that.

You were just *there*, regardless of what I brought to

therapy. You made me feel like there was space for all of me. That it was okay to be sad and angry and empty, that none of that took away from my worth in your eyes. I hadn't anticipated the effect that would have on me, nor how deep the grief it triggered would be, to realize that I'd never had it before.

I know that to you, I'm nothing. Or at best, I'm a number on a list, just another name in your professional diary. To me, you're everything. Don't think that I simply idolize you; I know you better than you think, I see a whole person, and at first it was difficult for me to accept you were actually real, flaws and all. People inevitably change when light is cast upon them; they seldom turn out to be the beautiful, perfect holograms you saw when you first looked. They crumble or grow distorted because nothing in life is pure enough to withstand real scrutiny – people and places and objects equally. Take the supernova. What looks so beautiful, like the moment something precious is created, is actually the moment of violent destruction. Nothing is ever how it looks at first, it's just how it is, and it was the same with you. And me.

When I try to determine what exactly you know of me, I draw a blank. I can't be sure. Once, I thought you knew and intrinsically understood everything about me, that you had preemptive powers to discern my every need before I could even begin to identify them myself. I was wrong, of course. But you know about the way I think. You know that emotion comes at me thick and fast. You know that I've been burned. You know that I don't love myself and that it leads to others taking what shouldn't be given away. And yet, you only know what I've told you. This is where we differ, you and I. You have told me exactly nothing about yourself, and yet I know – dare I say – everything. Even things you yourself don't know.

Let me explain. Beginnings.

It all started very innocently, and entirely by chance. I'd been coming to see you for a few months by then, so it must have been around Easter time. I was settling into therapy and found that it had become a lifeline. The sessions made me ask myself questions I wouldn't otherwise have raised. My awareness increased. What was my response in a given situation, and why? Could it be different in the future? It was exhilarating to realize that I may have a choice in the matter. But most of all, the thing that brought real change was the bond built between you and me. I trusted you. You showed me what I could do in a million little ways. You were never late, never distracted, always focused on whatever I brought to the room and for the first time, it made me feel like I actually mattered, that my feelings should be listened to and valued. By pretending you cared (and it *is* pretending) you made *me* care.

Back to that Easter. It was a beautiful Friday and we had a good session. I remember it clearly – I asked you lots of questions about yourself, which you gently deflected. I wanted to know about you because as the sessions increasingly began to have an effect on me, I felt intensely attached to you. I still do. Those feelings have played along the whole spectrum of human emotion, from neediness to admiration to attraction to love to dislike and even hatred.

To obsession.

After our session that day, I felt strangely liquid inside, like you'd torched me with your careful questions, setting fire to the long-held beliefs about myself that no longer served me. *Leah, could it be that you deserve your own kindness? That sounds like a very distressing experience, Leah. Even if he said you deserved it and you believed him in that moment, does it mean it was actually true? Could it be that you deserve to be loved?*

I walked the few meters from your office to Kaffebrenneriet on the corner of Parkveien and Bogstadveien, ordered a cortado and sat in the corner by the large windows, my back to the counter. It was loud in there, the baristas banging the portafilters against the countertops to empty the espresso grits, a steady chatter of the afternoon coffee crowd from nearby offices, and the occasional blue tram rambling past outside, heading uptown. I saw a flash of orange pass by the window as I raised the cortado to my nostrils, drawing its perfect bitter and burned scent into me, then the door opened, bringing a cool draft. Then I heard your voice.

A double tall white Americano, you said. I turned my head slowly, to double-check that it really was you. You stood, unaware, scrolling on your phone, waiting. When your coffee was ready you flashed a quick smile at the barista and it made me irrationally angry for a moment, watching you smile at someone as inconsequential as a random café worker when I was used to having your undivided attention. Your smile also prompted another wave of that liquid heat in my stomach. This was back when I sometimes felt confused by overwhelming attraction to you.

You took your coffee to go, and before I knew it, I'd left my cortado half-drunk on the narrow window table and scrambled after you out onto the street, struggling to get my jacket on. It was only March and the air was crisp, but the sky was a deep indigo blue and the days were getting longer. The promise of spring had changed the atmosphere of the town and even the facial expressions of the people. You walked slowly up Bogstadveien, easy to spot in your orange parka, and I hung back at a little distance, yet close enough to observe you. You stopped to look in a few windows, sipping at your coffee, and several times you checked your phone. About halfway up Bogstadveien, you crossed over to the other side. I followed. You turned down Rosenborggata, a quiet residential street, and I wondered whether it was where you lived – I didn't know anything about you back then. I hovered at the corner of the main street, pretending to look at my phone, and watched you approach a white, turn-of-the-century apartment building.

You stood looking up at the building for a long while, as if psyching yourself up to meet whoever was inside. You raised your finger to the panel of doorbells on the side wall, and it hovered there a while. I couldn't tell from where I stood whether you'd actually pressed one, and if so, which one. You glanced down the street in my direction, but wouldn't have been able to pick me out; I stood partially hidden in a wide doorway opposite the Peak Performance shop. Your face had changed, and you looked troubled and nervous. Suddenly you seemed to change your mind and came walking back down the street toward me, drawing your parka tight, burying the lower part of your face in the faux-fur hood. You walked straight past me and into the throng of shoppers and people taking an early Friday, heading home from work downtown. I let you out of sight and remained in the doorway for a long while. Then I headed back down in the direction we'd come, until I arrived back at Kaffebrenneriet.

The line was longer now, but I didn't mind waiting. My head was spinning with what I'd done and seen. It had been exhilarating seeing you out of the therapy room, and I knew even that first day, that I'd do it again. I couldn't have known then what I would find and what processes the slow discovery of Kristina Moss would bring about. Back then, you were still perfect to me, the way I wanted you to be. I wish I'd stopped there and then so you could have remained a shiny, flawless hologram. If I had, I wouldn't be writing these words. But equally, it is the imperfect, real Kristina I came to discover that has brought true empathy and a deep desire to be there for you like you've been there for me.

A *double tall white Americano*, I said when it was my turn to order, flashing the same barista who'd taken your order a quick smile.

31

Kristina

I slam the MacBook shut so hard the sharp sound makes me jump. I take a few moments to recenter myself in my unfamiliar surroundings. *It's okay*, I tell myself, but my heart is pounding and my hands tremble. In the minutes it took me to read Leah's words, everything I believed about our relationship and our journey into therapy, have come undone. She's betrayed me in the most fundamental way. The relationship between therapist and client necessarily has to be confined to the therapy room, and the therapist's personal life and preferences need to remain unavailable to the client. This is difficult for a lot of people, as the bonds forged are so deep and the intimacies shared so life-changing. To think that Leah blatantly disregarded the explicitly stated boundaries of our relationship and followed me around is profoundly disturbing. Had I known, I would likely have had to end our working relationship.

I try to determine whether there were any signs of her becoming unusually preoccupied with me, or especially interested in my personal life. She asked a few questions here and there; most people do. Right at the beginning, she would sometimes blush deeply and become visibly embarrassed by some of the things she'd tell me, especially if they were of a sexual nature. But there wasn't anything she did that set off any alarm bells or gave me any cause for real concern, at least not in terms of our therapeutic relationship.

I try to channel my feelings of empathy for Leah Iverson, for the person she is, a client I have always looked forward to seeing, and though it doesn't come easily, this situation is clearly complicated and Leah is very disturbed, significantly more than I was aware, it would seem.

Still, she betrayed me. I have the sensation that the relationship between us, the single most important aspect of the therapeutic process, has not only been irrevocably compromised, but also that it might have always been different altogether than how I subjectively perceived it.

I get up, still unsteady on my feet, but my mind is razor sharp. It seems to mean that Leah intended me to read *Supernova*, whatever this is, only in the event of something happening to her. But what did she think might happen to her?

I know that I won't be able to rest until I know what she meant. The strange thing I was left with in the years after my own traumatic experience was a heightened sense of danger. It's easy enough to explain in medical terms – my body and brain remained on high alert, resulting in PTSD and anxiety issues which I have been able to resolve. And yet I have been left with an ability to sense danger, and I sense it now, that Leah's words aren't just the ramblings of someone in a compromised state of mind, but rather, something potentially dangerous. To herself, but also to me. What did she intend with *Supernova*? *You have told me exactly nothing about yourself, and yet I know – dare I say – everything*, she wrote.

No one knows everything about me, not even myself. Not even now, after all the work I have done. All the years in therapy. So straight off, her statement is categorically untrue. She doesn't know anything about me, let alone everything, and I'm starting to feel I didn't know anything about her either.

I have to keep reading. I glance around, and the cabin is entirely silent, like a cocoon. I open Leah's Mac again.

32

Supernova

I'm hoping we can agree that it started pretty innocently, that day you happened to walk into Kaffebrenneriet to order a tall white Americano and I trailed you up Bogstadveien. It was a spur-of-the-moment kind of thing. It was such a rush to watch you when you didn't know that you were being watched. Back then, at that stage of therapy when it had become a focal point in my life, you were constantly on my mind. An hour on Friday just wasn't quite enough. Our sessions churned in my mind all week and I was always trying to conjure you up in my mind – your calm, encouraging way of being when I faltered, your gentle and unwavering support. I'd started to feel that you were like an invisible best friend I could carry around inside me, someone who'd always have my back even if you weren't physically there in that moment.

I'm not making excuses for my behavior; I don't feel like I've done anything wrong. I've come to understand what my role is in your life – it's not the poor, downtrodden client;

it's being your helper, your closest ally. Your savior, even. Of all the things you taught me, the most important thing was the realization that you can't ever outrun the past. You have to process it, to use your own jargon. Integrate it into the narrative of your life. And I'm going to help you.

It was an unseasonably warm spring, do you remember? Seen in the context of the autumns and winter we've had since, I don't think it's unreasonable to say that we're witnessing a shift in the climate in which every season presents itself more extremely. Hotter, wetter, drier, colder, darker. And that spring came upon us so suddenly after a relentlessly wet and stormy winter, giving us day after day of glorious sunshine and temperatures in the early twenties in mid-April. It breathed everything back to life, even me. It was like the whole city was buzzing with new love.

I did it again, two weeks after the first time. I waited for you at Kaffebrenneriet after our session, sipping a tall white Americano in the window seat. I'd gotten used to drinking my coffee just like yours by then. You didn't come into the café, but after an hour or so, you emerged from your office and walked past on the other side of the street. That day, you wore dark-blue jeans and a white and navy striped sweater with gold buttons on the sleeves. You looked young and carefree, more like a student than a Doctor of Psychology. You were so impressive to me back then – it was like I needed to drink in every last part of you so I could retrieve them later in my mind, and emulate them. North Face orange parkas? I got one, too, but was careful to never wear it on a Friday. White and navy maritime sweater? Check. These things made me feel close to you, like if I wore them, something of you would rub off on me.

Back to that day. You headed up Bogstadveien, like the last time. I followed at a distance, keeping your glossy, high ponytail in sight. If you'd suddenly turned around and noticed me walking in the same direction some distance behind you, it wouldn't be weird at all. I'd merely stopped at a café after our session and happened to also be walking up one of Oslo's busiest shopping streets. You took a right at the corner of Rosenborggata, like last time. That really caught my attention. You stopped at number 11 and hesitated by the doorbells. You stood looking up at the building for a long moment, as if psyching yourself up for meeting whoever was inside. I remembered the last time, when you'd suddenly turned back around and walked away, and I had to press myself into that doorway and hope you didn't see me.

You pressed the buzzer and disappeared inside. A couple of minutes later I went up to the door and read the names on the doorbells, but none of them gave me any clues.

Christiansen. Mikkelsrud. Tanum. Siemens. Olsen-Hoff. Rickards. Thiske. Ellingsen.

A lover? That was my first thought. It struck me like a bolt of lightening; the idea of you doing something sordid was totally irreconcilable with what I needed you to be. At the same time, I was intensely jealous at the thought of you having an illicit affair, and confused by those feelings. I knew you were married from the simple gold ring on your finger, and Google easily uncovered that your marriage was rather high profile. I'll return to it, of course. But back then, it wasn't Mr Moss who most held my attention. It was the suspicion that you were something other than I'd thought.

I fell into a routine of sitting at that café several afternoons a week, keeping an eye on the door to your office building across the road, waiting for you. Sometimes I'd get up and follow you for a while; other times I'd just watch you, committing what you wore to memory. After those first couple of weeks of sheepishly following you around, my fascination with you grew drastically. You might think that observing another person's day-to-day life might reveal them to be as underwhelming and boring as most people probably are, but oh, no – not you. Some parts of your life were as shiny and perfect as I'd previously imagined them to be. Your house, for example. Your husband. Your marriage. Your friends. (But only your new ones, right?) I'll return to all of those things.

The thing I hadn't anticipated was the fact that you clearly had some problems. Secrets. In our sessions, you'd encourage me to look where it hurt, to try to describe painful experiences, insisting that to process them, they must be brought out into the light. But what about yours?

The following Friday we had another tough session.

That day, you asked me to speak directly to myself as a child, to reconnect with that inherent goodness all children have and to consider whether I could find empathy with the little girl I once was. It didn't work like that for me because the little girl I saw was worthless and dirty, like a thieving street urchin. You were moved by the way I spoke of myself and you asked whether I would be willing to consider from whose point of view I was observing myself as a child. Could it be that it wasn't my own perception at all? What child perceives herself as inherently bad and unlovable?

Could it be that this was how I imagined my father saw me, as a way to comprehend the profound rejection of his departure? And if so, could it be that my interpretation of this was simply wrong and entirely unrooted in reality?

Your words hit me so hard it felt as though you prodded me with a searing prong, as though you knew me better than I could ever know myself. I felt at your mercy. But back then I felt at everyone's mercy. And now, here we are; the tables have turned, and it is you who are at my mercy, and it is me using all of myself and everything you've taught me, to help you. You see, Kristina, nothing is as it seems. Sometimes our worlds, which look beautiful, are actually on fire.

After the session I deliberated over whether to just go home. I had plans that evening, with an old friend from Karlstad who was in town. I felt torn – a part of me wanted to go home and relax for a few hours before getting ready for dinner. We were going to Sawan, the kind of fancy place I imagined you'd go to eat, and I wanted to try out a new look inspired by you. High ponytail, gold stud earrings, a whimsical flick of liquid liner. Another part of me wanted to indulge in my guilty pleasure of trailing you up Bogstadveien to Rosenborggata and observing you agonize over whatever it was that awaited you there. I decided on the latter. I felt unsettled and blue after our session and it helped a little to process while drinking a coffee as I waited for you to finish for the day. You appeared in the doorway, your face guarded and drawn. You looked a little sad, perhaps affected by the fact that you'd spent your day going deep into dark places with people like me. You walked slower than usual, stopping several times to look at your phone. You frowned, typed a response, checked your phone again, typed some more. You crossed the street absentmindedly and a car had to brake hard to avoid you. Its driver shouted at you but you didn't respond with aggression, or at all, really; you just stood there in the middle of the road, blinking. You raised a hand in apology, or surrender, and stumbled back onto the crowded pavement.

I wanted to swoop in and pull you into a hug. I wanted to take you home with me and make you tea and sit across from you, me listening to you, for once. I wanted to know what was on your mind. In hindsight, I wondered whether it could have been me. I would have liked to know whether I ever really affected you, Kristina. Whether you brought occasional thoughts of me home with you, into your real life.

That day, you didn't go up. You stood a while outside number 11, staring up at the building. Your finger hovered at one of the buzzers, then you changed your mind and rushed away, passing just meters from where I stood on the other side of the road, partially hidden by a white van. Tears were streaming down your face, and when you'd crossed Bogstadveien, you headed down a less-crowded side street and broke into a run, your hair flowing behind you on the soft breeze like contrails from a jet.

That evening, I began to understand that something had shifted in me. Something big. I could barely follow the conversation with my girlfriend at dinner; I had the sensation of sitting there trapped in my body, but my mind was far away. It was with you. All I wanted was to see you and talk to you and talk about you – it was as though anything other than you had just faded into uninteresting shades of gray. I was so worried about you and what I'd observed that afternoon. I was also feeling the first stirrings of anger, though I didn't recognize it as such at the time. It was like a dull ache in my stomach, that feeling you get when you've eaten something you know disagrees with you and you have no choice but to wait and see what happens. I was angry that you were more than what you showed to me, that you had a life outside of the therapy room, that you were affected by the highs and lows of life, like everybody else. It made me feel so anxious that someone who emanated such calm, such gentle compassion, was actually as intensely vulnerable as me. I'm over it now and that anger grew into an even deeper love, and a fierce need to protect you, and ultimately, to set you free.

33

Kristina

I want to howl and throw the laptop across the room. My face is wet with tears. I feel tired to the bone and highly agitated; it's as though an electric feeling of nervous energy rushes through me. I remember that day she's referring to. Elisabeth had taken another overdose and had just been released from hospital to another bleak women's shelter, and I was desperately trying to get in contact with the director at Villa Vinternatt, an old colleague of mine from when I did my psychology doctorate residency at a private hospital specializing in treating addicts like Elisabeth. He'd gone on to found Villa Vinternatt, and I believed its progressive arts program could be exactly the kind of thing that could bring lasting change to Elisabeth's life, so I tried to convince him to take her on the program. Instead, it led to her death.

I couldn't bear to sit across from the Rickards that day in their clammy overheated apartment, eating dry cakes and sipping sherry, which they always insist upon. I couldn't bear to listen to their reminiscing, their exaggerated stories of their only child's remarkable achievements, their musings about all the ways she'd be changing the world, if only she'd lived. I couldn't bear to sit there and look at the framed pictures the Rickards keep everywhere, on the walls, on the windowsills, on the kitchen counter, even on a shelf in the bathroom. Everywhere you'd look, Trine Rickards would look back at you, suspended in time, young and alive. Sometimes it feels good to be there with them, and speak of their beloved daughter as though she had only just left the room, even though she'd been dead for almost two decades. But that day I just couldn't bear it.

Out of the three of us, Trine, Elisabeth and me, I was the lucky one. I've had years of trauma therapy and built a good life for myself. My traumatized brain shielded me from reliving what happened and I have made my peace with it. Elisabeth wasn't so lucky – though she escaped, she didn't really; she was held hostage by trauma, and instead of facing it, Elisabeth tried to run from it through her addictions until she couldn't outrun it anymore and it ultimately cost her her life.

And Trine… No. I'm not going there. I never do.

So much grief, so many dark corners, so many things lost forever. I allow myself a few thoughts that never fail to center me. The view of the royal palace gardens from our kitchen windows, and the way being in my home makes me feel so held and so safe. The feeling of my husband's arms closing around my waist from behind, drawing me close. These are mindfulness techniques I use to select the thoughts I allow – I see my thoughts as floating past in little boats on a river. It's up to me which ones I pick up. If there are too many dark ones, I remain patient until a good thought comes floating downstream. It doesn't mean that dark thoughts are suppressed; it means that they are observed, acknowledged and released. I do it now, and it takes me a long while to build the image, because tonight the river runs red with blood and all the little boats are overflowing and jostling each other, snapping this way and that on a churning current. When my mind is finally calm, I keep reading.

34

Supernova

There was a day I remember later that spring when I felt particularly unhinged. I already lived for Fridays by then, but it was increasingly obvious that one hour a week just wasn't enough. I wanted more. It was midweek, and like I had started to do on a few occasions, I made my way over to Kaffebrenneriet when I took a break for lunch. I stood outside your office for a while, feeling numb with jealousy at the thought of someone else up there with you, bathing in your irresistibly soothing presence. I wished I could go up there and shove that person out of the door so I could sit across from you. Standing there, I felt tinged with bitterness – the more I knew about you, and the more I saw, the more I wanted. It's normal to get attached to your therapist; I've read all about it. But I knew that what I was doing wasn't normal. I knew it, but I couldn't stop.

I went across the street and bought a coffee. I sat in the window seat and waited for you to appear. I'd learned by then that you finish at four on Wednesdays. Four o'clock came and went and you didn't appear. Maybe a client had canceled and you'd left early and I'd missed you. I could have screamed. All I wanted was a quick glimpse. But in that moment, I had an idea. I would try to find out why you kept going to Rosenborggata, it would be like uncovering a mystery. And I would go to your house.

35

Kristina

My blood runs cold at Leah's mention of my house. My home is my sanctuary, the physical container for my life, the hub of my marriage. To think that she repeatedly followed me on Fridays to Rosenborggata, observing me as I weighed up whether or not I could face going up that day, is bad enough. The idea that she could have gone to my home is unthinkable, that she might have stood in my living space among my personal photographs and possessions, drinking them in and storing them in her illicit bank of information about me.

My head is throbbing and my stomach feels liquid and strange. I have to fight the urge to just flee from this disturbing place and Leah's increasingly insane narrative, but the need to read just one more section is too powerful. I have to know what she's done. And what she knows.

36

Supernova

A few days before I went to your house, on a Tuesday, I waited at Kaffebrenneriet from three thirty. I'd finished my tall white Americano by the time you arrived, just after four. By then, I knew that Tuesdays were exhausting for you, with clients back-to-back from ten until four, which is why I chose that day because I knew that you always stopped for a coffee after work, drinking it in the café instead of taking it to go like you normally do. It was a beautiful, hot day in late spring and I worried that you'd choose to sit outside on one of the little wrought-iron tables; one was free, but you didn't – you chose your usual seat at the back of the café, a barstool facing the wall. Your face was peaceful, serene, unsuspecting. I had a watertight plan I'd run through in my head over and over in the event of you suddenly glancing over to where I sat at a table just behind you. I'd simply smile shyly and say, 'Hi'. After all, why would it be strange that we should bump into each other there, at a popular café equidistant between your office and my house? It would only seem strange if I made it seem strange.

You didn't look over. Not then, nor any of the other times I observed you from less than two meters away at that same coffee shop. As far as I'm aware, you only ever saw me once outside of the therapy room, an episode I'm sure you'll recall. And even then, it didn't seem like you were remotely suspicious; you acted discreet and professional, like I knew you would, most likely assuming that us both being in that particular place was just a coincidence, albeit a big one.

You read the previous week's *A-Magasinet* and ate an oat cookie alongside your coffee. On the floor, next to your barstool, stood your Louis Vuitton Neverfull bag. It was exactly identical to my own, purchased especially for that reason. Extreme, I know. But I'm sure I'm not the first client who has tried to emulate your style; after all, it's quite the conformist Oslo West look you go for – inoffensive, quietly expensive, discreet. Like you. Tailored Prada, classic Louis, a glimpse of Hermès on your wrist.

Back to those moments. You'd placed your bag on the floor. Who would do such a thing, some might ask, but that's Oslo West for you. Nobody would steal your Louis Vuitton bag, because they all have their own. Lol. I pushed my identical bag close to yours very slowly. I'd endlessly rehearsed what I would do if I got caught, of course. It would be very obvious that I hadn't taken your bag on purpose, it was an honest mistake.

You seemed engrossed in an article, and I watched your back for a long while. You were close enough for me to be able to see the rise and fall of your chest as you breathed.

And I copied even that, syncing my own breath to yours. I got up to leave, while scrolling through Instagram on my phone, no doubt appearing distracted if anyone happened to be watching. I looped my hand through the straps of the Neverfull bag, yours, not mine, of course. Then I walked out. My heart thundered in my chest and my mind raced as I stepped outside into brilliant sunshine. No one said anything. Why would they?

I'd taken the car that day to ensure a swift getaway, and I reached it within seconds – I'd driven around the block at least ten times when I arrived to snare a parking space on Grønnegata, a stone's throw away from Kaffebrenneriet. My hands were slick with sweat on the steering wheel. I wanted to roll down the window and sing at the top of my lungs. It suddenly made sense to me in those moments why some people choose a life of crime. I fought the urge to laugh hysterically but settled for a smug smile at my own reflection in the rearview. The bag stood on the passenger seat next to me, just like its doppelgänger had done earlier that afternoon as I drove the few hundred meters home. Nothing appeared different, and yet everything was. Before I drove off, I fished your phone out of the bag. It had several notifications – WhatsApp, Messenger and Outlook, but Face ID was activated and there was no way I could access it, as I'd anticipated. I turned it off, and then I dropped it into a storm drain on the street.

At home, I carried the bag sagely and nonchalantly up the stairs like I had done every day for a couple of weeks. When I first bought the bag, the annoying flat-sharing girls on the ground floor had cooed over it when I bumped into them in the entrance hallway. *Oh, my God*, they'd chanted, *it is, like, soooo cool.* So, nothing new if I bumped into them again, but I didn't. I made myself wait for my cup of tea to brew, ginger and turmeric, what I imagined you'd choose. I took the bag through to the bedroom and upended it onto the bedsheet. Your keys, bingo. Your wallet. Louis Vuitton, too. Nice. And predictable. Like you, I thought, back then.

I slipped your driving license out and studied your photo for a long time. Like most people's, your expression was serious and unsmiling, like you feared they wouldn't let you drive otherwise. I took a picture of the photo with my phone; back then, I didn't have many pictures of you and I thought it would help to look at it when I craved your closeness between sessions. It did, for a while, but I assume you are familiar with the law of diminishing returns and how, once you get what you want, you always want more? I wanted more.

The bottom of the bag was surprisingly messy – I didn't have you down as a messy lady and I felt a stab of annoyance at this discovery. I had to scramble around amid old receipts, loose change, parking slips and empty chewing gum wrappers to reach the last few objects underneath. But, oh boy, it was worth it. There was a small, burnished-orange leather-bound journal. I opened it, assuming it was a calendar, so imagine my delight when I realized it was much more personal than that. It was almost full – page after page of your innermost thoughts and musings. I swear, my heart somersaulted. I put it aside, knowing I'd spend my evening drinking in your words, and that I'd cherish the little book forever. I was right about that.

I also found a Dior lip gloss, which I instantly applied to my own lips, and this, too, was an intensely satisfying moment. Several times, I ran the little wand up and down the length of my lips, thinking about how it had also touched yours. I closed my eyes and allowed myself an imagined scene in which you kissed me passionately, your lips slick with that same gloss, passing it from your lips to mine. You'd slip your tongue into my mouth and hold me close, so close I could feel the beat of your heart and the soft contour of your breasts. Back then, I often had fantasies like that, when the only language I had to describe feeling that close to someone was sexual or romantic.

With time, my attachment to you grew from the perceived sexual to the frenzied, obsessive friendship feelings of young girls, and then it deepened into a gentle, parental kind of bond, and that's when things really went wrong. In my mind and heart you were the very incarnation of perfection, though, like I've said, I knew you were human just like everyone else. But to the child inside, to little Leah who craved a stable, predictable, unconditional adult, you were perfect. So it hurt like hell to discover that you were its very opposite. That you were as hollow as Swiss cheese, vast parts of what makes a whole person, just gone. The rage I felt at first wasn't rational, I know that. But I feel it, still, when I revisit the memory of your persona disintegrating before my very eyes. I didn't stop loving you, in my basic childlike way. I never will. Now, I'm telling you this because I want you to know that there was a reason for my behavior, for all the questions I asked, for everything I did.

It was selfish at first, this need for you to be like a perfect hologram, so that I could feel safe. Naturally I felt angry when the bubble burst, but then as things progressed, I realized that you need me as much as I need you and the real healing, for both of us, will happen when all the cards are on the table. Mine, and yours. I need to fix you to fix me.

37

Kristina

I hold myself entirely still. There's a throbbing pain in my temple that burns and insists itself into my very brain. I steel myself to let in one thought at a time. It was Leah that took my bag and I try to take in the enormity of that fact. The lengths she went to. The depths of betrayal of the bond between us. At the time, I had no choice but to write the missing bag off as an honest mistake, the one that was left behind on the floor next to my chair was exactly identical to my own. There was no phone in the bag, no credit cards or any other identification. There was a generic set of keys and a cheap wallet with a couple of hundred-kroner bills, and some make-up. I handed the whole thing in to the police, and assumed that the person who'd taken my bag by mistake would do the same thing. But they never did. I bought another Neverfull bag with the insurance money and eventually forgot about the whole strange incident.

***

To think that Leah sat that close to me, close enough to smoothly exchange the bags, and I didn't notice her, is profoundly disturbing. But I know all too well that we don't often see what we're not looking for. I try to recall whether I ever felt like I was being watched or like someone was following me. I do remember the episode she referred to, and it is the only time I can remember ever seeing Leah outside of the therapy room. It was during the winter, months after the episode with the handbag, so by then, she must have been playing this game for close to a year. Eirik and I went skiing in Geilo, a rare weekend away together, and treated ourselves to a stay at Dr Holm's Hotel. On the second evening, we were at the after-ski hotel bar, drinking champagne and reminiscing about how we used to go away like that together all the time. We vowed to do it more often. We were just about to start our third round of IVF and were in that phase of really believing it was going to work this time. *Third time lucky*, we said and gently touched our thin champagne flutes together and smiled at each other in the soft light from the fireplace. Eirik had just been elected second in command in his party and the demands of a political career at that level were beginning to show. But I remember how close I felt to my husband that evening, how I noticed the new sprinkles of gray in his hair and how it only made him more handsome.

At one point in the evening, I realized I'd left my phone upstairs in the hotel room and went to get it – I wanted to take a few pictures of Eirik and me. I bumped into Leah in the corridor leading to our room and at first I couldn't instantly place her – this happens to me often when I see a client out of context. Then I matched the woman in front of me with the pretty Swedish writer I see every Friday at two. I smiled at her as she came toward me and as always, allowed the client to decide whether or not to acknowledge me. Leah looked shocked to see me there, but smiled shyly and whispered, 'Hi', and then she disappeared around the corner. I didn't give the episode another thought. I would have just assumed that she was there for the weekend like us; there wasn't anything particularly strange about that – Dr Holm's is a very popular weekend destination for the Oslo West crowds.

Thinking back, I realize she must have followed us there. That whole weekend, she must have lurked in the shadows, watching.

38

Supernova

Four days later, on the Saturday, I went to your house. I'd looked at your husband's party's event calendar and he was listed as attending a rally in Kristiansand that weekend. It said that there would be a gala dinner on the Saturday evening with local stakeholders and politicians, and I knew that you would be accompanying him to that, like you usually do.

On the Friday in my session, we had a moment when we were talking through some particularly difficult stuff I'd been dealing with, to do with compulsive thoughts of suicide and self-harming, when your eyes filled with tears. I asked you why you were crying, and you said you felt so moved by what I'd said and so empathetic toward me for having to deal with it. Your display of emotion, and the validation it brought, moved me so much, Kristina. It was in moments like that that I believed what we were doing in that room really had the power to heal me.

I walked out of there and straight home, not even

considering hanging around Kaffebrenneriet in the hope that you'd stop in. I lay on my bed and stared at the ceiling, tears rushing from my eyes. I felt so bad, then, for everything I'd done. For a moment, I considered calling you and confessing, laying it all bare so we could start over. But I knew it was already too late. I was in too deep. I promised myself that I would go to your house, satisfy my curiosity and then stop. I cried harder because I knew that even if I actually managed to walk away after that, there would always be these secrets between us now. I cried with confusion and jealousy, because in your diary I had read page after page about the worrying blanks in your mind, and about someone called Elisabeth, who sounded like another client, but not a single word about me.

I cried myself to sleep in the middle of the afternoon, and when I woke up it was close to midnight. I poured myself some wine and sat on the floor, letting the warm summer night into the room through the wide-open windows. I looked at your solemn face in your driving license picture and then I spent a long while reading through your journal again and looking at the strange drawings you'd made. I looked at the calculations too, and though math wasn't my strongest subject at school; it seemed to me like they were some kind of probability equations, page after page after page of them. I had to know more, Kristina.

I arrived early in the morning, around eight. I'd planned it very carefully, as you can imagine. I wore gray sweatpants and a baseball cap, and with me I had a bucket and a mop. The bucket was filled to the brim with various cleaning products. My face was scrubbed clean and not made-up and my hair was tied into a severe ponytail that emerged from the back of the baseball hat. I felt confident that if I bumped into a neighbor, they would just assume I was there to clean one of the apartments in the building.

I prayed you hadn't changed the locks after the incident with the bag, but the key slipped easily into the lock and I entered the communal hallway, which was much fancier than my building's, with soaring ceilings and ornate, freshly painted stucco. I didn't know which floor you lived on, so I crept upstairs and checked the doorbells until I found the one that read 'E & K Moss' on the second floor. I pressed it briefly, just to be totally sure that I wouldn't get a nasty surprise, such as a houseguest or an angry dog, when I unlocked the door. The apartment emanated the silence of a large, abandoned space. I slipped a key into the lock, and when it didn't work, another. This one unlocked the door with a smooth click.

I stepped inside, and couldn't help but take a sharp, stunned breath. Your home is exquisite, Kristina. The kind of home one would expect to see in interiors magazines, not a single detail left to chance. Your expensive handbags hung proudly from a series of hooks along the wall – Gucci, Givenchy, Hermès, Louis Vuitton – and it occurred to me then that you clearly have much more money than I'd thought, that you live inside an impenetrable bubble of serious wealth. I suppose I'd thought we were on the same level in that respect – I make a very good living, and I too, own a nice apartment in a snazzy part of town. But this – this was a different level. A huge gold mirror hung above an antique table on top of which stood an incredibly beautiful porcelain vase filled with peonies. I stepped closer to it, but felt afraid to meet my own gaze in the mirror – I think I irrationally craved that the person looking back at me would be you, and didn't want the disappointment of my own reflection.

The floor was laid with a warm, matte oakwood and I slipped my shoes off, feeling its smooth surface against my bare feet. On the wall of the corridor leading to the other rooms were several black-and-white, professionally-shot photographs, blown up big and placed in identical brushed-bronze colonial-style frames. I moved from one to the next slowly, taking in each one carefully, stopping to take pictures of them all on my phone. The picture of your niece and nephew is so beautiful. I wanted to know their names. And the one with you and Eirik on your wedding day. Everyone always says that a bride was radiant on her wedding day, but never was it more true than for you. I could have cried just looking at you, and maybe I did. He's a handsome guy, Eirik, but from a purely physical attractiveness perspective he pales next to you. Still, he has the self-satisfied smile of a man who believes he deserves you and knows he can afford to spoil you. Does he treat you like a trophy, Kristina? Does he make you feel like just another piece on the chessboard of his life? A queen perhaps, but a piece, nonetheless.

I liked the picture of you, Trine and Elisabeth, too. Back then, I didn't know what I know now, so I thought it was just a cute shot of three cute teenagers posing together, smiling innocently at the camera, arms flung around each other's shoulders. You're in the middle, of course. Now, I want to know how you can walk past that photograph every day of your life. Doesn't looking at those young, smiling faces fill you with dread and with the images of what was to come? Or do you think of yourself as so thoroughly healed that looking at them fails to provoke any emotional response? Then why do you cry on the street in Rosenborggata? Why do you fill your diary with all those detailed nightmares of crashing through forests echoing with laughing voices and the sound of gunshots? Why do you write out all those calculations, trying to work out if the outcome could have been different?

See, I get all agitated putting all of this on the page. It isn't easy, that's for sure. My mind is like a storm. I didn't know then what I know now. I didn't yet know what you'd been through or how much what happened to those three young girls would take from all of you. But even now, when I know everything, more than you, I still want to know how you can bear to look at all that innocence, every single day.

Are you ready to go back, further back, all the way back? Shall we go back to Carúpano? Yes, Kristina, I know. I know all about Carúpano.

39

Kristina

I pause, gauging whether I can actually handle this. I have naturally encountered a lot of people with serious mental health challenges over the years and have always been of the school that believes that even the most extreme manifestations of dissociation and emotional disturbance can be countered and healed with long-term psychotherapy. To be witnessed and tolerated in their most challenging incarnations can bring the broken pieces inside someone back together in the most miraculous ways; I've seen it over and over. In others, and in myself. I thought I saw it in Leah Iverson, too, but now I am forced to consider whether the healing I believed I saw was in fact just misguided preoccupation with me. I'm afraid of her now, of what she wants from me, and almost hope that she is dead – at least that way I never have to see her again.

It's obvious that these are the words of an extremely damaged individual. To break into the home of your therapist and steal her diary and take pictures of her personal photographs, and repeatedly follow her around – you'd have to suffer highly compromised mental faculties. What else could she have done? I'm not only furious, but afraid – I can only imagine how dangerous this might get if certain elements of the past become subject to the interpretation of a disturbed person such as Leah Iverson.

I suddenly understand Anton's rage and feelings of powerlessness. I tell myself that nothing she did or claims to know about me can hurt me, but I need to find out what she's playing at. And then I am going to return to my life and my husband and my work and all of this will fade away into a shocking, unsavory episode. But where is she?

I return to the document. There are over eighteen thousand words, over seventy pages. I don't want to know what more she wrote, or why; I just want to know where Leah is so I can leave all this behind. Wherever she is, she is clearly in need of psychiatric intervention, and I will make sure to get back in touch with her GP when I get back to Oslo to recommend exactly that.

I certainly won't let her invade my life any further. I will take this experience to my own therapy and attempt to learn from it. I will move on. Eirik will win the election. We'll get our baby. All of this will eventually feel distant and impotent. I have to believe that.

I look around Leah's cabin again and this time it doesn't feel like a comforting cocoon, but cramped and claustrophobic, rather. She'd clearly come here to write this stuff, all these weird and disturbing things about me, and fantasized about me reading her words. The space itself feels sullied, as though I'd stumbled upon the sinister lair of a twisted criminal.

I need to leave; coming here was clearly not a good idea. The sky is blustery and dark gray now and the snow is falling more heavily, not instantly melting as it touches the windowpanes, but settling in clusters across them, like iced spiderwebs. I bet the heavy clouds hide a most magnificent evening sky, far away from the glare of lights from the big city, and I wish I could see the stars when they appear, that they would light up the way back down to the car. I think about Leah's mentions of supernovae, especially the obliteration of the larger, brighter star by a little dwarf star stealing its matter, prompting them both to explode, as she described. Why did she choose it as the title for this strange and disturbing account? I close my eyes and imagine those thermonuclear explosions, the white heat, the rainbow fires of destruction shredding the blackness when stars collide.

I check my phone. No reception, unsurprisingly. It's just past 5 p.m. and I still have a headache from all the wine yesterday. My stomach growls with hunger, but I've left the cookies in the car.

I peer out of the window at the flurries of snow churning on the darkening air like static on an old television. I am dreading the walk back to the car through the woods. What if Leah comes back and I bump into her on the forest track? I realize I am afraid of coming face to face with her now. She lured me here and could come back at any time. She is clearly unhinged, and has not only extensively lied to me, but also stalked me in my personal time. She even had a restraining order out against her for assault. I need to get out of here right now. I choke the flame on the oil lamp, steeping the vaulted room in a deep twilight, a chill spreading through my bones.

I use the torch to get back to the front door without bumping into anything, pausing for a quick moment to listen before I step back outside – a visceral fear is taking hold of me but I have to find a way to control it and get myself safely back to the car. I place the phone on the floor for a second and shove my feet back into my boots, which I'd graciously left by the door like a polite guest, and the torch beam falls on something high up on the wall that I hadn't noticed before.

It's a long glass cabinet designed for a hunting rifle; its door is open, the weapon is gone. *Enough, Kristina, enough.* I hear the voice inside me as clearly as though it were spoken out loud. I grab the door handle and pull the door open toward me, but as I do, I can't help but unleash a scream of sheer shock – my hand comes back wet with something thick, sticky and cold, and even before I manage to direct the torch beam straight into my right palm, I know that it's blood.

40

Leah, days before

She can't stop shaking at the sight of him hammering on the cabin's door. Light snow is falling, settling in his hair. He's shouting her name, sending bursts of frozen air from his mouth. She watches from the window, and he suddenly realizes she's standing there. He stops knocking and shouting and holds her gaze. She turns her face so that the swollen, injured skin is clearly visible. He looks down at the ground, somber and sorry.

Hours later, when she's finally managed to get rid of him and the bright sky has faded to a dark ocean blue, she decides to go home. She finds her way easily enough back down to the car; the path is lit up by the moon and the walk through the woods soothes her after the stressful afternoon. She still feels wounded, somehow, by the way he screamed at her. But out here, she feels like a part of everything, unlike in her life among other people. She sits in the driver's seat and rubs her hands together hard a few times, breathing icy steam into the cold, dark space, then she starts the engine.

Several lamps flash on the dashboard and when she tries to inch back in reverse, a terrible crunching sound makes her realize something is really wrong with the car. She puts it in park and leaves the engine idling while stepping outside to take a look. All four tires are slashed.

She walks briskly back up to the cabin, but when she's almost at the first clearing, her foot catches on something and Leah comes crashing to the ground. For a long moment, she lies still, waiting for pain to crash over her, but it doesn't happen, only mild discomfort and the shock of actually falling over. When she sits back up, she feels a deep twinge to the left of her abdomen; she must have pulled a muscle trying to catch her fall. As she starts walking again, she feels a trickle of blood run down the side of her face and realizes the fall has opened a cut that was already there. She also feels a couple of achy spots on her legs and hips; she'll have even more bruises. She has no choice but to stay another day and tomorrow she can walk to the spot in the valley by the lake, where her phone usually picks up reception and call for help.

The afternoon is deepening into evening when she returns to *Supernova*, overcome by an almost feverish energy, like she has been every night since she got to Bekkebu, and the act of writing to Kristina instantly transports her away from her own circumstances. The day slips away as she delves deeper into her narrative; the shock of Anton hammering on the door, the slashed tires, the fall.

It's past midnight when she goes to the bathroom and runs a bath. There is a second door that runs from the corner of the bathroom to a more recent bedroom wing extension, and Leah goes through to her bedroom and lies down on the freshly made bed while she waits for the bathwater to fill the tub from the little cistern outside. After next week, the cabin won't have hot water again until the spring and Leah will have to heat big cauldrons of melted snow over the fire to take a bath.

In the bath, she closes her eyes and breathes the rising steam deep into her. She runs a natural sponge across her bruised collarbone, across her suddenly much-larger breasts, over the tight drum of her stomach, avoiding the tender points and the little cuts and grazes. She'll run disinfectant over the wounds, then sink into bed, hoping for a restful night and more clarity tomorrow. Maybe she will wake up to the sound of Kristina knocking on the door; she still can't help but hope it might happen. Since she started writing *Supernova*, the connection between them seems even stronger, like an umbilical cord of sheer energy.

She feels her eyelids growing heavy and the side of her face is throbbing; it's time to get up and go to bed. As she steps from the bathtub onto the bathmat, she has the strange sensation of a sharp twinge from within her womb. She feels woozy and holds onto the side of the bath for support. A dark drop of blood splashes onto the bath mat. Then another.

41

Kristina

It is the most disgusting, terrifying sensation and I instinctively wipe my hand down the front of my jeans, streaking them maroon. I shine the beam onto the door and its handle, and both are streaked with dried blood. The handle has significantly more blood on it, and some has dripped onto the floor below. There are also several patches of it on the floor, almost indistinguishable against the slate floor tiles, and I didn't notice it in the meager light of the little vestibule when I arrived – you'd have to direct the beam of a torch straight at it. There seems to be a trail leading to the bathroom. I step inside the bathroom and, shining the torch around, I spot another few small drops alongside the sink. There's a bio compost toilet I am familiar with from other trips to similar cabins. There's a bloody fingerprint on its closed lid and I shudder at the sight of it. There is also another door in the far corner of the room, impossible to see from where I stood before in the doorway of the vestibule.

I open it and realize that the cabin has been extended and is bigger than I thought. There is a pine-clad corridor with a door on either side and a floor-to-ceiling window at its end, with sweeping valley views. I shine the light onto the door on the left, which is ajar. I push it open with my foot to reveal a small but cozy bedroom with a built-in triple bunk, presumably for visiting children. I climb onto the bottom bunk and shine the light into the middle and top bunks in turn, but they are empty and neatly made up. There is a cupboard, also empty, and there are no signs of bloodstains anywhere in this room.

I go back out into the corridor and shine the light onto the second door, the one on the right. There is a rusty smudge on its door handle and I cover my hand with my sweater sleeve before grabbing it. The door doesn't open easily, I have to lean against it to get it to budge inwards into the room, as if something is blocking it on the other side. Is she in there, dead? I pause for a brief moment, but find that I am strangely freed from fear or hesitation in this moment and know that it's because I am high on the adrenaline surging through my veins.

The door gives enough for me to squeeze through and as I send the torch light around the room to get my bearings, I can't suppress a cry – it is as though the sound is torn from my insides and will now remain an eternal echo in the room.

42

Leah, days before

The blood stops as suddenly as it started. She has heard of sporadic bleeding in pregnancy; it doesn't have to mean anything at all. She prays; she doesn't know what else to do, and though she's never done it before, she knows how to ask for mercy.

Please, please let the baby live.

She conjures up the baby in her mind the way she constructed the characters in her book; she gives it little details that make it feel more real – a fuzzy little patch of strawberry blonde hair atop a soft pink skull, tiny fingernails, a slightly upturned nose, slim, almost see-through wrists. She breathes life into the imagined child, until she has a vivid image of it there inside her womb, fingers and toes moving, heart fluttering.

Please, please live.

She's in bed, with her legs elevated on a tall stack of pillows. She's waiting, for Kristina, for morning, for the dull ache in her stomach to stop. She brings her phone out, and realizes there is, unusually, a single bar of reception. She does something she has never done before: she dials Kristina's number, which she knows by heart. It rings for a long while before she picks up, and when she does, tears begin to flow from Leah's eyes at the sound of her voice. There was a time when Leah believed that Kristina could fix everything, and a part of her must still believe it, and maybe it's true, because there is something so soothing in the silence that unfolds between them on the crackly line that Leah feels her heart resume its normal beat. In the end, she puts the phone down and lies back against the pillows. She prays again, feeling new hope and energy flow through her after hearing Kristina's voice. Maybe now she'll come.

She falls asleep. When she wakes again, she feels strange, as though her limbs are weighted down, and she has the sensation of being submerged in water. She blinks in the dark, getting her bearings, taking in the outlines of her surroundings; Bekkebu, she's at Bekkebu. Fragments of the day before return to her. The screaming, the slashed tires, the fall, the blood, the email. It is completely dark outside but she can make out the glow of the moon through the gauze curtains. She tries to sit up but a searing pain across her abdomen stops her. Then she realizes she is bleeding again.

43

Kristina

At first I can't makes sense of what it is I'm looking at. The bedroom is small, but neat, with pine walls and a big double bed with a white padded headboard and white bedsheets, gathered into twisted piles. There's blood on the bed, as well as traces of it on the floor, half cleaned up with a big pile of bath towels. The door nudged against these when I tried to push it open. The bedsheets are gathered in a mound on the bed, and I give them a little tug to make sure she isn't under them, though there is nothing there, only some streaky, brown bloodstains. I push a large cupboard open with my foot but there is nothing but towels and sheets and a couple of ski jackets inside it.

There is no sign of her but I think about the empty gun cabinet in the vestibule; whoever has killed or injured Leah is armed and still on the loose.

'Jesus,' I whisper. I'm about to turn around and leave the room when I notice something sticking out from under one of the pillows. I unfold it and recognize Leah's handwriting from the note she pressed into my hand in our last session. I read it, and it's instantly clear who killed Leah Iverson.

44

Kristina

It wasn't going to be like this.

I've fought and fought so hard to find a way to be me. To be someone else. To be anyone at all. But I can't. Even my own child couldn't bear to remain inside me. And I can't do this. I can't bear it anymore because the thing is I just don't get any breaks I don't get a breather or a break or just peace it never ever stops. It's like I'm roadkill, ripped open and exposed and bleeding to death in the road and my dark thoughts are vultures, feasting before my pebble-sized racoon heart has even stopped beating. The thoughts the images the words the pain and the endless black aloneness which is different from loneliness because it isn't a perception, it's a statement of fact. The only time it ever stopped was when I tried to be different, to undo me, and become someone else, someone sane and beautiful and whole and worthy but no one is really like that, even if it looks like it; the shiny perfection we see is just another symptom of the darkness inside isn't it and anyway we

can't ever be anyone other than who we are, can we – not
really

   I felt the exact moment when the baby died
   It was like the flip of the smallest switch
   I knew it even if I couldn't bear to know it
   Lights out
   I wanted the pain to come, then. I needed to see the blood
and the evidence of it but now I wish I hadn't. I wish away
the inevitability of what will happen next. The darkness.
The simple, simple answer. The shame. I am so sorry I'm
so very sorry

   I want Kristina to know about Supernova, I want people
to read it, for Elisabeth, for Kristina, for me, for Trine, for
all of us, could it be that if people did it could turn all of
that destruction into something beautiful?

   Even now it's the word I can't let go of. The images. A big
star and a little one, together in a celestial dance. The little
white dwarf star stealing material from the big one until it
has too much, too much to carry and to hold, drawing both
stars into a gigantic thermonuclear explosion so bright it
can light up anything, anything at all.

   And afterward, a black hole, a rip in the lining of the
heavens.

   Lights out
   I'm going to the lake, it's so beautiful, there is nowhere
more beautiful in this world, not to me, so I'm going there
and I will stay there forever until I become part of it,
disintegrating into its deep, cold water, infusing it with the
very essence of me.

   Ask Linda and Anton and Kristina to forgive me. Most of
all Kristina. It wasn't meant to happen like this, none of it

***

I crush the note in my hand, then smooth it back out – I'll need to hand it over to the police. I glance around the sad room one last time and immediately wish I hadn't – I know I'll never forget this.

I rush back down the pine corridor and through the bathroom and the vestibule with the empty gun cabinet; I've seen enough and I need to get out of here. I burst from the cabin into frozen air, bustling and wet with thick, swirling snowflakes. I'm crying with shock and the horror of the afternoon and the tragedy of Leah's last hours – all those hours she waited for me before she went to the lake. To think that she wrote those words after losing her baby, and waiting, hoping, that I'd come help her – I can't bear it, in spite of everything.

My cries holler into the blizzard, settling against the wall of trees, against the iced lid of the lake deep in the valley. She's down there, below the surface. Jesus Christ, the poor woman is in it. I didn't help her, just like I didn't help Elisabeth, in fact. I might as well have shoved her into the icy, black water. I haven't cried like this in years. Like a trapped animal. Like a hurricane gathering wild speed, screeching through the night. I scream until my voice bleeds dry, until I start to cough and splutter. I take a few stumbling steps away from the cabin and turn around to look at it, but already it is almost swallowed up by the snowstorm, only a dim haze from one forgotten oil lamp still lit on the windowsill discernible through columns of whirling snowflakes. I've left it burning – will it catch fire and raze the cabin to the ground? I decide I don't care, I just keep stumbling through the snowstorm. I need to get away from this place more than I have needed anything in my life. Now.

I try to remember the direction I came from but my mind is in overdrive, throwing random thoughts and images at me, and my heart is pounding. *Which way?* I scream the words out loud, but this time my voice doesn't carry; instead it peters out mid-holler to a pitiful squawk. The cabin lay to my left as I approached, on the edge of a rocky promontory overlooking the lake. No. It lay to my right. Or did it? The air is murky gray, with particles of pure white rushing at me on a bitter wind like confetti, and there is just no way of making out the path that leads back down the hill to my car.

I'm shaking with cold and sheer dread, and I spin around on my heels, rubbing at my arms; I'm not dressed for a dash through deserted, mountainous woods in a blizzard.

I grab my phone from my parka pocket, but there is still no reception. I find the compass function and though I am only just able to make out the hazy green glare of the screen, I begin to follow the needle north – I am certain I headed south on my way up here – I have a vague memory of the opaque sky being brighter to my left as I emerged from the clutch of the woods into the cabin's little clearing. I want to run as fast as I can away from the horror of Leah's cabin and her terrible words, but I have no choice but to inch forward slowly, until I reach what must be the path, a sliver of space between towering rows of pine trees. I can see more clearly here – the snowstorm is hampered by the density of the trees – so I pick up my pace and rush down, down, away from that place and the terrifying reality of what I've just read.

I'm in a forest in the foothills of a long range of mountains that stretch from Skien in the south across much of Telemark to Kongsberg and into central Norway beyond, in the middle of a blizzard on the first day of November. *Stay sharp, Kristina. Just get out of here and get home and all of this will eventually fade away into just another bad memory.* The wind is bitterly cold and carries the scent of deep lakes and mulchy earth and ancient trees.

I stop for a moment, pressing my fingers to my eyes, before looking around at more static whiteness, more blurred outlines of trees. The path has opened out into another snow-drenched clearing. I am breathing so hard I feel as though I might black out. I can feel the downward slope of the path and its uneven surface of slippery roots and jagged rocks poking out of the earth, concealed by fresh snow, but can't see anything. How much further? I'm about to keep walking when I notice something beside me, breaking the almost complete whiteout of the hillside clearing. It's the blonde wood and charcoal metal barrel of a rifle, emerging from the snow like the mast of a sailing boat rising on the horizon. I reach for it, then decide against it: it could go off in my hands. Next to it is a huddled mound; at first glance I assume it's a fallen tree. But it isn't a tree; this is instantly clear when I kick it with my foot, revealing the outline of a hand, a sickly shade of ice blue, then a shock of long brown hair atop a rusty patch of blood-stained snow. It's Leah.

Part II

EXPOSURE THERAPY

45

Leah, days before

It had always been the words that saved her. They gave her something to hold onto when she felt too little and too weak to go on. But they can't save her now, nothing can. The violent contractions stopped a long while ago, and the blood, too. She is empty again, emptier than ever before.

She runs through everything in her mind, but her mind doesn't work the way it usually does, there are vast chunks of nothingness, like black holes thoughts get sucked into and disappear. Is that what it feels like for Kristina? It makes sense that the brain would simply erase what it can't bear to contain. *Supernova*. Yes. The big star and the little one, locked together in destruction. The beauty of them burning each other out.

She wants everyone to see these fires. She wants them to watch her burn.

Since the baby went, since she realized what the blatantly obvious answer to everything was, she has read back through everything, all the way up to the end of *Supernova*, and only the silent blackness of the night ahead remains. It's time. She'll send *Supernova* to Kristina and then she will go to the lake.

Supernova, back to *Supernova*, she needs to be quick, now. But how? There is no reception, though she has very occasionally been able to catch a faint signal in this newer part of the cabin. She composes the email, using all her remaining strength to sound vaguely coherent. But the document won't attach, even when she moves around the room, painfully slowly, holding the phone up in the hope of a single bar of reception. By the lake, there's a patch of occasional reception near the jetty, which is anchored to the surface now by ice. She'll bring the phone, send the email, then take it with her into the lake.

Just one more thing to write, to be read by whoever comes to Bekkebu next and finds her gone. She starts writing, but keeps stopping, erasing, trying again; the words don't come out right. Some words she crosses out because she doesn't mean them.

~~I'm sorry.~~

She imagines the dark water of the lake closing over her head like the velvet blackness of the night sky and maybe when she really gives in to the lake and death, the glimmer of stars will reach her all the way down at its bottom. Maybe it will be like a supernova, when death itself is more beautiful than anything in life. She doesn't want to die, she wants to live, but not this life, the life that can now never be separated from that other life, the lost life.

But what if there is a message waiting for her when the phone recovers reception? Maybe Kristina has left her a message. Maybe she is on her way, maybe she will come tomorrow. Would it make a difference now? She thinks about the phone call, days ago now; how she still didn't come.

Leah gets up and stands a while at the window. She's still a little unsteady on her feet after days in bed drifting in and out of dreamless sleep, and she feels a deep ache in her womb that travels all the way up to her heart. Her reflection is mirrored in the little grid window and Leah studies her sad, bruised face and its mournful expression. She finds it easy in this moment to access the empathy for herself that Kristina always speaks of.

She stands at the window a long while looking out at the beautiful night with crystal clear skies awash with billions of stars. She's about to put clothes on and get ready to go when she hears a sound. Footsteps approaching. A muffled cough. A series of firm knocks on the door as knuckles strike the thick timber.

46

Kristina

She's buried in fresh snow which I brush easily away from her face, but the back of her body is welded to the ground by older layers of snow that have hardened into solid ice. There is nothing but a fleshy crater where the left side of her sweet, familiar face was. Her right eye is intact but grotesquely rolled back in her skull. The rifle points its cruel black mouth straight at her.

On impulse, I touch her hand with my own, as though my touch might make her leap back to life, but she's cold as ice and as hard. I scream, and it is my screams that suck me from these impossible moments, back in time and into the blank patches of my consciousness. It isn't Leah I'm looking at, it isn't Leah at all anymore, there's nothing Leah about these mangled remains. I can smell the bitter, rotting-egg smell of gunpowder trapped in the pit of my brain – it must have been there all along, stored away. I can see the strange maroons and grays and purples hidden inside skulls, blasted open and exposed, like the vivid wet cores of smashed melons. I know these images; they were just removed from my consciousness like words with correction fluid, invisible but nonetheless still there underneath, black on white.

I become aware of my own high-pitched, uncontrollable screams ripping through the air and force myself to physically clamp my mouth shut with my left hand. Whoever did this to Leah could still be roaming the woods. But she did it herself. She wrote that. No, she said she was going to the lake. She must have changed her mind. Or someone must have hurt her after she'd already written the note. Anton – it must be him. And he could be on his way back up here, right now.

I have to get help. The snow is still falling heavily, and there is nothing visible to mark the spot where Leah lies; she'll be covered again by the time anyone can get here. How am I going to direct the police or emergency services to the exact place? I point the phone to the grotesque remains of Leah, my hand shaking violently, and open the camera function. I take several pictures, but have to stop and retch, spitting mouthfuls of bile into the snow at the harrowing sight of Leah's shattered face, even more brutal in the light of the flash. *It's not her, it's not her*, I tell myself out loud, fighting the urge to start screaming again – *it's not her. This isn't real.*

I can't control the wild gallop of my heart or my shallow, panicked breath, and I begin to run, hurtling down the steep incline of the narrow path, stumbling over slippery rocks and partially buried roots coiling from the earth, and it must be under one of the bulbous roots my right foot slips and catches, bringing me crashing to the ground, and it must be against one of those sharp rocks my head strikes because in an instant the white night is replaced by solid blackness.

47

Kristina

I'm in space. Silent technicolor explosions tear into the velvet backdrop of the universe, sending soundwaves across light-years, tearing my skin clean off and melting my insides. My consciousness drifts into vast clusters of swirling green gas. It goes from green to ocean blue, then deep indigo, before it gathers again, drawing together into bulbous clouds of electric blues and pinks and neon orange that collide and burst into white flames, streaking and pulsating across the black.

No. I'm not in space. This isn't air, it's water. The water is black and so cold that my limbs have grown stiff and numb and I sink slowly, slowly, like a statue thrown into the deepest part of the ocean. I try to move my hands and feet but they are entirely unresponsive to my commands. I hear something, a muffled sound traveling slowly through the water, but can't discern what it is or where it is coming from. It grows louder and then louder still, and it seems to be a siren, with prolonged wails followed by silence, but then I realize it is music. Rising and falling, closer and closer, until it is crystal clear, a warm, trembling vibrato, produced by an expert hand. I feel overcome by emotion listening to the cello, and just then, it seems as if I reach the bottom of the sea, my body settling onto something firm after all the falling. Like the water, it's cold and dark. The bottom is entirely smooth so this must be a pool rather than a lake or an ocean.

I'm aware of something foreign in my mouth – a pebble, a rock, a snail, a fragment of metal? I try to spit it out but my mouth is filled with water. I push whatever it is away with my tongue, and it finally slips from my mouth. Slowly, I feel about the bottom of the pool, and my right hand seems to regain some of its movement and I realize I'm not in water at all, but on the ground. I'm so cold, colder than I've been in all my life, the kind of cold I know to be dangerous. Some life and movement seeps back into other parts of me. I wave the toes of my right foot and they move. I try the left but a wild pain crashes over me, like I've been struck by an ax. I clench the muscles in my jaw and they tighten. I try to open my eyes, but they won't. I touch a hand to my face and the right side feels almost normal, but the left is a swollen, unfamiliar landscape of tender bumps and stinging cuts. I rub my right eye gently and after, I'm able to open it a little to look around.

I'm face-down on the ground, shrouded by a layer of fresh snow. I vaguely recall stumbling through a snowstorm, my foot catching on something, falling. The terrible reality of the afternoon returns to me – *Supernova*, the remote cabin, finding her note, then Leah herself. I remember the terrible gaping mouth of the gun. Leah's one rolled-back eye, her violet lips peeled back, the meaty hole in her face.

How long have I been unconscious? It's unlikely to be more than a few minutes, but the snow is still coming down heavily. I pull myself up and feel around for my phone, but it's nowhere to be found; all I can make out in the meager light is the unbroken shroud of bone-white snow, except for a spray of blood above where my head landed. I turn my head slowly and now I can make out the mound I mistook for a fallen tree, I've clearly been unconscious for long enough for the snow to cover her again. I shudder at the thought of the two of us out here in the night, side by side in the clearing, struck still, snow falling silently onto us until we are entirely covered and one with the landscape.

There is a strange feeling in my mouth and I run my tongue around it. A tooth toward the back of my lower left jaw is missing; this must be what I spat out when coming to. In its place is a disturbing hole and fresh blood surges to its surface as I probe it with my tongue.

A searing pain tears into me, shooting up my leg when I try to flex my left foot gently. My ankle is broken, without doubt. If I hadn't regained consciousness when I did, I don't think I would have lasted a half hour in this cold. I'll die out here if I can't get back to the car, but how? I remember the long walk up to the cabin through the woods from where I parked; it took me at least fifteen minutes of brisk walking to reach it, on uneven terrain, and that was before the snowfall. There is simply no way I could make it back, not with a broken ankle, in the dark, in an unfamiliar place. I could fall again, or get impossibly lost, and either way, I'd freeze to death before morning, my body entombed in ice like Leah's. I don't want to die.

'I don't want to die,' I whisper out loud, and even my voice hurts. I begin to cry because the pain in my foot is so intense. My mind darts to a wild animal caught in a trap and left to die. I bring my hand to the racoon trim of my parka jacket and cry even more. My head spins.

I very slowly drag myself up so I am standing on my right foot, using an upended tree trunk for support. I run my hands across my torso and over my head and find everything more or less in its usual place, with the exception of some very sore points at the left side of my skull and jaw, and quite possibly a broken rib. I can't help but cry out loud as my fingers travel across the bruised side of my face. My fingers are so stiff with cold, their tips are numbed beyond any real sensation. With the exception of the broken ankle, I don't think I am dangerously injured, though the state of the left side of my face is worrying. An image of Leah that last day comes to mind – how I must resemble her now, eyes bruised shut, covered in bloody scratches, terror etched on my face.

I have no choice but to try to return to the cabin. Maybe I'll be able to find some bandages and something to splint my left leg with, and tomorrow morning I might be able to drag myself back down to the car in the daylight. Or at least find my phone and call an ambulance. I'll light a fire and eat whatever I can find in Leah's cupboards, then I'll sleep. Everything will be better tomorrow; I have to believe that.

I burst into tears again at the thought of my own bed at home, and how every night I fall asleep next to my husband, drawn close into his warm embrace. But not tonight. How could I have been so stupid to come to a remote cabin by myself? Telemark is a big county, with thousands of cabins scattered across remote and mountainous terrain. Nobody can find me here.

I try to hop up the slippery path in the direction I came, but I can't place any weight at all on my left foot, and after less than a couple of meters, I fall back down. I scream with the pain; it is unlike anything I've felt in all my life. I make myself get halfway back up so I'm on my hands and knees and begin to drag myself up the path. My hands claw at the slushy snow and the sharp rocks underneath, tearing at my skin, and I also have a nosebleed, making droplets of blood drip onto the snow as I inch forward. The snowstorm has momentarily eased up and the dense clouds have parted to reveal patches of inky black sky. Pinprick stars twinkle merrily and it feels as though they are taunting me – a lone, broken woman crawling on her hands and knees across snow-covered rocks, up an inaccessible forest track to an isolated cabin.

I keep going. I have to, or I die.

'I don't want to die,' I whisper, over and over. I really don't want to die, not here, like an animal, no, not at all, and the truth of that makes me want to both cry and laugh at the same time, because nothing could be a stronger sign of how far I've really come. How incredibly far I've succeeded in removing myself from the rock-bottom hell of my life as it once was, how I've turned trauma into triumph, building a valued life for myself with my husband who adores me. I think of my husband and my home every inch of the way.

The white porcelain Jonathan Adler vase Eirik bought for my birthday, filled with a riot of tulips. Five inches forward. The antique hand-painted silk lamps we bought in a tiny shop on a back street of Montmartre many years ago, casting our living room in a cozy, homely glow. Another five inches, the sickly taste of blood at the back of my throat. Our deep bathtub, big enough for two, the feel of the mosaic wall tiles beneath my fingertips as I soak, eyes closed, a glass of red on the shelf to my right. Ten inches forward, a wave of pain. The way it feels to be pleasantly trapped beneath my husband in bed, his skin on my skin, his hands in my hair, his voice murmuring into my ear. Five inches more.

I become aware of a strange sound, a low, animal-like grunting echoing up and down the narrow shaft of the path, slicing through the trees. It rises into a wail, then a high-pitched keening, and I realize that it is coming from me – the pain tearing through me manifested in sound. I don't want to die, but in this moment I am convinced that I will. I have no strength left in my hands, my fingertips are raw and feelingless, my head is pounding and strangely light, like everything that normally fills the conscious mind has seeped out into the white night. What I want now is to lie down. To give my body to the earth. To be cocooned in dark silence, to feel some peace.

'I don't want to die I don't want to die I don't want to die,' I try to keep whispering out loud but the words die on my lips. *Come on, Kristina. Come on.* I can feel a voice speaking to me inside; it's so strong, it's physical, like the rush of blood through my veins. In my mind, I see a girl. A young girl. She's in the woods, like the broken woman on the snowy hillside in Telemark. She's going to die, and she knows it. But she doesn't. She is going to get out of there and build a beautiful life. She will leave those woods. But still, the woods won't ever really leave her.

I inch forward. I follow the girl. She's crashing through the forests, screaming. She doesn't want to die. She wants to become whatever it is she'll become, if only she lives. She wants to see her parents again. She wants to lie in the narrow bed in her childhood room, following the slight tear in the wallpaper with her eyes in the soft darkness, just one more time. I follow her desperate sprint in between impenetrable patches of shrubbery, across clearings, across streams, alongside a dirt track, into a tiny hamlet with a single meandering mud track alongside which sit squat gray brick houses with tin roofs and black gashes for windows. She screams. People come, rubbing sleep from eyes, muttering in a foreign language.

She lives. She goes home. I open my eyes.

The cabin is there, just yards away, its middle window still lit up invitingly by the oil lamp I forgot. I drag myself over to it, then through the door, collapsing on the floor, shaking and retching. The gray slate tiles feel warm and smooth beneath my fingertips. Fresh blood rushes from my nose onto the tiles, dripping onto the dried blood stains already there. I close my eyes. I thank the girl that was me in my head for showing me how to live.

48

Kristina

I drag myself into the bathroom and crawl onto a turquoise Berber rug between the bathtub and the compost toilet. Its lid is shut and I manage to pull myself up onto it. I'm shaking uncontrollably and my fingers are a strange shade of gray-blue. I blow on them repeatedly and after a while I feel some warmth return to them. I manage to slowly peel off my jeans, though the pain as I graze my left ankle is so intense it momentarily takes my breath away.

I inspect my ankle and foot in the faint light from the oil lamp on the shelf above me. The skin is unbroken, but grotesquely swollen and bruised. I very gently run my fingers across where the fracture seems to be, and even the lightest touch provokes an onslaught of pain. I open the bathroom cabinet where I discover that Leah thankfully kept an impressive supply of painkillers. There's ibuprofen, paracetamol, codeine and, impressively, oxycodone. I take two dry – there's no water in the tap – Leah must have a summer cistern or get it delivered in tanks for the warm season. Cabins like this one often don't have water in the winter – the pipes would freeze. In the cupboard I also find sterile compresses and bandages. I manage to stand up for a moment, catching sight of myself in the small mirror. My face is swollen and almost unrecognizable. The skin is broken in several places, with mud and pine needles pressed into the cuts and scratches. I spit on my finger and rub the dirt away gently before sticking the compress over the entire side of my face. I hold my own gaze for a long moment, almost mesmerized by the terror in my own eyes. *It's okay*, I tell myself. *It's going to be okay.*

I lower myself very gently to the ground and crawl into the main living space, and when I take infinite care to not brush against anything with my ankle, the pain is just about manageable. Like I thought I remembered, there are some scraps of kindling in the wood basket by the hearth. I choose the longest and firmest pieces and press them gently in place to support my ankle in a splint, while winding the bandage tight. When I finish, the pain has softened somewhat, probably a combination of the bandage and the Oxycodone. I sit by the side of the hearth, in the exact place I imagined Leah before, singing to herself and drawing warmth into her body. I layer four logs with kindling in between and place some scraps of old newspaper into the gaps between them. When I strike a match it takes immediately, sending big flames leaping into the chimney.

I sit here for a long while, feeling warmth return to my limbs. Occasionally I look across the room through the little grid windows at the dark night beyond. All the clouds have disappeared now, leaving a huge moon hanging high in the sky. The snow has stayed on the ground and the little clearing sparkles in the moonlight. It must be getting late, though how late, I can't tell without my phone. Nine o'clock maybe? Eirik might be back at his hotel after dinner. Maybe he's trying to call me. My phone will ring from under a thick cloak of snow, if it even works still.

The shock and fear have given way to numbness and an almost overpowering fatigue. I decide to look for coffee. I need to think, and I don't feel ready to lie down to sleep in this place, among Leah's possessions. The very thought of it makes my skin prickle into goosebumps on my arm.

Once I have fully regained my warmth, I make my way over to the kitchen nook, supporting myself on bookshelves, backs of chairs and the side of the little Chinese cabinet as I go. There is instant coffee and a kettle, but I don't understand how to make it work without electricity. I follow the cord from the little countertop refrigerator down to the floor, where it disappears into the large, humming generator, almost as big as the appliance itself. I realize there are plug holes around its sides and connect the kettle. In a cupboard I remember seeing several bottles of Imsdal bottled mineral water, and pour half of one into the kettle.

I drink my coffee black by the side of the hearth, gazing into the flames. It is utterly delicious, and for a long moment I feel a strange calm, considering the circumstances. It could be even worse, I suppose. I made it back to the cabin. I have firewood and coffee. I won't die from these injuries. All I have to do is get through the night. But what if whoever killed Leah comes back for me? Or did Leah kill Leah? My mind is spinning. She left a suicide note saying she'd drown in the lake, and yet she ended up shot on a hillside. I take several deep breaths. *Control yourself, Kristina*, I say to myself. I am safer here than anywhere else in this moment, no one knows I am here. All you have to do is get through this night.

I let my eyes travel again across the numerous books that dominate the room. Several copies of Leah's own novel are displayed on a shelf, I hadn't noticed them before, in Norwegian, Swedish, English, French, Portuguese and Italian. I could choose any one of them and make my way to the windowless, cozy sleeping alcove tucked away in the corner of the room, reading until I am able to fall asleep. And tomorrow will bring light, hope and rescue – I have to believe that.

And yet, inside, I know what I crave. I try to resist, because I decided I couldn't bear to read another word she wrote, and don't want to know of any more ways Leah might have infiltrated my life. None of it matters now – she's dead in the most tragic of circumstances and her misguided actions will have no further impact on my life.

What did she hope to achieve by following me around and writing about my life? I try to run through all the possible scenarios, but my brain is dull and uncooperative. It also feels impossible to spend the long night here alone, and choose not to know what she was trying to tell me. I inch across the room to the sofa and settle myself into it before opening Leah's MacBook and opening the document. She would have been pleased to know she has my full attention now – that's what she wanted.

49

Supernova

You'll be familiar with exposure therapy. It may come as a surprise to you that, so am I. According to *Psychiatric Times*, exposure therapy is defined as, 'any treatment that encourages the systematic confrontation of feared stimuli, which can be external, such as feared objects, activities and situations, or internal, such as feared thoughts or physical sensations'. Consider this entire account exposure therapy, Kristina.

I'm getting ahead of myself. I've mentioned Carúpano. I bet it horrified you. I'm not doing this to torture you, I only want your life to be perfect. Selfishly, I suppose I need you to be perfect, and the only way you can be perfect is if you're whole.

What we're going to do here is to rewrite the stories you tell yourself. You see, like any good journalist, I've done some research and some fact-checking, and it would seem things aren't quite how they looked at first glance. Your dissociative amnesia came as a surprise to me. A trauma therapist marred by trauma; you couldn't make it up. A doctor of psychology dedicating her life to the extensive exploration of the inner life, and yet your own remains steeped in shadows.

I've been thinking about how to best do this, and came up with the idea of a 'guided walk through the mind' approach. Bear with me, I've actually done a lot of research into this. It'll be a bit like that meditation bit in yoga; I know you like a bit of vinyasa flow, you told me yourself in your diary. See, I pay attention.

Let's start off with the mental image of a large, beautiful house. It's modern and sleek, in a good part of town. The house is your life. Your marriage is one room, your friendships another, your career a third. Your past is downstairs, and behind one of several doors is Carúpano. But you've nailed that door shut and plastered over it, making it indistinguishable from the smooth white walls. We're going to open it.

How? And why? I can almost feel your questions, across whatever time lapse separates us. How did I know? It wasn't that hard. It's pretty public knowledge if you know where to look. But I know more than them. More than everyone, including you, it would seem. Why, is arguably more interesting. I want to put you back together. I believe that if we build a picture and reconstruct what happened, then the white patches in your mind will become colored in, and you'll be able to move on. Here goes.

Your mother is a delight, isn't she? Not sure I understand why you're cold toward her; at least that's how she feels.

She told me herself. It was easy to get her to talk. I must say she's a talker, unlike you. It was difficult to find my angle of approach; you can't just turn up on someone's doorstep and get them to divulge intimate details about their family members without rousing suspicion. You need to establish a connection over something they care about, build a sense of trust. Finding out where she lives was obviously easy; I must say I love how almost everyone in Norway's address is listed on 1881.no, from the moderately famous to the very wealthy. Bærum, huh? I suppose I should have guessed you'd grown up somewhere fancy. You have that rich-girl privilege; that's the thing about you I find hard to acquire as my own. As you know, I didn't grow up like that and it's hard to fake when you don't know all the nuances and cues of privilege.

Your house wasn't fancy, though, and that's where I lucked out. I spent some time on Google and discovered that the row of semi-detached houses where you grew up were scheduled to be demolished by the council to allow the new E18 motorway extension to bypass Sandvika. Most of the residents had accepted this and taken the generous payoff, but a few refused to budge, delaying the expansion of the new road. Your mother was pictured on the cover of *Bærum Budstikke* with two neighbors, holding a poster reading 'E18 over my dead body'. Passion and fury – great. I had my angle. All I had to do was call her and tell her the truth – that I was a journalist freelancing for several national newspapers interested in speaking with her. She may have mentioned it to you – I even succeeded in getting them some coverage.

We got on well, your mother and I. So well that she quite

happily chattered on about her family and her kids when I prompted her about what a fantastic place it must have been to raise a family. She told me of your father's impressive career as a leading geologist and that it had been hard, sometimes, to be married to a man who is more interested in rocks than in sex and conversation. This made me laugh, genuinely, and it made me wish I could laugh with my own mother like that. Yours is very different from mine, though you've probably already concluded that a long time ago based on what I've told you in our sessions. Yours is funny, a little scatter-brained, full of energy and with tons of plans for the future. She's trusting, too trusting, but I guess that is not so strange when you've been married to a man more interested in rocks than sex or conversation for over forty years. Everyone needs someone to talk to, and someone to feel close to.

She told me all about your impressive and exhausted sister, both surgeon and supermom, fighting tirelessly on that battlefield of career and children. Then she told me about you.

She is, in fact, practically a hero, said your mother. She lowered her voice when she spoke of the terrible trauma you'd endured in your late teens, and of how you'd turned your life around and become a highly respected psychotherapist who contributes to international research and has made a name for herself, specifically in the field of trauma. I gently encouraged her; I know how to make people talk. She made more coffee, reassured herself that I wouldn't speak of this to anyone, and of course I reassured her – the empty promises of a stranger. She dropped her voice as though you were there somewhere in the house and might walk in to learn of your mother telling a stranger the things you don't even talk to your friends about. Or your husband.

Her hair dropped out, she said. *Her skin broke out in scales. She lost her period and it never returned to normal. Personally, I believe that it was the trauma that robbed her of the chance to have children.* I asked, carefully, about the trauma, and she told me that you and your two friends were held at gunpoint in Venezuela. *She went there with her two best friends, Elisabeth Eliassen and Trine Rickard.* This rang an instant bell and I felt exhilarated; it was the feeling of discovering a crucial piece of a puzzle. Rickard – it was one of the names on the doorbells of the building in Rosenborggata 11, where you go on Fridays after seeing me. And Elisabeth – the name in your diary. *They thought they had to travel across the world to that dangerous country to find themselves. Only Elisabeth and Kristina came back, but they didn't come back as themselves.*

She spoke for a long time; it was clear that she needed to get something off her chest.

Everything she told me became part of the backdrop. I didn't yet know what to do with it, or where I was going with any of it – I just wanted to be close to you. At that point, I was driven by needing to prove my illusion of you as perfect, because if it was possible for you, then it might be possible for me. I didn't know, then, that it would be up to me to piece you back together.

It was your mother who first told me about Elisabeth. She spoke of a sensitive and beautiful little girl with natural charisma and a love of the arts who'd lived just next door – she pointed to the left, and my eyes traveled through the windows into the gardens outside, yours and Elisabeth's separated only by a low hedge, and it was almost like I could see two little girls out there, running through sprinklers, chasing a ball, playing hopscotch.

She turned out badly, said your mother, her face grief-stricken.

After, I went home and hit Google, as one naturally would. It wasn't hard to find the old articles about the three girls from Bærum who were held hostage in Venezuela back in 2003.

'The Trine Rickards Tragedy,' read *Aftenposten*'s headline. 'The nineteen-year-old aspiring vet was traveling around South America with close schoolfriends, Elisabeth Eliassen and Kristina Hellerud, when she was shot at point-blank at a private address on the outskirts of Carúpano on August 24th. *It was, quite simply, an execution*, says Jorge Aruelo, police chief in the Eastern Venezuelan region of Sucre. A local man with an already extensive criminal record, including several drug-charges as well as assault, Xavier Miguel Rodriguez, was apprehended at the scene and will face trial for first-degree murder.'

'The murder of innocence,' read *VG*, dated three days after the attack. 'One life lost, another two shattered. The surviving girls of the Carúpano shooting, Elisabeth Eliassen and Kristina Hellerud, of Sandvika, Bærum, are receiving trauma therapy in Caracas after Thursday's brutal attack. They are receiving support from the Norwegian foreign office in Venezuela, and are expected to return to Norway later this week.'

I opened a third article, this one in *Dagsavisen*. 'Rickards, who recently turned nineteen and was a graduate of Sandvika Gymnasium, had spent most of the summer working at 7-Eleven in Bekkestua to save money for the trip of a lifetime, traveling around South America for six months. Excitement turned to tragedy just two weeks into the trip, when the Norwegian trio decided to hitchhike in the notoriously dangerous northern Sucre region, after several scheduled buses failed to showed up. The girls were picked up by Rodriguez, who brought them to a house party at a private home near Carúpano. According to the witness statement of Elisabeth Eliassen, they stayed for several hours, taking drugs and drinking alcohol with Rodriguez, his brother and several others. At one point in the evening, Rodriguez, an unidentified second man and the three Norwegian girls retreated to a gazebo in the grounds of the house, bordering the surrounding jungle. It was here Rodriguez brought out the weapon and threatened the girls when they refused to perform a sexual act on himself and the other man. The girls tried to run, but Rodriguez fired the gun straight at Trine Rickards, who was killed instantly. Elisabeth Eliassen and Kristina Hellerud managed to run off into the jungle in the commotion that followed.

'Hellerud was recovered several hours later, disorientated and dehydrated, a few miles away in the Macarapana area. She remains in hospital care and is said to suffer from cognitive impairment as a result of the incident. Elisabeth Eliassen managed to reach the main road and flagged down a vehicle. She was brought to the Hospital General de Carúpano, where she was reunited with Hellerud the following day, before being transferred to Caracas at the insistence of the Norwegian Consul General, Einar Johannessen.'

I was so shocked to learn what you'd been through. It changed everything. I had to know more. I suppose I wanted to know how it had affected you and how you could have survived something like that and gone on to seem so whole. I pored over the images of teenage you and your two tragic friends. Blonde-haired, blue-eyed Trine, tiny next to you and Elisabeth who are both so tall, smiling in every picture. Trine was obviously the goofy one, unable to resist a peace sign behind your head, or crossing her eyes, or sticking her tongue out.

What kind of monster could point a gun at her head and pull the trigger?

Elisabeth seemed more concerned with striking a pose; she was probably quite aware that she was the most physically striking out of the three of you. You seem insecure and more anonymous than your friends in the pictures, and in more than one, you were looking at Elisabeth in the moment the flash went off, as if to gauge how to pose, whether to smile.

I spent a lot of time thinking about what your mother said, and what happened to you. I thought about it so much that it almost felt like I, too, was there and that I'd shared the experience with you. I could practically feel the fear you must have felt crashing through that terrifying forest, all alone, the sound of the gunshot reverberating in your head. I saw what you must have seen – the girl crumpling to the ground, a spray of blood lingering for a moment on the air that had held her, fragments of her skull landing on your skin. I could smell the sweet scent of rot on the air, the sulfur of the gunpowder, the cruel murderer's rancid body odor. I built these images in my mind obsessively, not really understanding that my preoccupation with them was just another of my brain's escape fantasies.

I was even jealous of your trauma, Kristina. It's true. I think what I mean by that is that I craved a tragic story of my own, something as big and shocking as the Carúpano shooting, that would explain why I have spent so much of my life feeling so empty, so ravaged by grief, so utterly alone. I had an absent father and a self-obsessed mother who doesn't like me very much, and a failed marriage to a man who rejected me in myriad little ways every day, but those things aren't exactly reasons to feel so broken. Or are they? You always made me feel like my feelings were valid, whatever they were. When I think back at how you used to make me feel, I miss you so intensely that it takes my breath away. I wish we could go back to that time when I'd sit across from you in our sessions and drink in your kind, attentive presence, when you were all I needed, and entirely mine for fifty minutes each week. I wish I hadn't done what I've done.

For a while, knowing about Carúpano made me even more obsessed with you. It was so moving and impressive that you'd moved on from a tragedy of such magnitude and built a good life for yourself, a life in which you managed to offer support to others who suffered trauma. I put two and two together and realized that you paid a weekly visit to Trine Rickards' parents, presumably out of the kindness of your heart. It wasn't hard to understand the conflicting emotions around those visits, and why you clearly sometimes couldn't face going. I assumed that you'd be haunted by impressions and memories of that terrible night all those years ago, the images that came so easily and convincingly to my own mind when I thought about it.

What I didn't know back then was that I'd conjured up memories you yourself don't have. Cognitive impairment, said *Dagsavisen*, but what did it mean?

I'm getting ahead of myself. I was overwhelmed by sympathy for you and your plight; I couldn't stop thinking about what your mother said. That your hair fell out, that you couldn't have children, that you had basically hauled yourself out of the flames and soared into the sky like a phoenix, like a hero: those were her exact words. I also thought about the other survivor, charismatic and beautiful Elisabeth Eliassen, clearly the ringleader out of the three of you, and wondered what her life might be like now. *She turned out badly*, your mother said, and when I thought back to that conversation, her choice of words made me angry, because it was exactly the kind of thing my mother might have said about me. *She turned out badly*, meaning – *she turned out different to me*.

I became curious about this woman who, like you, had survived unimaginable trauma but 'turned out badly'. I made a mental note to find her.

50

Elisabeth, June

The group has fallen silent without Elisabeth noticing. She's been lost in thought, staring at the strange imagery of the painting in front of her. She realizes that Arne, Villa Vinternatt's visual arts therapist, has stopped in front of her and has clearly asked a question.

'What?' she whispers.

'Do you want to share something about your painting with the group?'

'Um.'

Arne watches her carefully. His face is kind and open, but when he turns to study her newest picture, done during the morning's two-hour session in watercolor, his eyes change expression and he frowns.

'What do you think this picture is trying to tell you?' he asks.

'Umm.' She stands up, takes a couple of steps back and stands shoulder to shoulder with Arne, considering her work. She glances around the room, at her fellow residents craning their heads to get a clear view, and catches Joel's eye. He raises an eyebrow slowly and gives her a little encouraging smile.

'It seems to me that this picture is quite different from most of the images you've produced here in these sessions, Elisabeth,' says Arne.

'Different how?'

'Does anyone else want to contribute? Does anyone have an idea why I believe this picture is a clear departure from Elisabeth's general style?'

'It's certainly more explicit,' says Gina, an older woman with scraggly black hair and teeth stained an impressive shade of yellow.

'Continue,' says Arne.

'Well. In most of Elisabeth's pictures, the themes seem to be pretty abstract. You might see bloodstains, I might see the inside of a jam jar, Joel might see something else entirely. But this... This is, like, obvious.'

'What do you see, Gina?'

'Well. A river. Of blood. A dark, busy forest. Uh. Lots of life somehow. Bugs, bats, those faces among the trees.'

'Faces?' Elisabeth blurts it out, her eyes returning to the painting, and only then does she see them: faces indeed, distinctly human, and ghoulishly twisted into terrifying grimaces that bleed into the dense foliage of the forest.

'Elisabeth?' says Arne. 'You sound surprised.'

'No. No, just I didn't realize that they were so obvious, that's all.'

'Can you tell me about this?' Arne points his finger to the top right-hand side of the picture, where a little brown bird, painted meticulously and in more sophisticated detail than the rest of the scene, flies in between deliberately childishly drawn, yellow five-point stars.

'Um... No.' She has rarely felt this tongue-tied in a group therapy session; usually Arne's art sessions are her favorites, but today she feels strangely discombobulated and dissociated, entirely unable to decipher any meaning in her own imagery. The task they were given was to 'paint yourself in nature'.

'Would I be correct in assuming the bird represents you?'

'Yes. Yes, maybe.'

'It looks like a happy bird.'

'Yeah.'

'And yet, the scene it flies over is very disturbing.'

'Yeah. Yes, I guess it is.'

'A blood-red river, threatening faces among dense trees, a real sense of danger.'

'Mmmm.'

'But the bird is free.'

'Yeah,' says Elisabeth, blinking at sudden tears in her eyes.

51

Kristina

I shiver lightly at her words. My mother. I can't believe Leah has really gone that far, seeking out people in my life and striking up contact with them, but she clearly has. The problem is, Leah is certainly mistaken if she thinks that she could uncover some deep, dark secrets about me by speaking to my mother. There are no deep, dark secrets to uncover. It's all right there, on the internet, like Leah herself says.

Could she really have gotten to Elisabeth, too? I can't imagine it would be possible; Elisabeth spent the last eighteen months of her life in a rehabilitation facility with limited visitor access. I think she would have mentioned it to me if someone had come around asking about me, no doubt about that. But what if she didn't?

Leah was clearly completely destabilized, and I have truly failed at picking up the signs of how disturbed she really was, but how much damage has she managed to do? Leah speaks of missing pieces of puzzles, of unlocking the doors to the past, as if my life was some fucking story to be reconstructed for her twisted entertainment. I hate her smug, misinformed voice and find it impossible to reconcile with the Leah Iverson I thought I knew. The reality of what she has done is shocking: she sought out my mother, who, like Leah said, likes the sound of her own voice, and possibly poor Elisabeth too. It explains a lot. Everything, in fact.

I don't know why Leah became obsessed with what happened to us in Carúpano, but I think she's right about the preoccupation with someone else's tragic experience being a way for the mind to escape its own reality. I see it sometimes in clients who become unusually preoccupied with events that ultimately have nothing to do with them, such as a plane crash or a terrorist attack.

What happened to us in Venezuela was a terrible tragedy, one that has defined my life in many ways, but still, I have built a life beyond it. I committed to my own healing and I was able to move on past trauma by accepting its presence and integrating it into my experience. It's true that I was more fortunate than Elisabeth in the way my mind and body processed the attack – I haven't been forced to endlessly relive what happened or been haunted day and night by what that man did to us.

Why is Leah hell-bent on dragging this back out into the light? I feel sick at the thought of her seeking out Elisabeth; she was a very vulnerable woman, and especially in the last months of her life. She would have been easily won over by someone as devious and convincing as Leah. She might have told her things that were untrue, or irrelevant, or dangerous, or all of those.

Elisabeth was confused and unreliable in the months before she died in August. More than once, she relapsed with both alcohol and marijuana, and I had to use my professional relationship with Villa Vinternatt's founder for leverage to allow her to stay on the program after breaking the strict policy on total sobriety. She also showed worrying signs of distorted memory and reality perception. She'd ruminate over her relationship with Andreas and make it sound like it was the greatest love story in the history of the world, when in reality it was a disastrous five-year descent into hell, defined by an endless cycle of co-dependency, addiction and chaos. She'd paint and draw obsessively, and her incredible talent was clear for everyone to see, but her art gave an insight into the turbulence of her mind – she'd paint blood and violence and that jungle she wasn't ever able to leave behind.

She began to say worrying things, and at times she took her underlying anger out on me. One of the last times I saw her, she called me a 'Fucking golden girl who lives in a fucking golden bubble with my fucking golden husband,' and I had to work hard, then, at controlling my own reactions to her. I knew that what she said really had nothing to do with me or my life, and everything to do with how deeply disappointed and ashamed she was about the mess she'd made of her own life. I knew that it wasn't my fault that she couldn't find healing and peace.

Loving Elisabeth in those last days required merging friendship with therapy, but I loved Elisabeth; she was my best friend in spite of everything, and I tried everything in my power to save her. I really did.

I feel overwhelmed with dread thinking about Elisabeth

and how she ended her life, and the thought of Leah insinuating herself into her life is unbearable. Highly unstable herself, she might have directly contributed to the way things turned out for Elisabeth. Looking back, I can see how she might have influenced Elisabeth; toward the end, she went from being seemingly content and more at peace than she had been for many years, to becoming so angry and so bitter. At the time I suspected that her treatment at Villa Vinternatt was making her question everything and that her new pursuit of art had brought all those feelings to the surface. I tried to redirect her focus to the future, to everything she could still become. But she refused to let go.

My head and the bruised side of my face throb with increasing intensity. My fingers hurt and still feel strangely numb. My stomach aches and growls. And my ankle hurts so badly the sensation of it almost goes beyond pain, like if you put your hand into a flame and watch the skin burn but feel a wild heat rather than pain. It must be late in the evening by now, but it's hard to tell because the moon is hidden behind thick clouds and I can see from where I'm lying on the sofa that the snow is falling heavily again. I close the computer to preserve the battery; it's just gone into power-saving mode and I doubt I have more than another half hour of power. I haven't seen the charger anywhere, and it's not like I can easily move about to search for it. I need the bathroom and it takes me at least ten minutes to get there. I find that the easiest way to move around is to sit on the floor and very gently push my way backward.

Still, I cry with the intensity of the pain and by the time I return to the sofa, I'm trembling with exhaustion. How will I ever make it back down to the car? And how will I get through the night, with nothing but Leah's insane account for company?

52

Supernova

Many days have passed since I wrote this account up until this point. In the meantime, terrible things have happened. When I first started this, it felt powerful and exhilarating, like all the pieces just magically slotted into place. It just flowed, at long last. Night after starry night, the words came rushing out, just how I intended them, like a piece of music masterfully coaxed from an ancient instrument. For every day that passed I lost hope that you might come, that we might sit across from each other here in this room, like I'd envisioned, finally united in truth. But for every day that passed, it mattered less, and a slight hope began to grow, that writing this account of the truth might come to matter just the same. But then the baby left me, Kristina. I can't bear it. It made me realize the outcome will be different now. There will be no happy ending. I can't, won't, can't, stay. But I decided to finish this, first. Why? Because I wanted someone to know the whole truth. My truth. We're arriving at a crucial point here, something I've been staving off and also building up in my head. Perhaps what's happened to me in the meantime can bring the right rawness to what happened to you.

Someone once told me that when it comes to writing, you start off with an earthquake and then work your way up to the climax. It's strange, how something seemed to loosen inside me once I started writing to you, and on some level, I must have known all along that we'd end up here. Back there. I meant what I said about exposure therapy, that it will help you, so I've tried to rebuild what happened. I feel I know these scenes so intimately it's as though I was there myself. I wish I could see your face as you read my words. I wish I could know if I got it right. If I helped.

You run excitedly towards the dirty grey Mazda sedan purring impatiently by the side of the deserted road, exhaust rising into the night sky. You scoot across the back seat and try to get a glimpse of the man behind the wheel, but you can only make out a smooth brown neck and longish black hair curling at the tips. You feel a wave of trepidation and fight the urge to slip back into the night, but you immediately feel silly – after all, there are three of you. Elisabeth and Trine rush into the car, giggling and breathing exaggeratedly after the little dash up the cracked tarmac towards the car. Trine's bare legs squeak against the leather seats. Elisabeth mutters, 'Hola,' and, 'Gracias,' and then all three of you giggle again, a hollow nervousness creeping into your voices. The man steps on the gas and the car surges off, fast.

When someone had finally stopped, you'd squealed and clapped your hands, it felt like you'd been standing there for hours in the hot, dusty air. You know that hitchhiking in Venezuela is a bad idea, but you also know that you need to free yourself from the over-protectiveness of your parents back home, and that young people need to have adventures. Wild adventures – that was the whole point of this. Besides, Elisabeth and Trine are convincing co-travelers and you know better than to question their plans. Mostly, you just do what they say.

You glance at them now, watching shadows chase across their faces as the car speeds north towards the coast, bringing those sandy palm-fringed beaches you've been dreaming of closer.

Carúpano, Elisabeth had said as she got in the car, and the man had nodded, so presumably he'd understood. It isn't far, less than thirty minutes, but the bus you'd planned on taking never came. While you waited, you drank tequila from a roadside shack and danced in the violet twilight with your best friends, well aware of the stares from the men populating the plastic chairs to the side of the makeshift bar. You smoked cigarette after cigarette, stubbing them out with the heel of your flip-flop. After a long while, feeling warm and woozy, you started walking, leaving the few lights dotting the steep hillsides of the little crossroads town behind. Then it got dark. Elisabeth and Trine had stuck their thumbs out every time a pair of headlights appeared in the distance, but not a single car had even slowed down, before this one.

The car stops. The jungle has grown denser and stands like mountainsides on either side of the road. A long sliver of moonlight spills down the empty road, making it appear liquid, like a river snaking through the forest. You glance down at your hands, held gingerly in your lap. A childhood memory flashes through your brain, random but clear;

those same hands gripping the handlebars of your first bicycle, purple and white streamers flying behind you as you tore down the streets. You look at Trine and Elisabeth, but they are both quiet and serious, now, like you. Your eyes have adjusted to the darkness and you can make out a narrow dirt track disappearing into the forest from the patchily asphalted main road.

The man turns around and only now do you finally see his face. It is a beautiful face, with soulful black eyes set beneath thick brows, and full lips spreading out in a slow smile at the sight of you. His cheeks are sweetly dimpled, and a long scar runs from the outer corner of his eye all the way down to his stubbled jaw, as though a tiger had clawed him. A small snake is tattooed on his throat, its red serpent tongue flicking upwards to the man's chin. You can't help but take a stunned, sharp breath of air. He'll come back, this man, in your dreams and in your waking moments, and maybe you know already now that you'll never be free of him. You'll write about him in your diary in twenty years' time, when you'll be a respectable, married woman with a beautiful home and a rewarding career. You'll write about that first moment. About desire coursing through you like a white heat. You won't feel desire like it again, not ever, not with anybody. Is it even real, such a sudden and uncontrollable explosion in the synapses, at the mere sight of a stranger? In your own words – *an instant surrender of everything I knew, everything I thought I was*?

I'm on my way to a party, he says, in almost fluent English, nodding towards the dirt track. *It's an awesome house. Overlooking Playa Hernan Vasquez. My brother and a couple of friends are there. Come and have a few drinks with us.*

Trine shakes her head almost imperceptively. Elisabeth says nothing, but looks at you for direction. A glance passes between you, and she *knows*, she'll always remember the look in your eyes. At the time, she would have called it the look of desire, or love, even, but much later, she'll realize it was the thrill of danger.

Yes, says Elisabeth. You coyly break the man's glance; you know instinctively to leave him wanting more.

How does it make you feel, how *his* life turned out?

53

Kristina

I close my eyes. I have to. I feel myself disappearing down into the empty spaces inside myself, back in time, back to the place I never allow into my thoughts, there is no point anyway – there's nothing but a milky nothingness there.

But now it is as though the scene Leah describes colors in the white patches in my memory. Where my brain has always drawn a blank when it comes to *him*, I now suddenly and distinctly remember the serpent tattoo on his throat, his soulful eyes and deep dimples, the scar on his cheek like a river on a map. In spite of Leah's extremely limited understanding of dissociative amnesia, it's true that huge patches of my memory were simply erased. I spent my early twenties in intense therapy to heal and to try to retrieve the memories of what happened in Venezuela – like Leah, I believed back then that remembering would be the only way to move on. In the end, Ingvild taught me that acceptance was more important than full recollection, and besides, we knew what happened because Elisabeth was there.

I open my eyes briefly and they flood with tears. I close them again and now I see *him* clearly in my mind's eye. I can't recall the rest of the scene – the car ride and the words he spoke, what we were wearing and what thoughts might have run through my head, but Leah has succeeded in sending me back there, to Carúpano. The forest that surrounded the futuristic beach house set high above a pristine bay we were brought to was as dense and ancient as the one surrounding this cabin. Instead of being snow-covered and silent, the jungle of Carúpano was sticky warm and buzzing with a plethora of sounds. The sounds of lives lived in the undergrowth, in the trees, in the air above them, a ceaseless chattering of a thousand species. This I remember. And the deafening gunshot.

'Why?' I whisper into the cool air of the silent cabin. 'Why are you doing this to me?' I have to know why. And, Elisabeth – what have you done?

54

Elisabeth, July

The dining room looks and feels very different. No longer witness to the chattering of residents and clinking of cutlery, the commissary tables and long benches are gone and replaced with row upon row of white sheets like sails awaiting their ships. The exhibition, titled 'Recovery Reframed', is the first of its kind in Norway and seen as a groundbreaking attempt to rehabilitate some of the country's most prolific drug addicts by restoring their art careers left in ruins by addiction. Similar programs have already met with great success in New York and London, and Oslo is keen to follow suit.

The management of Villa Vinternatt is busy organizing the installation, and the stress of it all is etched on their faces. Carpenters are still busily constructing the gallery while staff meticulously pin small white description cards to each piece in an attempt to make some sense of what the artist is trying to convey. The media has taken quite an interest in the story and several journalists are expected to attend the vernissage, hoping to speak to the artists themselves.

Elisabeth is one of the most high-profile artists in the group and her series of five paintings all center on the recurrent theme of blood. She smiles to herself as she stands back and looks at her work, knowing that a part of her is on the canvas, her blood, guided by the brush strokes of her memories. Memories so dark that the only way she feels she can survive sometimes is to get them out of her physically. Nobody knows that she cuts herself. The inside of her mouth hides the lacerations; it's one of her many secrets and it brings her a strange thrill to know that her blood is there, unhidden, on the canvas for everyone to see. Her haunting imagery sees wild animals, scared, trapped and abandoned, fused against a bleak swirling landscape of rich earthy tones. Bloodshot eyes, bloodied mouths, bleeding wounds, blood-emptied open bellies.

Her thoughts are interrupted by a junior counselor asking her to change as the guests will be arriving in the next thirty minutes. Elisabeth makes her way back to her room and rifles through the few items of clothing in her wardrobe. It actually hasn't occurred to her that it might be nice to wear something special on a night like tonight. She throws on a navy chiffon blouse and the only pair of trousers she owns that aren't sweatpants, adding a flick of mascara and a touch of lipstick. Perfume is banned at Villa Vinternatt because it contains alcohol, as if she would glug her favorite Chanel, and the thought makes her smile impulsively at herself in the mirror. Her palms start to sweat as she heads back to the dining room, the hum of voices rising up the stairwell from the formal reception rooms downstairs.

All the artists are asked to stand next to their work, like schoolchildren awkwardly showing their finger-painting skills at parents' evening. Elisabeth guesses it is mainly so that the press and members of the local community can more easily tell the druggies from the staff. Elisabeth wishes Kristina were here tonight. It feels almost impossible that she isn't – all these years later, Kristina remains her main source of support and comfort, more so than her elderly mother. But Kristina is in Hamburg at a conference about rapid eye movement therapy. Elisabeth asked her if there was any way she could move it around or even not go so that she could be there tonight, but Kristina had to go. Elisabeth understands, of course she does, but glancing toward the wide double doors at the throng of people waiting to be let in, she has to swallow hard at the thought of Kristina not being among them.

The members of the local community hover at the entrance, like vultures circling high above carrion; nothing like ogling the inner thoughts of a bunch of junkies. It was only a few years ago, under the old management, that the residents were nicknamed the Vintanutters, a term that still endures many years later.

Elisabeth goes through the motion of explaining her pictures and answering the usual questions from well-meaning people who have no ability to understand what she's been through.

'What made you take heroin?'

'It looks like real blood; well done. How did you manage that?'

'Why don't you paint happy themes?'

'Do you think you'll return to drugs?'

'Do they lock the doors at night here?'

'You don't look like a drug addict.'

'I suppose prostitution must have been part of that whole life, eh?'

She turns away from the man asking the question mid-sentence and walks out of the room. In the next room, where the larger sculptures of some of the residents are displayed, she catches the eye of a young woman, a tall, attractive woman in white jeans and a blue-and-white striped blouse. The woman smiles at her, and she smiles back in passing; she's on her way to the bathroom to splash some cold water on her face and get a moment's peace.

'Hey. Hey, wait,' says the woman and Elisabeth turns back around to face her. When she does she is struck by a sudden familiarity, and then it occurs to her that the stranger in front of her bears a slight resemblance to Kristina. It's something to do with the smooth bronzed skin, the understated style, the gold stud earrings and the chocolate-brown, expensively highlighted high ponytail. 'Are you Elisabeth Eliassen?'

'Uh, yes?'

'I'm familiar with your work. I really wanted to speak with you. My name is Ella Victor, I'm a journalist at *Dagbladet*.' Elisabeth shakes the woman's hand and lets herself be gently led by the elbow back through the throng of people to her canvases in the next room.

'Your work is fantastic,' says Ella Victor, looking past Elisabeth and gazing to the pieces strung from the ceiling, focusing intently on each one in turn. 'You've really captured the essence of something quite frightening here.'

'Thank you,' Elisabeth replies, blushing slightly at the praise. Sometimes she thinks her work is so dark that nobody could ever see past the darkness and see beauty there, too. She looks at Ella again and there is something about the way she stares at her that makes her suddenly afraid – it's not Kristina she reminds her of now, but one of the animals circling her in her dreams. She takes a big sip from her glass of orange juice and feels like laughing out loud at her own ridiculousness.

'Shall I tell you about this one?' she says, pointing to the middle canvas and Ella nods enthusiastically, any trace of imagined threat gone from her eyes.

55

Supernova

You moved on. You healed. I get it. It's what people do. You did your own long years in therapy and it made you reflective and aware of your own reactions and contributions – I suppose those are the things we all hope for when coming to therapy. Your training taught you real insight into yourself, I imagine, to the point where your inner life became subject to understanding and empathy, and perhaps this was one of the things I sensed and which so drew me to you. You know how to forgive yourself. You believe that you deserve it. I want that for myself. Especially now, as you will come to understand.

Let's move on, so much ground to cover. Another thing that impressed me about you was your obvious ability to maintain, and thrive in, a long-term partnership. As you know, this isn't an ability we share. It feels as though whatever I do and whomever I do it with, I leave nothing but pain and destruction in my wake. Take Emil, for example, that guy I dated last year; you might remember him. A good man, and someone who was endlessly patient with all my whims and insecurities and issues. I dropped him over and over, until he was so bruised by me that he'd lost all sense of himself. Still, he'd come back for more. Like a dog.

I guess it was just me replicating the behavior I'd learned from Anton, and even earlier, from my father, hooked on the emotional rollercoaster ride of loving men who have nothing to give you except rejection and abandonment.

I lied to you about Anton. I lied to the whole world about Anton, didn't I? We hurt each other; it went both ways, that's the truth. Before I came to therapy, it was me who hurt him. But last Friday, before our session, it was Anton who hit me. It was him who did it. He punched me in the face and that was actually the first time he ever physically laid hands on me. By doing it, he actually turned my lies to truth.

And because of my book, I got trapped in a web of lies about what happened between us. Much of that book was made up; it was partially fiction, after all, but everyone thought it was a precise account of our relationship and hailed me as a domestic abuse survivor, when the truth was a lot more nuanced and rather more boring.

So I let everyone believe that I left Anton in the end, that he attacked me and left me in fear of my life. I adopted the persona of the brave but downtrodden abuse victim because I just couldn't bear the truth that sat beneath the surface of my skin like a never-ending itch, impossible to escape. It's what I told you, even. *I realized that I had to leave to survive*, I'd say, smug as fuck. I lied because I was too ashamed to tell the truth, even to you. In the book I preached about self-love and the need to protect the flame burning inside myself when I had no fucking concept of either of those things. I still don't. But they sounded good, and they were what people wanted to hear.

Who would want to read a story about a cold marriage from which the main protagonist actually doesn't want to leave, where she deep down welcomes constant rejection and cruel ridicule because they are the only things that confirm what she believes to be true about herself? People want happy endings, stories of strong women who overcome abuse and build shiny, wholesome lives.

But it was Anton who left me and I'd suppose you would say that it triggered that underlying wound of my father leaving me. It unleashed a wild, primal grief. He'd been indifferent and cold toward me throughout our marriage, occasionally throwing me an intoxicating little bone of affection. I was obsessed with really winning him over and mistook my hurt over the fact that he had one foot out the door for excitement. I bent over backward trying to make him stay, compromising myself more and more; I couldn't bear another man walking out on me. I begged him to stay, but he didn't even react, just looked the other way. I would have preferred being hit to his indifference. I'd never known shame like that. Or anger. I can still see his look of surprise when I slammed my fist into his face, breaking his nose. I clawed at his skin and pummeled him and pushed him down the stairs. Then I threw myself down them, too, breaking my collarbone and giving myself severe concussion. I told everyone I got a restraining order against him, so nobody would suspect that the actual story was rather different.

Nobody believed Anton's version of events, especially after the book came out. We didn't speak for years. But

I'd go by his apartment sometimes at night and watch the shadows of his flickering television from across the street. I'd lie in bed and dream of him holding me, making love to me, hurting me even. I just wanted to be held, Kristina.

Then I got what I wanted. He came back last year. Because I'd lied about Anton being physically abusive, I couldn't exactly tell you that I was seeing him again. I was in therapy then, of course, and I just couldn't find a way to tell you. I'm still not quite sure why I lied to you about this, but I had fallen in love with the victim role and wanted you to feel sorry for me. And I guess it was hard to admit that I was so pathetic. I couldn't tell you that the more therapy I had and the more I began to grasp the underlying patterns that led to my behavior, the more I lost interest in Anton. A man suddenly committed to staying was unfamiliar and uninteresting to someone as messed up as me. I began to seek thrills elsewhere. I began to sleep with men who were willing to act into the never-ending cycle of hurting me and leaving me – it's what I know.

And now, it's all over. So much is lost. I'm afraid of myself.

But for you, it's different. You don't court drama and pain and rejection and abandonment. You have a solid marriage. And you've held onto it. Without drama, and with what appears to be an above-average level of happiness. Just look at all those interviews your impressive husband gives. He never fails to mention you. It's like he thinks he's married to a saint. His rock, he calls you. His inspiration. *I'd be lost without her*, he said recently. *Me too*, I thought, scrutinizing the photograph of the two of you – a classic Norwegian shot of an outdoorsy couple climbing some mountain or other, beaming at each other, a broody and barren valley rolling away behind you.

It must be nice to be loved like that.

Someday, your husband will be prime minister if he has his way. And it seems to me that this guy mostly has his way. You'll be propelled to the forefront of our society then; the intriguing other half of Norway's leader. The media and the public will be interested in you – you're rather different from those who have gone before you. Much younger, with a fresh look and a rock-solid education, a respectable career and a winning, unassuming way of being. You have made yourself so inoffensive, so inconspicuous. You've built a life so ordinary, but so beautiful.

They'll find out about your past, of course. It's not like it's a secret anyway – a simple Google search will give it away. It's a long time ago now, but your past will without doubt be brought back out into the light when your husband ascends to the very top of the political hierarchy. Perhaps you'll give a tell-all interview to avoid any rumors and to elicit even more sympathy. People will cry for you. You will cry for yourself, too, like I already know you do. At night. Right now, probably. Sometimes when you're driving. On Friday evenings, walking back home, your eyes locked hard on the blur of pavement, not noticing your surroundings, or me, twenty yards behind you.

You'll realize by now that I've done quite a bit of homework. Learned to talk your talk. According to betterhealth.com, dissociation is, 'a mental process of disconnecting from one's thoughts, feelings, memories or sense of identity. The dissociative disorders that need professional treatment include dissociative amnesia, dissociative fugue, depersonalization disorder and dissociative identity disorder.'

I want you to understand that you were the victim. To really understand it. I believe that you blame yourself. That's where the anger comes from. And the control issues. Did you think I didn't notice them? The way you arrange the tea bags is a dead giveaway. The way the photographs were hung at your house, I just know you obsessed about the distance between them. The calculations in your diary move me to think that you're trying to work out the mathematical probability of what happened to Trine Rickards.

I've wondered whether you really can't remember, or if you have become so good at control that you don't allow your mind to be whole? Either way, it must be lonely. Especially now that Elisabeth is dead. It must be so hard to not know why *she* died. I imagine you believe she committed suicide because of the endless cycle of addiction. That she just couldn't stand it anymore. Except that wasn't why. I tried to tell you. I tried to talk to you about it. I wanted to be there for you. Haven't you always said to me that the truth is never ugly, unlike lies, and that we will live better if we live by it? She committed suicide because of you. Elisabeth died to protect you. She loved you so much because you're worth that much love. But before she died, she told me what she'd been carrying for so long. And I need you to know, because otherwise it will keep hurting you in myriad ways – you need to know and then you can be free. This freedom is my parting gift to you.

56

Kristina

I take a break here. I'm sick of Leah Iverson playing some fucking cat-and-mouse game with me. My mind is spinning and I don't know what to think or feel about anything anymore. In spite of everything, I feel sorry for her; it's terrible to think of her sitting here in this cabin, losing her baby and clearly having some very dark thoughts and, by all accounts, a serious mental breakdown that resulted in the delusions that make up *Supernova*, only for Anton to return to kill her. I know he did, and either he made her write that note or she wrote it before he got to her. I glance out the window at the black night. Could it be that he'll come here again? He could turn up here tonight, and might try to cover up what he's done to really make sure it looks like suicide.

I shiver violently and my pulse is so high I keep bringing my hand to my throat to feel it. I feel strangely light-headed. A part of me wants to try to get to the kitchen nook and drink the bottle of wine in the fridge. I'm desperate to numb my mind but I equally know I need to stay sharp to get out of here alive.

I reread the last few sentences over and over again. I almost want to laugh. *She committed suicide because of you. Elisabeth died trying to protect you.*

For a moment there, I was getting worried about where she was going with all this. Now, it's merely laughable. *Oh, Leah, how could you have got it so wrong?*

57

Elisabeth, July

She loves many things about being here and this surprises her every day because she hadn't anticipated relaxing into her surroundings or feeling at home. She can't recall summer ever being more beautiful than here – the vast neon-green lawns rolling down toward the steely water of Drøbaksundet, which in turn leads to the inner Oslofjord. So close to the capital, but light-years away. The incredible orange and pink roses growing on scraggly bushes alongside the path leading to the beach. The emerald forests climbing the hills behind Villa Vinternatt, unmistakably stern and Nordic, nothing at all like the dense, humid jungles that haunt her.

In the afternoons, after lunch, she likes to sit out in the garden, sketching, even when it is chilly like today. Just basic charcoal sketches on plain notepaper, depictions that don't need to carry any meaning at all. She especially likes to capture the elegant line of a bird wing caught in flight, or held close to a little bony body, or touching its tips against the surface of the sea. Today, she is drawing a small sparrow perched on a bird feeder hanging from one of Villa Vinternatt's enormous oak trees. It twitches its wings, draws them close around a fat, fluffy belly, stares at her with its black pinprick eyes. She spends a long time on the texture of the feathers; it's hard to capture their lightness and near-translucency in contrast to the sturdier, coarse feathers underneath.

When she moves her gaze from the bird to the path running from the terrace at the back of the house through the garden toward the beach, she notices that a woman is walking to her. There is something familiar about her, and Elisabeth narrows her eyes trying to place her. One of the new members of the rehabilitation team? The woman stops in front of Elisabeth and she turns the drawing over: she's self-conscious about her work until it has matured. The bird scrambles up into the upper branches of the tree.

'Elisabeth?' asks the woman. Elisabeth nods, still unable to place her. She doesn't think they've met before, but the woman reminds her of someone. She is tall, though not as tall as Elisabeth, and has thick chestnut-brown hair streaked through with lighter strands piled on top of her head in a deliberately messy bun. Her skin is a beautiful, smooth, sun-kissed brown, and she has wide-set hazel eyes with flecks of green. Elisabeth realizes that it is Kristina the woman reminds her of – it's in the way she carries herself, and in the style of clothing – quietly expensive and classic; Hogan shoes and Gucci belt, Mulberry Del Rey bag, the uniform most of her friends seemed to adopt in high school. Elisabeth herself likes to dress less conformist – *like a crazy bohemian artist witch*, Kristina sometimes jokes. *But that's what I am*, Elisabeth would respond.

'Yeah?'

'My name is Ella Victor. We met briefly the other day. At the vernissage.'

She remembers, then. Of course. The journalist; they'd spoken for a while and she feels stupid now for not remembering, but all the years of drug use have taken their toll on her brain.

'Ah. Yes. I do remember.'

'I wanted to stop by and speak with you again, if that's okay. I really loved your work. I've never seen anything quite like it before. Such emotive pieces.'

'Thank you.'

Ella sits down on the bench next to Elisabeth and for a long moment they sit in a comfortable silence.

'What were you drawing earlier?'

'A bird.'

'Could I see it?' Elisabeth looks over at Ella and there is something about the warmth in her eyes and her kind smile that makes her trust her. She nods and flips the notebook over to reveal the unfinished sketch of the bird.

She glances down at it and sees it as if for the first time; it's really good. 'Wow,' says Ella. 'I was wondering how I could support you.'

'Well, you could buy a picture from the vernissage, I guess. If you wanted. They are for sale. You'd have to ask at reception.'

'Sure. I'd love that. Seems like a good cause to support; I love what they are doing here.'

'So... who are you?'

'I'm sorry, Elisabeth. I should have explained. I work freelance at the moment, and I'm thinking about writing a non-fiction book. About art therapy and trauma.'

'Oh.'

'When I saw your work, I wondered if you might be interested in contributing to the project.'

'Oh.'

'I'm thinking of choosing ten or so promising artists who have experience with trauma and who incorporate it into their art as part of their healing process.'

'Oh.' Elisabeth feels her cheeks redden, she always feels numb and speechless when asked about her past or her artistic process. 'I don't know... I don't think...'

'You could be anonymous if you wanted.'

'Umm.'

'It would be my goal for the book itself to be cathartic for the participants.'

'I'm not sure I'd fit that description. About, uh, trauma and using it for healing...'

'Oh. Okay. Well, of course no pressure whatsoever.' She's going to get up and politely bid this woman goodbye, but maybe because she seems so gentle and trustworthy, or maybe it is because she reminds her of her best friend, Elisabeth surprises herself by speaking of the things she never speaks of anymore.

'I paint a lot of blood,' she whispers. 'The way it is such a symbol of death and destruction, but really it is the very essence of life. The other day... I painted actual blood into one of the paintings. One of the ones in the vernissage. Watching it merge and darken with the paint and become part of a thing of beauty – it made me feel good. Like everything ugly could become beautiful someday.' When she stops speaking, she's surprised and also moved to see a sheen of tears in Ella's eyes.

'That's the picture I want to buy,' she says.

Later, in the night, she sits on the windowsill and looks out at the shimmering, moonlit sea. She considers painting, or maybe finishing the bird sketch, until she gets tired enough to hope for sleep. She'd felt light after speaking with Ella, and it took her by surprise. It had felt good to speak to someone not paid to care for her, someone who knows nothing about her history, other than that she is obviously a recovering heroin addict.

Though Elisabeth has spent years in therapy and various rehabilitation programs, it is different speaking to a friend, and most of her friends have dropped away by now. Many have died of overdoses, a few have managed to stay clean and understandably have to cut out everyone from that old, dark life of using and abusing, and then there's Kristina. Where Kristina comes across as so infuriatingly perfect and calm and centered, Ella seemed a little rougher around the edges, a little more real. Still, Elisabeth misses Kristina and cherishes her monthly overnight stay away from Villa Vinternatt at Kristina and Eirik's house.

It's just hard, sometimes, to be around Kristina. The two of them started life side by side with very similar family backgrounds, and they went through the same school system and moved in the same circle of friends. They went through the same traumatic experience in Venezuela. And yet Elisabeth spiraled downwards, all the way to rock bottom, and stayed there. Kristina found a way back up, and though Elisabeth is happy for her, and impressed with the success she's made of her life, she can't help but feel a little bitter and jealous. Kristina Moss, the mind doctor who was saved by the dysfunction of her own mind. If she could remember what really happened in Carúpano, she'd be on her fucking knees. Elisabeth remembers, and keeping it secret is like bleeding slowly to death from an invisible wound.

58

Supernova

Everything that has happened is because I love you and wanted to be like you and wanted to keep feeling what being near you made me feel. It doesn't excuse what I've done. I've done bad things.

The image in my mind when I think of you and the way you live is this: a charmed, honed life, nothing left to chance. An inner life picked to pieces and analyzed inside out. Back to the house analogy – I want to take it even further. If you were a house, you'd be a sleek modern one with symmetrical lines and huge floor-to-ceiling windows looking out at an equally unblemished landscape. The house would have carefully arranged sections of expensive furniture – glass tables, flattering mirrors under warm lighting, soft leather chaise longues, never-sat-on white sofas. Other than that it would be empty. But under the house, where its foundations should sit on impermeable rock, is a vast, black space. The house sits precariously on a couple of wobbly stones, and far below the world you pretend to live in is another world. A dark one.

Now, we need to move forward. I'm so tired, so empty, wrung inside out. I can't know what you will do with these words. Perhaps you've already abandoned them. In a way it wouldn't surprise me if you had, I could imagine you might simply walk away and never look back if you suspected that something might compromise you in any way. It's not a bad thing to be self-protective but I'm not going to lie, I hope you're still reading. And listening carefully. We are going to be covering a lot of ground here, both past and present, and you will come to see that your life is enmeshed with mine in many more ways than one.

Onto the next thing. The big thing. Kristina, we need to talk about your husband.

59

Kristina

I can feel Leah's hands reaching for me through time and space, closing around my throat and squeezing tight. She's like a determined little dwarf star that sidles up to its unsuspecting neighbor and sabotages it until they both go up in flames. I can barely breathe. *Onto the next thing. The big thing.* I don't want to know what she is going to say about Eirik; I can't bear the thought of Leah having uncovered something sordid that will destroy my marriage. Because she's right about one thing – my life is built on unstable foundations, like most people's lives, and I need my husband.

My head is literally spinning with an onslaught of thoughts. My mother, Elisabeth, Venezuela. And now, Eirik. I realize that the dread I felt as I got deeper into the *Supernova* document is precisely this – that Leah would stop at nothing, that she'd go from my mother and Elisabeth to Eirik, bringing my whole life crashing down in some misguided attempt to get close to me.

I move a little, positioning the MacBook more comfortably across my lap, taking care not to graze my left ankle against anything, and yet a terrible pain chases up and down my leg. The battery is down to nineteen percent. It's still relatively early and I'm nearing the end of the document; I should be able to get through it before the battery runs out. The question is whether I can bear to read another word. It is profoundly disturbing how wrong I got it with Leah Iverson. I look out the window at the sky, still opaque with white clouds.

I'm still staring at the frozen, white world outside, about to return to the screen, when a peculiar blueish light sweeps across the snow outside. A comet? I push myself back up against the cushions to a more upright sitting position but the shift hurts my ankle so badly I cry out loud. The light appears again, bouncing across the dark shapes of trees at the edges of the clearing, then shining straight into the window. It remains there, held in place, its unbearably bright light projected directly onto the timber wall behind me. It is, without doubt, the beam of a very powerful flashlight.

60

Kristina

I'm a calm person. I'm calm even now. I'm not someone who gives into wild panic or irrational thoughts. This isn't true. I'm terrified. *Calm down, Kristina*, I tell myself, slipping quietly from the sofa and onto the floor. The beam of the flashlight is roaming the little cabin, as though whoever is holding it is inspecting it from every angle before deciding what to do. I push Leah's MacBook under the sofa and begin to crawl toward the entrance. When I first came here, I noticed an ancient pickax hung in the space between the bathroom and the front door. It could be there for decorative purposes, or it could actually be that Leah used it to split firewood – either way, I'm glad it's there.

Stop, I tell myself. Whoever it is, they're way more likely to help me than to hurt me. Unless it's Anton. He might have just come out of police custody and headed straight here to cover his tracks before the police realize what he's done. I'm in no doubt he'll kill me in cold blood if it's him, and in my current state that won't be difficult.

The beam from the flashlight is being moved alongside the length of the wall as if whoever is holding it is walking slowly around, inspecting the cabin. I drag myself across the floor, trying hard not to cry with the pain from my ankle. Whoever is outside seems to be moving toward the front door. I am obviously unable to outrun anyone, so what do I do? What part of a normal life might prepare you for something like this? Do I unhook the pickax and hold it in my hand just in case, risking looking utterly insane in the event it's just a random neighbor who may have heard my screams earlier or seen the unfamiliar car parked at the head of the track leading to the cabin? But there are no neighbors. The track is used only for Leah's cabin.

If not Anton, who? Who else might have known Leah was here and come looking for her? Her mother? Could it really be Linda, unsettled after being contacted by the police about Leah's whereabouts? From what I've heard about Leah's mother, she is primarily concerned with her own pursuits and would be unlikely to get in her car in Årjäng and drive for hours and hours just to check whether her daughter is okay.

My heart shudders in my chest and I pause for a long while, listening. There are no sounds coming from outside, not even the gentle rustle of swaying trees. I pull myself up by the door frame and unhook the pickax from the wall.

Calm down, Kristina, I tell myself. Surely a crazed killer wouldn't announce his arrival by shining a powerful flashlight in front of him? And surely the odds of encountering a murderer the one time you find yourself trapped in a remote cabin in the middle of the woods are fairly slim. I turn around and look back into the living room, but the roaming beam is gone and only the murky night lies beyond the windows. Could I have imagined it? Is this the beginning of a total loss of my faculties? My head, like my heart, is throbbing; I hit it badly when I fell and could be concussed.

I hear something. A sharp cough. A man's voice muttering. Then the muffled thud of footsteps on snow, approaching. I tighten my grip on the pickax's wooden handle, biting into my bottom lip to stop myself from crying out loud. Then someone grabs the door handle and shoves it hard without knocking, and because I must have forgotten to lock it when I dragged myself into the cabin earlier, it shoots open inward, bringing a surge of icy air.

Part III

POINT-BLANK

61

Kristina

The pickax is wrenched from my hand by someone much stronger than me and dropped to the floor. I am picked up, gently, and carried. I am held. I am rocked back and forth, my face pressed into a broad chest, the sound of a hammering heart beating directly into my right ear.

'Jesus Christ, Kristina,' says my husband, over and over. 'Jesus Christ.'

Eirik has placed me on the floor by the hearth on top of a sheepskin rug and a thick down duvet taken from Leah's bed. He swiftly and expertly examines me, running his fingertips across my bruises and my bones. I watch him, feeling a flood of love rush into me, as if it were being injected directly into my veins. His hair, still wet from the snowstorm, glows in shades of chocolate and amber and coffee in the flickering light of the flames. His face is serious and concerned and I have to fight the urge to laugh. It must be shock. He found me. Eirik found me here against all the odds. I'm not going to die up here by myself.

'Broken,' I hear him say.

'What?'

'The ankle is broken, in two different places. I think your cheekbone is fractured, too.' My husband's eyes shimmer with tears and he looks around the cabin. He runs his hand through his hair and presses his thumbs into his eyes. He must have driven straight here after I messaged him. I feel giddy with love for him, this man of mine who drove through the night to my rescue, like a hero.

'Happened.' I see his mouth forming words and I hear them without being able to understand what he says. It's as though I am separated from Eirik by an invisible membrane, like hearing him speak through water.

'What?' I whisper. My voice is raw and painful. He says something again and I can't quite make it out. I close my eyes. Eirik kisses my neck, my face, my hands, and I sense his warmth. *Don't leave me*, I want to say, but I can't get the words to come. 'Please,' I whisper.

'Jesus Christ, Kristina.'

'Please…' *Please just hold me*, I want to say, but still, the words won't come, but it doesn't matter now, because my husband understands, and very gently lies down behind me, enveloping my body in spoons. I close my eyes for a long while, and my mind feels blurry and strange, as though it has simply crumbled now I'm safe and don't have to stay on high alert. I clutch Eirik's big, impossibly warm hand at my waist. I feel dizzy and nauseated.

After a very long time, I open my eyes. Where we're lying, we're facing into the living room. I can make out the outline of Leah's MacBook on the floor underneath the sofa, and just then, I remember her words, the terrible words I read just before the flashlight shone into the cabin.

Onto the next thing. The big thing. Kristina, we need to talk about your husband.

I need to think. And I need to know what Leah wrote next.

'Water,' I whisper. I need Eirik to get up off the floor so he doesn't happen to catch sight of the laptop. 'Please can you get me some water?'

He places me gently on the sofa, then sits down and places my head on a pillow in his lap. He strokes my hair, kneading out knots with his fingertips, tracing patterns on my scalp. I try to muster all my focus to gather my thoughts, but the fuzzy dense feeling remains. I sip water and watch the flames still dancing in the hearth. I think about Leah's MacBook on the floor, just centimeters from my body.

'What time is it?' I ask. Eirik pulls his phone from his pocket.

'Eleven forty,' he says. 'No reception up here. In fact, not since I parked, next to your car.'

'How did you find me? I don't understand?'

'Honey, we need to talk.' I turn around so I can see his face. He smiles gently at me, his fingers still buried deep in my hair. 'Something very strange happened earlier this evening. When you messaged me, I had just walked through the door at home – my last two meetings and the dinner got canceled, so I caught the four o'clock flight back to Oslo. I figured I could always fly back to Bergen on Tuesday morning and I was going to surprise you. I knew you have had a lot on your plate recently and I knew you were feeling stressed about the situation with Leah Iverson, after everything you told me on Friday night. I was really worried for you. I was standing in the hallway, quite shocked to read that you'd set off to find Leah, and that she'd written about you, when the doorbell rang. It was a man, asking for you, and when I said you were out, he grew really agitated and so I went down to street level to speak to him. He seemed completely out of it. A young, kind of squat guy with these light-blue eyes. Quite a scary-looking guy. He said his name was Anton. I'm assuming that's the ex-husband?'

I nod. 'Yes,' I whisper.

'Okay. Seemed totally nuts.'

'What did he say?'

'He said... He said he was going to fuck you up since you'd called the police on him.'

'Uh. I don't. I don't understand...' I am trying to get my mind to compute that Anton came to my house.

'Then he literally ran off. Krissy, I was terrified for you. I called and called and called and you didn't pick up. I called the police, but without any other information there wasn't much they could do. I didn't know if he might have guessed you'd have come here to look for Leah, so I decided I had to find you before he did. Now, where is this woman? Leah.'

'She's dead.'

'What? How do you know?'

'I found her, outside. He's killed her.'

'Oh my God. How do you know?'

'I— she's shot. When I came here, I thought she'd committed suicide. She left a note...'

We stare at each other for a long moment.

'Wait. What? She left a suicide note?'

'Yes.'

'So she shot herself?'

'No. I don't think it would be possible. It was a big hunting rifle; she wouldn't have been able to turn a weapon like that on herself. Besides, she wrote that she was going to drown herself in the lake.'

'Wait, are you sure?'

'Yes. It's so tragic and shocking. She lost her baby. I think the shock of it massively destabilized her, and…' I have to pause for a moment, my voice is raspy and weak.

'Where is the note? Can I see it?'

'Yeah. Of course. But Eirik, there is something I just don't understand… How did you find me?'

'I found you on Find My iPhone.'

'Ah.'

'Clever, huh? When I'd got the coordinates, I went on Google Earth and screenshotted the map so I'd be able to find it even if reception was bad. There was only one cabin, so I knew this must be where you were. But Jesus Christ, how remote is this place? Why did you come here alone? I need to know what's happened. I've been so afraid.'

'I'm sorry, honey,' I whisper. And I *am* sorry. Eirik must have been terrified.

'Where did you find the note? And why did you she write about you?' I think of *Supernova* and the MacBook on the floor under where we are sitting. I don't know why, but I know I must keep its existence from Eirik for now. *We need to talk about your husband.*

His hands have stopped moving in my hair; he's waiting for me to answer. My heart is hammering so loudly it feels like he'd hear it if I open my mouth to speak. I take several deep breaths, calm my mind down, and tell myself that I have the tools to handle this.

'That guy. Anton. He told me that she was unnaturally preoccupied with me. And that she'd been writing about me,' I say. 'Like she wrote about him. I decided that I wanted to speak to her about it.'

'Why didn't you tell me this on Friday?'

'I don't know. I guess I forgot.' *Because I didn't know about* Supernova *yet.*

'And had she?'

'What?'

'Written about you?'

'I don't know. I've looked around but there's nothing. Just the note. And my diary.'

'Your diary? How did she get hold of that?'

'Honestly, I just don't understand it. She must have taken it from my office during one of our sessions.'

'Jesus, that's so creepy.'

'Yes.'

'You shouldn't have come here by yourself. You could have died out there.'

'I know.'

'So what happened after you found the note?'

'Well, first I found some bloodstains. In the bathroom and in her bed, and the note was on the pillow. She said she couldn't face the rest of her life after she'd lost the baby. By then, I was shocked and afraid; it had started snowing heavily and I worried I wouldn't find my way back down to the car. Then I found her, shot. It was so horrifying and

I couldn't help running away and then I fell badly on the steep part of the track. I was knocked unconscious.'

'Oh, baby.'

'I'm sorry. I'm sorry for everything…'

'Shhh. I'm here now.'

'Do you think you should go out there and do something? Bring her inside, or—'

'Honey, I can't bring her inside. It's best for the forensic team to be the ones to move her. But you're right, I should go out there. Is the weapon still out there? Did you see it?'

'Yeah.'

'I'll go out there and secure it, and cover her with tarpaulin.' I nod, trying not to think of the gruesome task Eirik has ahead of him, but when I close my eyes I see her, outlined beneath a shroud of snow, one hand curled like a claw. 'And tomorrow morning I'll go for help first thing, it's going to take at least two men to get you out of here. It would be straight-up dangerous for me to try to get you down to the road in the middle of the night in a snowstorm. The safest place until tomorrow morning, is right here,' he says, and his fingers start moving again, gently tracing little shapes on the skin behind my ears, before moving down to my throat and collarbone, pressing his fingers against the soft and firm parts of me under his fingertips.

Eirik detangles himself from me and places my head gently back down on the sofa.

'If I don't go deal with her right now, I'll talk myself out of it,' he says, stretching his limbs and staring out the window at the stormy night.

'Be careful,' I whisper. He nods and listens intently as I explain where I found her.

When he has gone I have to fight the urge to get the MacBook back out and quickly read the next section – I have to know what Leah was about to say about Eirik but I don't want to risk him bursting back into the cabin and asking questions about what I'm reading. I'm glad I don't because he returns after less than ten minutes carrying the rifle, his face pale and twisted into a terrorized grimace. He places the rifle back in its cabinet, then I hear him in the bathroom, retching.

'She did this herself,' he says, when he emerges from the bathroom after a long while.

'What? Why do you think that?'

'She removed the shoe and sock on her right foot and pulled the trigger with her toe.' I try to picture this scenario. Leah, so desperate she got the hunting rifle from its cabinet, took it outside, selected an apparently random spot on the hillside just off the path, and fired it straight into her own face. But I can't.

'Are you sure?'

'Completely. Jesus, what a sight. That poor woman. I saw something similar once, when I was in the military. A guy in my barracks blew his brains out with a rifle. Same thing, used his toe.

'I... I just can't even—'

'Shh, my love. You're safe now. You need to sleep. Everything will be better tomorrow.'

62

Kristina

I fell asleep easily moments after settling closely against Eirik in the comfortable, deep sleigh bed in the sleeping alcove, my whole body heavy and aching. In the middle of the night I wake with a start and the sudden movement sends waves of pain up my leg and I have to bite my lip not to scream out loud. Eirik shifts slightly beside me. I push myself up against the pillows into a half-sitting position and feel about on the nightstand for the painkillers he laid out for me before we went to sleep. I take two ibuprofen and an oxycodone. I can make out a faint milky glow from the window high up on the wall, and realize it is still snowing.

This sleeping alcove seems to have been made by integrating a storage space into the cabin, and not originally intended for sleeping. I don't understand how it could be possible to get this bed here, then I realize it must have been built in place. I lie back down and close my eyes, waiting for sleep to carry me away, but it doesn't. My mind is racing with disjointed, strange thoughts. I keep seeing myself running through the forest, the snowflakes biting my skin, those last terrifying moments before I fell to the ground, my screams hollering down the hillsides. This image bleeds into the other image, and I'm *her* again, the kid running for her life in the Venezuelan jungle.

The familiar nausea rises in me, the way it always does when I can't control my thoughts and they go to where I can't allow them to go, not ever, if I'm going to stay alive, if I'm going to stay Kristina; success story, survivor, wife, psychotherapist.

The contours of what Leah has actually done are becoming clearer. But did her snooping around kill Elisabeth? It was as if one of the blank patches in my mind disappeared when I read her words, rebuilding the scenes in Venezuela. The dirty Mazda. The clifftop house. Xavier, with the bottomless eyes and the slashed cheek and the warm hands and the rough stubble deliciously turning the skin around my mouth raw as he kissed me. The gun glinting in the moonlight.

Of course they will find out about your past, Leah wrote, *it's a simple Google search away*. Except it isn't. It's true that if you were to look, you'd find old media coverage of what happened in Carúpano; it was all over the newspapers for weeks. You might find some quotes from the witness statements I gave at the time, though my name was Kristina Hellerud then, not Kristina Moss, so you'd probably only make the connection if you were specifically looking. You might see the picture of me arriving at Gardermoen Airport, being met by my parents and the foreign secretary at the aircraft steps.

Do you ever think about how his *life turned out?*

He, too, must return to that night. For the first time, I try to imagine what his life might be like, and find that I can't. Another blank. What game is Leah trying to play?

Tears are flowing down my face and I snuggle closer to Eirik. I'm facing him now and though the light is dim, my eyes are used to the dark and I can make out the outlines of his peaceful face. His hair is cut shorter than usual, and I realize I haven't noticed this until now. His eyelashes are long and fluttering slightly as his eyes shuttle back and forth beneath his closed eyelids. His jawline, which was always strong and clearly defined, has softened slightly, and this makes me feel a flush of empathy for him. All those late nights at the office, too many dinners out of a delivery box. And all the while, I've been at home, waiting and waiting with dinner, until I inevitably give up and eat alone, scrolling on my phone. I don't mind so much most of the time, I'm used to it by now, but lying here like this, next to my husband in the dark, I am filled with such conflicting emotions.

I am overwhelmed by relief and gratitude that he managed to find me and came straight here. What would this night have been like without him? I also feel that deep, constant love for him that I've been able to hold on to throughout the years of our relationship and marriage – fourteen now. And I feel something else, something new and frightening. Looking at my sleeping husband, I feel a sliver of fear run through me for how little we actually know of another person, how little we can ever know of what goes on inside their head. Life, and love, are like therapy sessions at the end of the day – we only know what someone says and shows. But what about the things they choose to hide, and go to great lengths to keep hidden?

What have you done? I mouth the words in the dark. Could Leah have followed Eirik around like she followed me and found something out about him that she now wants to tell me about? She was jealous, that much is obvious. Obsessive. And yet, I felt that she and I had a good therapeutic relationship and that we made solid progress over the years she came to see me. Was it all fake? Did Leah play a role in our sessions while attempting to inch ever closer to me, motivated by obsession, or is it more complex than that? I wish I could go through to the living room and read the rest of *Supernova*. I *have* to know, but more than that, I have to tread carefully. There is something about the measured tone and the controlled patience of Leah's revelations that make me take her extremely seriously.

I very gently run my index finger across Eirik's thick eyebrow, smoothing the wiry hairs into place as I go. He barely stirs but purses his lips. *I love you*, I think. And – *I need you*. And – *What have you done?*

63

Kristina

'Honey? Honey, wake up.' His words reach me, but slowly and buffered through a dream. I try to open my eyes but it is as though they've been glued shut. 'Krissy, can you hear me?'

'Mmm.'

'Wake up.'

'Mmmm.' My right eye cracks open. My husband is sitting on the side of the bed, eyes puffy from sleep, dark stubble chasing up his neck, face serious.

'Jesus, Kristina. You had me really worried there. You wouldn't wake up.'

'Sorry. I… My head hurts. Uh. What time is it?'

'Just gone nine. I didn't realize it was morning; it's almost completely dark in here. Look, sit up. Bit of a problem.' Eirik helps me to sit up, positioning me carefully against the pillows and the wooden headboard.

'Ow.' The pain is significantly worse today than yesterday.

It feels as though I have been pummeled and then run over by a freight train.

'Look,' says Eirik and points across the living room to the windows facing out to the valley and the little lake far below. But we can't see any of that, in fact we can't see anything at all, because we are snowed in. When I was a child, we'd stay at my grandparents' cabin in Valdres and we'd get snowed in fairly often, waking up in a muffled, hushed cocoon. My father would have to dig us out and sometimes Camilla and I would toboggan off the roof of the cabin, which would only be a meter or so above the ground. I didn't realize it could happen as far south as Telemark, and especially this early on in the season – it's only just November.

'It's fucking crazy out there. I'll have to dig us out.'

Eirik half carries me as I limp over to the sofa. He places a large mug of freshly brewed coffee on the table in front of me.

'My poor girl,' he says, leaning in to plant a kiss on my cheek. Then he goes back to the front door and begins the slow and cold task of getting us out of here. He is wearing light jeans, a cashmere jumper and a lightweight down jacket, hardly the attire for unearthing an entire building devoured by snow, but it's not like he thought he'd have to do that when he set off from Oslo yesterday. As the cabin is built on a slight slope, the snow will be deeper at the back of the building where the door is, so the windows facing onto the valley might be a better bet.

'Try the windows, babe,' I say. I sip my coffee and focus on taking deep, even breaths. The combination of the strange, unsettling situation we're in and the terrible pain in my ankle is making my anxiety, which I have managed well for over a decade now, rear its ugly head. It's like the bubble of boiling water in the pit of my stomach. And it's like that moment after you realize you've seriously hurt yourself, before the pain crashes over you. A prolonged wince. I am itching to get back to *Supernova*, but I have to wait until Eirik has managed to get outside.

'Did you tell anyone you're here?' I ask. 'As in, is there anyone who might come and look for us if we don't return?'

'Like who?'

'I don't know? A friend? Bjørn?' Bjørn is Eirik's older brother, and they're close enough to speak several times a week.

'Nope. After that weirdo came to the house and I couldn't get hold of you, I just got in the car.'

'Thank God you did.'

We smile at each other and in this moment, I am overwhelmed by my love for this man. I know in my heart what a good man he is, and I'm furious with Leah for planting even a sliver of doubt about my marriage in my head.

'But babe, how are you even going to get back down to the car? It must be, what, two meters deep?'

'Yeah. Jesus. You're right.'

'You'll have to make your way out through a window and then dig the front door free from the outside. Then we'll have to focus on how to get you to the car or at least somewhere with phone reception.' Eirik nods and pulls his iPhone from his jeans pocket as though he might suddenly have reception in this most remote of places.

'Fuck, I only have twenty-six percent battery.'

'Where's the charger?'

'In the car.' We stare at each other. For a moment I almost feel the urge to laugh.

'You couldn't make this up.'

'Nope. Okay, no time to waste. Operation window leading to operation evacuate invalid wife imminently commencing.'

I smile at him and he smiles back, and in spite of everything it feels good to be here, alone with my husband.

It was his determination that won me over. Back then, when we met at the student union bar at Oslo University, he wasn't so special. He didn't yet possess that easy authority that he does now – that came with money and power and age, but he embodied a grittiness I hadn't seen before in a Norwegian boy my age. When you grow up in one of the richest countries in the world, where the school system is rather relaxed, and you're statistically speaking unlikely to have faced any real challenges in your early life, it's perhaps understandable that Norwegians often seem to be unusually laid back. Some might call it lazy, but it isn't that, exactly; it's more an ingrained belief that life doesn't have to be a struggle and so why sweat it? It's an easy enough attitude to cultivate in a country that has organized itself in a way that means life isn't too much of a struggle for most people. A lot has been achieved in terms of gender equality and bridging the class divide. People are fairly compensated for the work they do, there is little unemployment and a livable minimum wage. We leave work at four on the dot and most people have access to nature and use it frequently for recreation.

There is no reason to be fiercely ambitious, or work into the early hours – those qualities aren't expected or particularly celebrated. And yet, that is what my husband is like.

He needs to be top dog and best at everything. Those qualities could have impacted Eirik's likability but the reason they don't, at least not in my eyes, is that he only compares himself against himself. He doesn't gloat or make unfavorable comparisons to others, he merely acknowledges his victory and moves on. I wonder what he will do once he breaks through the ceiling of his own ambitions. Will he be able to just enjoy it and not chase the next achievement, or will he always be chasing the next thing?

He pursued me with the same quiet determination he goes about getting whatever he has decided he wants. He isn't forceful or flamboyant or overtly persuasive. But he's patient and secure in his own offerings. *It's a long game, Krissy*, he often says, and I think he means everything: life, and love, and his career. He seems to have been able to settle into our marriage without growing restless after a few years, and has always made a point out of idolizing me. This is something I have struggled with at times, because by repeatedly claiming that I am 'perfect', and 'the ideal woman', and 'ridiculously clever', he is actually subtly stating his expectations of me. I know he doesn't do it consciously but we have had many talks over the years about how I feel that those kinds of definitions feel like attempts at control. And yet I am lucky, because I have never had to doubt my husband's love or devotion. He has never given me any reason to grow suspicious of his actions or motives. But what if I haven't been looking in the right places? What if he has grown bored and unfulfilled in our marriage and started chasing the next thing, as is his tendency otherwise in life?

I swallow hard several times, trying to dislodge the raw hoarseness at the back of my throat. I watch Eirik unhook the window clasps carefully, running his palm against the blueish, densely packed snow outside. One window thankfully opens inwards, and I assume this must be intentional in the event of getting snowed in. Eirik begins to dig, using a metal mixing bowl from the kitchen, emptying the snow into the kitchen sink as he goes along. It is slow and painstaking work. He shrugs his jacket off, having grown hot from the physical effort of the digging and when I complain that I'm getting colder, he comes over and puts it on me, gently slipping my arms into the armholes as if he were dressing a child.

The last of the firewood is gone and to get more, we'd need to access the woodshed to the side of the front door. It occurs to me that if Eirik hadn't come to my rescue when he did, I would likely have died here, even though I made it back to the cabin. I wouldn't have been able to dig my way out of a window, climb through, and make my way down to the car in shoulder-height snow – I can barely stand up. I shiver at the thought that if I hadn't had the sense to message Eirik when I did, mentioning that I'd gone to Leah's cabin, he wouldn't have found me. I would have gone through all the firewood and when it was gone I may actually have frozen to death in my sleep. If that had happened, how long would it have taken for someone to find me? It could have been years. We've all read the stories here in Norway, of dead bodies found in the beds of abandoned and remote cabins.

What would my parents and Eirik and the police have concluded happened to me in the absence of a body? Would Anton perhaps have been investigated, considering I called the police expressing concern about him just before I came here? And what would have happened to my clients? Some of them may have experienced real shock and substantial setbacks at my sudden disappearance. Several tell me they live for our sessions; at least that's how it feels for them, that our weekly hour is the one place they feel seen and heard.

'Look, honey!' shouts Eirik. I follow his pointed finger out the window where he has succeeded in making a narrow tunnel through the snow, at the top of which is a sliver of blue sky.

64

Elisabeth, August

'Thank you for coming all the way out again this week.' Elisabeth smiles at Kristina, who looks tired and a little pale, and pours two mugs of steaming black coffee from the thermos. They're sitting on a blanket on the beach below Villa Vinternatt. The huge Color Line passenger ferry, bound for Kiel, fills the narrow sound between Drøbak and Hurumlandet, and many smaller leisure boats float languidly on the water. It's a beautiful day, and Elisabeth is glad; it feels easier having this conversation out here rather than inside one of Villa Vinternatt's austere common rooms.

'That's okay. It's good to get out of the city for the afternoon.'

'How have you been?'

'Yeah, good. A little tired. This summer has been quite full-on. Eirik has worked nonstop and I've been keeping busy with the research paper I'm submitting in September. But, you know, I guess I would have liked to get away for a couple of weeks. We talked about going to Cannes, but then he had to work. What about you?'

'I'm good. Better and better,' says Elisabeth.

'You look and sound good, sweetie.' Kristina places a hand on Elisabeth's and smiles at her. 'The work you are doing for yourself will serve you for the rest of your life. So many people would have given up, but you're a fighter.'

'Uh-huh.' Elisabeth looks out at the deep-blue water, sunlight trapped on little wavelets.

'Is everything okay, Elisabeth? You know I can speak to them if there is something you need that you're not getting here. Are the therapy sessions working out okay? Is it just once a week? Maybe twice would be—'

'I don't need any more therapy.' Elisabeth speaks more firmly than she intended and feels Kristina's surprise at being cut off. 'Sorry. Just that I've had a lot of it.'

'Sure.' Kristina takes a sip of coffee and her eyes follow Elisabeth's out on the water. She waits for Elisabeth to speak and Elisabeth is envious of her ability to just sit in loaded silence.

'I was wondering if we could speak about what happened. In Venezuela.' Elisabeth speaks quickly, then wishes she hadn't thrown it in there quite so bluntly. She glances quickly at Kristina, who looks as calm and composed as ever, but Elisabeth has known her all her life and can tell by the vein pulsating visibly on Kristina's neck that she is agitated beneath the surface.

It's no doubt a surprise to Kristina that Elisabeth has chosen to bring up the shooting. They haven't spoken about it in over a decade; there didn't seem like anything more to be said, and Kristina never recovered her full memory and made her peace with that. She moved on. Why would Elisabeth drag the terrible tragedy back out into the light, when it would change nothing? Trine was dead and gone forever. In the last few weeks, since the vernissage and since the meetings with Ella Victor, who has visited twice more, Elisabeth has begun to question her decision to not speak up about certain things. After all, she put an innocent man in prison, where he remains to this day. How is she supposed to carry that for the rest of her life? She is starting to wonder whether by keeping secrets, they are what eat away at her and stop her from being really free.

'You know you can talk to me about whatever you want, Elisabeth.' Kristina is looking straight at her now, and her brown eyes don't flinch or give away even slight anxiety.

'I suppose I feel that we never talk about it, though.'

'I suppose we don't. I'm not sure I personally feel that anything can be gained by going over it again now, but if you need to talk about it, of course we can.'

'Well, the thing is, since I've been here and really returned to the art, I've realized how much what happened influences me. It is the backdrop of my mind. The images are always there. I paint them sometimes, like all the pictures with swirls of red that are meant to look like bloodstains. They encourage that here, to bring what we see in our minds to the paintings.'

'That sounds like a very healthy approach.'

'Yes, but... The thing is, I think I need to speak about Carúpano differently. I've come to realize that it is harming me not to talk about it more explicitly. In my art. And in my life. I've been asked to contribute to an art book about trauma. You know, the experience written about and chronicled in writing on one side of the page, then depicted on the other side. I want to be more explicit in my image-building. I don't want to just paint blood patterns and frightening foliage forever.'

'I'm not sure I follow.'

'I can't move on until I tell you what really happened back there.'

'Elisabeth, what do you mean? We know what happened. Everyone knows—'

'Nobody knows.'

'What? You know, you were there. I know, I was there, too.'

'You don't.'

'I can't recover those memories, Elisabeth, God knows I've tried. I wanted to process them fully to recover but came to understand that accepting I won't regain full recollection is enough. I live with it now, in peace. But I *know* what happened.'

'There are things I never told you. I didn't tell anyone.'

'What are you talking about?'

'What really happened.'

'Elisabeth, you're worrying me. We know what really happened. We've been over it endlessly…'

'But it wasn't the full story. When I saw you there, in Caracas, in the hospital, that first time, *afterward*, when I saw how frail and broken you were, and realized that you actually had no recollection of what had just happened, I made the decision to tell the story a certain way. But it wasn't the whole truth…'

'Elisabeth, listen to me.' Kristina's voice is crystal clear and controlled, and Elisabeth can see how hard she has to work to control the anger and fear running through her. 'Stop, please stop. Jesus, Elisabeth, please just stop. You have to let it go now; we're thirty-six years old. Hashing out some minor detail you haven't told me about isn't going to help me, or you. What happened has dominated your life for almost twenty years. You have to let it go.'

'Let it go? That's surprising advice coming from a psychotherapist, a Doctor of Psychology, especially one who specializes in trauma. Don't you think I have read about this stuff? Don't you think I know all about integrating trauma to process it properly?'

'Of course. I'm just saying that going over and over what happened in Venezuela isn't serving you. Look at your life, Elisabeth. You are in the process of rebuilding it. I love you and want you to get better. I think the way to do that is accept that what happened can't be changed. It can never be changed. We can only attempt to move on.'

'But it wasn't what happened.'

'Elisabeth. Please, please stop.' Elisabeth can tell that Kristina is about to get up and walk away, and she might never get another chance to broach the subject with her.

'I can't carry this anymore.'

'What... What is it?' Kristina looks alarmed at the tears rushing down Elisabeth's face, but she can tell she is listening intently now.

'I only did it to protect you,' she whispers. Then she speaks of Carúpano, slowly at first, stumbling for words, then faster and faster as the images leap back to life, the images she has never spoken of and when she stops, Kristina gets up and walks away, straight into the water, soaking the hems of her white jeans. It is several minutes before she returns, tears streaming down her face, which bears a strange expression; pinched and pained, like she's just bitten down hard on her tongue and is trying hard to not scream out loud.

'Can I ask you something?' asks Kristina.

'Of course.'

'Have you spoken about this to anyone? Your therapist here, or your mother, or—'

'Never. And I think that is the problem. I need to speak the truth, and then maybe I can really let it go. Can you imagine carrying something like that for almost twenty years?'

'Well, yes I can, because even though I can't recall the events in a coherent way, I certainly carry them, too. And I don't think there is anything to be gained by coming out with this now. It would crush the Rickards. That kind of shock could actually kill someone, and it would massively compromise me—'

'Wait, what? Of course it won't.'

'It would most definitely compromise me. And Eirik. Can you imagine the effect on his political career? You have to understand that you can't just suddenly drop a bomb like that on my life.'

'But why would it compromise anything? We were the victims, we were just kids,——'

'Exactly. And we are going to leave it at that, Elisabeth.'

'No.'

'No?' repeats Kristina, incredulously, and Elisabeth sees something ugly then, in her eyes.

'You don't get to decide how I talk about my own trauma.'

'It directly affects me.'

'Yes.'

Kristina stares hard at Elisabeth for several long moments, and it occurs to Elisabeth that her friend doesn't recognize this Elisabeth who answers back and challenges her after so many years of being a downtrodden mess, pathetically grateful for the smallest of charities. *I did it for you*, she thinks. *Now I'm going to put me first.* Perhaps Kristina senses how serious she is, and how steely her resolve is, because she subtly changes her approach. Kristina begins to cry again, and doesn't attempt to wipe away the tears that run down her face and hover at her chin before dropping onto her jeans.

'I'm sorry,' she whispers. 'What you've told me is obviously a very big shock. I think I just need to process this.'

'Of course.'

'Elisabeth, could you please do something for me? Could you please hold off a little bit before speaking about this? Just so I get a chance to really take it on board. I think that's only fair – this does primarily affect me.'

'Okay.'

'Just a little while, okay? Can you promise me that? Of course you deserve to speak your truth and I can only imagine how hard it must have been to hold all of this for so long to protect me. I was just thinking that maybe you and I could do some processing exercises together at the weekend when you come to ours. Eirik is away again. It could be really healing for both of us.'

'Really? Uh. Are you sure you still want me to come?'

'Of course, Elisabeth. This doesn't change anything at

all. But please just promise me that for now, you and I will work through this together, just the two of us, in the first instance.'

Elisabeth nods, and returns her gaze to the water, but the sun has disappeared behind a cloud and the pretty deep blues of the sea have turned steely gray and obscure.

65

Kristina

He stands on a chair positioned underneath the window and scrapes furiously at the mouth of the tunnel, dislodging big lumps of snow that come crashing into the cabin. The slash of blue sky grows wider, casting a patch of brilliant sunshine on the floorboards. He whoops like a kid. I can't help but laugh. I watch his look of triumph as he judges the tunnel wide enough for him to pass through, and he instantly clambers onto the chair and hauls himself onto the window ledge. My husband disappears through the hole and sticks his head back down into it from the top.

'I made it!' he shouts. His face is red and elated, and though he is forty, he looks about fourteen in this moment. He squints in the sudden bright sunlight and pumps the pickax up and down, like an actor who just received an Academy Award. 'Are you okay? This is going to take a while. Just stay where you are on the sofa, I

should get through the door in an hour or so. Maybe two.'
He shouts.

'Okay,' I say and smile up at him from my icy tomb. I'm
huddled underneath a duvet and two woolen blankets and
still, I can't help but tremble with cold.

'I love you,' shouts Eirik, and then he disappears from
sight. I wait for several minutes, until I can hear the faint
repetitive thud of the scooping bowl hitting the top layer
of snow outside the front door. Then I turn over onto my
stomach slowly to not prompt another onslaught of pain,
and slide Leah's MacBook back out from underneath
the sofa.

I hesitate for a long moment, trying to breathe calmly,
trying to maintain my composure in case Eirik suddenly
reaches the front door – I'd only have a second to slip the
laptop back under the sofa and face my husband. I'd need
to make sure nothing about me would betray what I've
read. And I fear what I'm about to read; I fear Leah will set
about reducing Eirik to something other than what he has
been to me for almost fifteen years, in just a few devastating
sentences. I can hear him outside, but the digging still
sounds distant, so I can assume I have a little more time. I
have to know where she is going with this – I have the eerie
image in my mind of Leah as my executioner, dropping
an acrylic rope around my neck and pulling it tighter and
tighter, watching me. And then – the moment that changes
everything. Because sometimes it is a single moment that
changes everything.

I just happened, for the briefest of moments, to let my
eyes roam around the cabin, and perhaps it is because the

room is now brilliantly lit up by the sunlight streaming through the hole Eirik made that I notice it – it would have been harder to spot last night or this morning in the meager light. On a top shelf, close to the hand-carved, exposed supporting beams, several small picture frames are lined up. From what I can see from here, a couple are photographs from nature, places I don't recognize – a beach, a mountain, a forest-fringed lake. One is a drawing of a middle-aged woman leaning her face against the palm of her hand and staring into the distance – Leah's mother? The last is a little oil painting, an abstract in beautiful shades of vermilion, maroon, scarlet. And it is unmistakably one of Elisabeth's paintings, not dissimilar to the one I have at home.

I have to swallow a scream and fight the urge to launch myself from the sofa and grab the picture, but I'd have to climb onto a chest of drawers to reach it, and it's not like I'd be able to do that, let alone move over there.

It is like finding another piece of a puzzle and realizing that it alters the whole picture in every single way. I feel like I am looking right at the answers but can't decipher them. This casts *Supernova* in an even more sinister light. She stalked me. She claimed to know things about me that seem impossible for her to have found out about. She infers that she knew things about my marriage and my husband. But could it be that Leah Iverson somehow also directly contributed to Elisabeth's death? Elisabeth was my best friend, and now she's dead. I get a sense, in this moment of what she has done, and how.

I'm so worked up that I can no longer feel the pain in my leg or the icy cold air of the cabin. I'm running out of patience, and battery, and time. I feel a strange sensation in my left hand and realize I've dug my nails into my skin so hard I've pierced it, making dark beads of blood appear. I suck at the cut and return to *Supernova*.

66

Elisabeth, August

Elisabeth feels strange to be somewhere other than the ordered, predictable world of Villa Vinternatt, even though she comes here overnight once every month. Kristina picked her up in the late afternoon after spending the day in Drøbak with Camilla and the kids, and they got stuck in unusually heavy traffic heading into Oslo on the E6. They talked about what had happened since they'd last seen each other less than a week before, but Elisabeth fell silent as Oslo came into view, a gray blur in a wide valley, held in between dark pine forests on one side and the shimmering fjord on the other. She spent her whole life in this city and its outskirts, but since what happened with Andreas and getting sober and living at Villa Vinternatt, Elisabeth feels trepidation at returning, as if bad memories will spring forth from Oslo's streets, chasing her down.

At Kristina's house, she slips her shoes off and places her weekend bag down on the gently heated wooden floorboards of the impressive hallway, and stands a moment looking at the familiar pictures on the walls. Elisabeth is always momentarily taken aback by just how grand Kristina's apartment is, but then again, she is married to a wealthy politician and has a successful career in her own right. She remembers living in a similar apartment just down the road when Andreas was alive, though the circumstances were certainly different. Theirs had been a world of painting, passion and wild drug parties.

Elisabeth stops for a moment in front of the black-and-white photograph of herself, Trine and Kristina, taken at graduation from high school, just weeks before they set off for South America. Kristina comes back into the hallway, having gone ahead into the kitchen.

'Look at us,' says Elisabeth, softly.

'Yeah,' says Kristina. 'Come.'

Elisabeth follows her back into the kitchen. On the granite countertop is an opened bottle of red wine, an Italian amarone. Outside it's raining lightly, a relief after a relentlessly hot August. Elisabeth feels suddenly excited about the coming fall and what it might bring. The vernissage at Villa Vinternatt had gone beyond all expectations, and many of her paintings were sold that same evening. She'd had several additional commissions in the months since, as well as an interview request from one of Norway's major newspapers, *Dagbladet*. Elisabeth also can't wait to get properly started with the art book curated by Ella Victor. Ella had been to see her twice more at Villa Vinternatt since the first time and on both occasions they'd ended up talking for hours and hours, and it had felt like a beginning friendship. It was nice to laugh with someone and to discover common ground. It was fun, Elisabeth realized. Such an easy, light word – fun, but how important and difficult, too.

She'd been in contact with Ella again by email just days before about the book. Elisabeth found it easier to talk that way, and Ella had been so pleased to hear that Elisabeth would be willing to take part in the project and her preliminary thoughts. She glances at Kristina, who is placing pieces of cheese and fat olives and serrano ham on a metal Alessi tray. She feels momentarily guilty for having agreed to do the book and for having decided that the only way she can really move on is to deal with the full truth in the only way she knows how – through her art, and with real honesty. Kristina was very clear about her feelings when they spoke on the beach below Villa Vinternatt, and while Elisabeth understands and wants to protect her and please her, she can't do it forever at such a high cost.

She watches Kristina pour two large glasses from the bottle – strange: she knows Elisabeth is required to stay totally sober at all times, including when on leave like now, to continue to be eligible for Villa Vinternatt's residency program. Elisabeth remembers how angry Kristina was last winter when she was caught drinking smuggled whiskey with Joel and one of the other guys. *I put my professional reputation on the fucking line for you*, she said, a vivid red stress rash appearing on her neck.

'Is Eirik home?' she asks, looking around as though he might suddenly appear. Elisabeth assumed he wouldn't be; in the past five years she's only seen him a handful of times as his political career has skyrocketed. It's strange to her that the undeniably charismatic but rather immature man Kristina met at university has morphed into this political powerhouse often on the cover of Norway's major newspapers.

'No.'

'Oh. Yeah, I thought you said he was traveling for work. Is someone else joining us?'

'No.' Kristina smiles, a warm, carefully honed smile, the kind Elisabeth imagines she gives her clients when they say something particularly disturbing and she wants to make them feel secure. She slides one glass across the countertop to where Elisabeth sits on a bar stool.

'But... You know I can't drink. Obviously.'

'Well, I was thinking to myself this morning how far you've come. It isn't at all obvious, actually, at this point, that you shouldn't be allowed to unwind and have some fun with your best friend.' Fun, that word again. Light. Dangerous.

'I...' Elisabeth begins to respond but is so surprised she actually has no words.

'Look. I work with this stuff. On a daily basis I see clients struggling with grief and addiction and trauma. I know about these things, probably more than anyone else you'll ever meet. And I know you. I know your personal strengths and weaknesses and in the past year I have seen, firsthand, your incredible strength and ability to pick yourself back up. You should be proud of yourself and feel free to celebrate.'

'By breaking my sobriety? Kristina, I'm sorry but this has really thrown me.'

'Obviously no pressure. It was just a suggestion. I think it is also important to take steps back to normality when it comes to sobriety. I don't believe that complete abstention is necessary forever; true healing can only come when you find balance.'

'But the rules...'

'You're right, Elisabeth. Maybe this was preemptive of me. Just, I've had a tough week at work. I've been looking forward to seeing you. I just wanted us to have some fun. Like in the old days. You know, a couple of girlfriends on the sofa, watching *Sex and the City* reruns, eating crazy amounts of cheese and enjoying a couple of glasses of nice red wine.'

Elisabeth feels a warm, cozy feeling spread out in the pit of her stomach at the description – she knows that is how they could have been, in another life. She looks at Kristina, noticing the way she emanates calm and trustworthiness, as always. Maybe she's right. If someone as knowledgeable and experienced as Kristina says that balance is the goal and that occasionally allowing yourself a little bit of fun is necessary, then why shouldn't she?

No, she thinks, and realizes that this thought came from deep within her, as though spoken by her very core self.

'No,' she says, her voice low and trembling. 'No. Thank you, but I'm not ready for that. Let's do all that, but I'll stick to iced tea.' In the past, whenever Elisabeth has come to stay at Kristina and Eirik's, Kristina has gone out of her way to prepare delicious non-alcoholic alternatives for her. Home-brewed iced Kusmi tea with fresh blackberries and mint leaves, or decaf espresso tonics with juicy, thick wedges of lime.

'I don't have any, I'm afraid,' says Kristina, and retracts the offered wine, pouring it into her own glass, filling it all the way to the brim. She takes a sip from it and laughs. 'Why don't you take this through to the dining room and I'll see if I can rustle up something yummy.' Kristina hands her the tray and takes another big gulp of the wine.

Elisabeth takes it and heads to the dining room, passing through two other huge, spotlessly clean rooms – a drawing room with heavy damask sash curtains and impressive modern art, and a library with custom-built color-coordinated shelves and a French marble fireplace with a gaping black mouth.

She sits down where she usually sits and waits for Kristina. She's a little different today, she noticed it when they were driving – she seems preoccupied and jittery, though she is good at summoning a calm presence. But not that good; Elisabeth has known her since they were three years old. *I've had a tough week at work*, Kristina said and this comment makes Elisabeth suddenly angry. *You've had a tough week at work? You should try to take a walk in my shoes, golden girl.* She instantly feels guilty for these thoughts; Kristina has done more for her than anyone else, and they are bound together by so much shared history. Kristina walks into the room, carrying her own wine glass and a beautiful non-alcoholic cocktail laden with fruit and ice and fresh mint.

Elisabeth smiles at her, hoping that Kristina will eventually forgive her for what she is going to do and say in Ella Victor's book. She also hopes that someday they will sit across from each other like this, on even terms, not as addict and her friend-slash-therapist-slash-savior, but just as friends.

'Try this,' says Kristina, placing the berry-red drink on a jade-veined marble coaster in front of her.

67

Supernova

We're coming up to a really important part. I know why Elisabeth committed suicide. It wasn't your fault. And I know how much guilt you must feel. Elisabeth never blamed you, I know she didn't. But I think you blame yourself and that's why you will always be haunted by it. I worry that you will have stopped reading, that all of these revelations coming at you hard and fast will have scared you off. Somehow I think you're still here, all ears. I wonder what will shock you the most, the truth about Carúpano and Trine and Elisabeth, or the truth about your beloved Eirik and what he's done. Don't worry, we'll get to all counts soon.

So. We've done your mother. We've done Elisabeth. We've talked about exposure therapy and now we're going to take all of this to the next level.

Okay. Carúpano. Not going to lie, this part packs a fucking punch.

***

Like Xavier said, the house is stunning. Built into the cliffs above the sheltered bay at the eastern fringes of Carúpano, the villa has several levels, with two separate rooftop pools. There are people everywhere, dancing, laughing, openly doing coke. One couple is clearly making love in a dark corner of the main living space. You walk through the room on Xavier's arm and take the beer he hands you. You begin to sway to the music when you reach the dancefloor outside. You've never been anywhere like this before. This is what you dreamed of, all those long months dragging past during your final year of school in a safe, underwhelming suburb of Oslo. You look at Xavier. You smile. You get high.

Occasionally, you scan the crowd for Elisabeth and Trine and spot them both on the dancefloor, moving energetically with a couple of guys, the usually reserved Trine pumping her fist in the air. You laugh and Xavier closes your mouth with his own, playfully touching the tip of his tongue against yours.

After a while, you edge towards the edge of the crowd, time for a break. Xavier takes your hand and leads you through the main space, down a flight of stairs, then another, along a long corridor, to a bedroom. The crowd is thinning, some must have left, some might have retreated to the bedrooms on the lower levels. The heavy bass throbs through the house like a pulse. You don't need me to tell you what happens next. When you emerge from the bedroom, your hair messy and your eyeliner dragging sweetly upwards at the corners of your eyes from laughing so much, you seamlessly rejoin the others on the dancefloor and they pretend like you'd been there all along. Elisabeth and Trine are red-faced from all the dancing, beads of sweat running down the sides of their faces glinting in the white light of a high, full moon.

Let me show you somewhere special, says Xavier. *Come*. The three of you walk behind Xavier and one of the other guys who'd danced with Elisabeth and Trine, away from the house, away from the beach, into the jungle on a narrow track. Perhaps he senses a change in atmosphere, a charged current of beginning fear, because Xavier turns around and smiles widely, pointing up at the hillside, clearly visible now after a sharp turn. Up there, nestled in verdant forest, is a wrought-iron gazebo. It's beautiful, like something out of a fairytale. You step inside and settle in a circle on the floor, around a large round mirrored table. The other man, Xavier's friend, plays tinny hip-hop music on his phone. You look out over the gently rippling Caribbean, then back at Xavier. You can't stop smiling. The other man pulls a little Ziploc bag from his pocket and cuts five long lines of coke on the table clearly intended for this purpose.

Puro, he says, and winks at you.

Muy puro, adds Xavier.

After another hour in the gazebo, laughing and chatting, Trine grows quiet and visibly tired, and Elisabeth whispers straight into your ear.

We need to get going. It's the middle of the night, she says. *Our hostel might not even let us in.*

Soon, says Xavier, when you nuzzle his neck and ask him if he can take you to Carúpano.

The three of you confer quickly in Norwegian and agree that you need to be a little more forceful with Xavier, it really is time to go.

Let's play a game first, says Xavier's friend. He's a scrawny guy with a blandly handsome face, and although he's quite a bit older than the rest of them, Trine had seemed quite taken with him on the dancefloor, though nothing seems to have happened between them. Xavier pulls you down gently next to him on the dirt floor and you let yourself be drawn close. Xavier laughs and pokes you playfully in the soft hollow between your breasts, so you laugh, too. But then the man pulls out a gun and places it on the stone slab with a loud clang.

Let's go, says Elisabeth and stands up, but you tug gently at the hem of her dress and she sits back down.

None of you have ever seen a gun before. And why would you have? Naïve, spoilt, sheltered little girls from average families in the richest and safest country in the world usually haven't and never will. Later, much later, you'll be asked to identify the weapon. They'll show you image after image of handguns; small ones, big ones, black, bronze, silver, guns with wooden details, guns with silencers and guns without. You won't be able to take more than a single glance at them without starting to sweat and shake. Which one? They'll ask, and you'll close your eyes and shake your head lightly. Your mind will be blank, entirely empty, like the still surface of a lake.

The man, who will never resurface after this night, and whose name you'll never recover, removes something from the back pocket of his low-slung, mud-splattered jeans and holds his palm out for you to see. The bullet glints in the incandescent light of the full moon. A single golden cylinder, an object of beauty, like an amulet. He flicks the hand holding the gun, and the weapon splits open to reveal the chamber with six empty holes. You can't help a sharp, audible intake of breath at the sight.

Hey, chill out, Xavier says. *He'll go first.*

The man slots the bullet into the chamber and stares at you all in turn with small, strangely burning eyes, buried in the folds of heavy eyelids. He spins the barrel dramatically and it hurtles around its axis until it suddenly stops with a soft 'click'. Then he hands the gun to you, the ringleader. (Yes, you were the ringleader, Kristina, even though you might have claimed it was Elisabeth. It was always you, the others revered your natural authority, your calm, centered way of being.)

No, says the man. *She chooses.*

You hold the weapon entirely still in your hands. You'd have felt power, trepidation, fear, exhilaration. A heavy silence settles over all of you. Did you try, in those moments, to work out the probability of a bullet burying itself in your brain if you were to raise the gun to your head and pull the trigger? It was one of the most moving things I discovered about you, back when I was discovering everything about you – your meticulous penciled probability calculations. You turn the gun over in your hand, its dangerous body cool against your sweaty palm. You hand it to Xavier.

You go, you whisper, taking in his handsome face as his expression goes from suspenseful to shocked, then quietly impressed. He takes the gun from you, slowly, and laughs softly under his breath. You can see a thick vein pulsate on his neck. You can still taste him in your mouth. Never was anyone more alive than Xavier in those moments (your own words, again). You glance around and your eyes meet Elisabeth and Trine's terrified ones. They are both enraptured and horrified. You raise an eyebrow and Xavier takes it as his cue. With his right hand he lifts the handgun and presses its mouth to the soft hollow at his temple. He places his left hand in yours, his gaze not leaving yours for a second. Then he smiles slowly, that same smile he gave you when he first looked at you in the car, a smile that seems to wash his face in light, making a tough-looking guy look soft and easy to love. He raises an eyebrow almost imperceptively and everyone holds their breath. You give the faintest nod and Xavier pulls the trigger.

A soft click. A collective whoosh of released air from five pairs of lungs. Laughter. The sharp sting of tears in the corners of your eyes, quickly dismissed. Xavier's tongue probing your mouth, the cheers of the others, another round of cocaine.

Just one more time, says Xavier. *Come on, ladies, seems only fair.* Elisabeth wants to leave. Trine is too tired, too high, to protest.

Yes, you say. *Just one more. Then you take us home.*

Xavier nods. The other man picks the gun up off the dirt floor where Xavier dropped it after the first roulette. He flicks the barrel open and shows it to the four of you, as if to prove the bullet is still there. Then he spins it, and it turns rapidly around itself with a soft whirr that merges with the murmur of the waves far below you, until it audibly clicks into place.

You choose again, says Xavier, placing the gun back in your hands. Did you ever feel more alive than in that moment, Kristina? I doubt it. Do you think you ever will again? I'll never know why you chose her. A crystal-clear demonstration of the hierarchy in your trio, perhaps. An attempt of showing off to Xavier. After all, you could have handed the gun to the second man, a random stranger. But you don't. You hand it to Trine.

It's not even real, you whisper. *It's just a game.*

Trine emerges from her coke-haze to find her eyes locked on yours. She can't quite decipher your words. Elisabeth says something. *Let's go*, probably. Trine tries to do as she's told, to lift the gun, but she's started to shake uncontrollably, the sound of her teeth chattering audible to the others.

Stop, says Elisabeth and tries to stand up, but Xavier gently and firmly pulls her back down.

Come on, ladies. We have to finish what we started. Last round. You laugh, but your voice sounds hollow and strange.

If you want to play this game, you should go next, says Elisabeth. Everyone falls silent. A long moment unfolds between you.

You're right, you say. You reach for the gun, which lies nestled in the space between Trine's jittery, trembling knees.

No, whispers Trine. *You chose me. But you hold it.*

You glance at Elisabeth, then at Xavier, their faces are unreadable. Suddenly none of it seems funny or exciting and you fight the urge to just get up and bolt into the clutch of the jungle, merely inches away. Finally, you look at Trine. She has stopped shaking and appears strangely calm. You can make out the beat of her pulse on her throat. A slight smile plays on her pink, full lips and she gives a little nod as your hand closes around the gun.

Another collective intake of breath. Metal and moonlight. You struggle to lift the weapon to Trine's temple, it feels impossibly heavy, and you press it very hard against her temple to stop your hand from trembling violently. A wince. Then, another little nod.

68

Kristina

'Kristina? Honey, what's happening? Kristina, what the fuck? What's going on... what are you doing? I don't understand? What are you reading?'

I needed to stay composed. I needed to keep this from my husband, but I have entirely lost control of myself. I am racked with sobs, waves of grief shooting to the surface like molten chunks of lava erupting from a volcano.

'Babe,' he says and sits down next to where I am crumpled on the floor by the sofa. He reaches out to take the laptop from my hands, but I'm clutching it tight. 'What's happening? Why are you on the floor?'

'I'm sorry,' I whisper, trying to come up with some kind of explanation for this meltdown. Eirik has never seen me like this in all the years we've been together – I pride myself on having found the perfect balance between showing emotions and controlling them.

'Whose laptop is that?' asks Eirik and when our eyes meet, I notice something cold in the way he's looking at me.

'It's mine,' I say.

'Yours is at home. On the kitchen table. I used it to find your iPhone before I left – they're synced.'

'This is my work laptop. I... I'm feeling so overwhelmed because I just read through my patient notes for Leah Iverson. It's just so sad, what happened to her. I think I just needed to cry it out.'

'Can I see?'

'No.'

'Kristina.'

'No.' Eirik reaches for the laptop again, more forcefully this time, but I wrench it away from him and try to move away, but he's so much stronger than me, and the movement brings another crash of pain and I cry even harder. 'Eirik, you're hurting me. Please. Let go.' When I speak calmly and slowly to him, he snaps back into himself, realizing what a strange thing it is to do, to try to wrestle your badly injured wife to read her professional notes.

'Sorry. I'm sorry, Krissy. Just, I guess I felt suddenly irrationally suspicious of you when you said it was your laptop when your laptop is definitely at home.'

'You know I have two.' Thank God everyone seems to have the same MacBook.

'Yes. Look. I'm sorry. You look... Terrible. Can I do anything? Shall I make you a coffee?'

'Yes, please.'

Eirik goes over to the kitchen nook and I place the laptop on the table. I don't know what I would have done if he hadn't bought my lie about it being my work laptop and insisting on seeing it. I watch him make the coffee and we sit in silence, the air filled with the loud whine from the kettle as the water gets closer and closer to boiling, and the groan of the refrigerator too. Eirik kicks the side of the refrigerator and it instantly stops. The kettle boils and snaps off. It's totally quiet except for the sound of Eirik stirring milk into my coffee, the spoon scraping against the porcelain mug. He looks up and realizes I'm staring at him. When our eyes meet, I suddenly grasp hold of a vague sensation I had moments ago – there was something about the way he nudged Leah's refrigerator and knew how to make it stop. Something familiar.

69

Kristina

Eirik hands me the coffee. I blow on it, sending ripples onto its surface.

'What is it?' asks Eirik, and again, I catch sight of something cool in the way he is looking at me, as though he is trying to analyze my thoughts. I remind myself that he can't and focus on making my face soft and relaxed. I feel uncomfortable holding his gaze, it suddenly feels like the gaze of a stranger. I glance around the room, careful to avoid Elisabeth's picture – I don't want Eirik to notice it. I'm wondering how he got through the barrier from the main road to the private track leading to the parking space for Bekkebu; I locked it behind me.

'Nothing,' I say and wince exaggeratedly. 'I'm in quite a bit of pain.' This is true. But also, I'm afraid. For the first time in my life, I'm afraid of my husband.

70

Kristina

Eirik returns to the digging, and for a long while I just sit in silence, staring at the timber walls, at Elisabeth's picture, at the laptop on the table in front of me. I know that what Leah wrote is true. I already know what happened; Elisabeth told me before she died, but I don't remember it. I don't want to remember, that's the truth. I can build the images Leah describes in my mind, like any reader could, but still it is as though they are being constructed by her descriptions, rather than drawn from my own memories. I don't have any memories of my own from those moments, the last of Trine Rickard's life. Until now, because Leah unleashed them.

The thing she said about the single bullet glinting in the moonlight like something beautiful. I can see it. The feeling of the gun's barrel, snug in my hand, so heavy. I can feel it. The sound it made, tearing the night to shreds. I can hear it. The moments after, when I opened my eyes. There was nothing there. I saw nothing at all. A black hole, a white patch, a cloak of nothingness.

I hear a sound. It's Eirik, standing right in front of me, speaking.

'What?' I whisper, my whole body feeling weak and strangely numb.

'Look, I've managed to free the front door. It's just after noon. I was thinking I'd get some more firewood out of the shed, and once I've got the fire going, I'll try to make my way down to the car. I should have phone reception there. At least now the door is free.'

'Okay,' I say. I think about the strange moments that passed between us before. I was afraid of him. But am I just disorientated and in shock? This is my husband. I've known him inside out for fourteen years. I smile at Eirik and he smiles back. Still, something is different about him, in the way he watches me. He places a glass of water on the table in front of me, next to the laptop, and kisses the top of my head lightly.

'Kristina?' he calls from over by the front door.

'Yeah,' I say, leaning forward to see past the doorway. He pushes the door open to show me the tunnel he's dug outside. In his right hand is the pickax. I feel another surge of fear. *What have you done?* I think, looking at him.

'I'm getting the firewood, okay? Do you need anything?'

'No. I... Actually, I wondered about something.'

'What?' He's halfway out the door but turns back to look at me.

'Did you ever meet Leah?' I've spoken without properly thinking through the consequences, unusual for me – my impulse control is good. Her name hovers in the air between us. I watch Eirik very carefully. There is no reaction other than a very slight clench of his jaw.

'Leah Iverson?' He repeats her name, as though I might be referring to some other Leah than the Leah who owned this cabin, who stalked me, who killed herself, who set in motion a devastating chain of events, who insinuated that there could be some juicy stories in store about the man in front of me.

'Yes.'

'No, of course not.'

'Okay.'

'Why? Did she ask about me or something? She might have been aware of who you were married to.'

'No. No she didn't.'

'I knew who she was, like I said. I imagine most people would. She was pretty high profile, wasn't she?'

'I guess.'

'Okay. Well, see you in a minute.' Eirik holds the pickax up and waves at me, then he disappears outside.

Eirik drags the sofa with me on it closer to the hearth, as close as it will go. If I reach my hands out, the heat from the flames is so hot I have to retract them after a moment. He carries me to the bathroom and waits outside while I go, then back to the sofa.

'The fire won't go out for a long time; I'll be back way before it does. But do you think you can manage to toss a few more logs on if it starts to die?'

'Yeah. I don't even have to get up.'

'I think the nearest hospital is in Notodden, they might choose to send an air ambulance.'

I ponder this for a moment, the surreal thought of being

airlifted away from Leah's cabin. 'The moment I have reception, I'll call the hospital and the police.'

'She'll be buried completely by now,' I say, and imagine what would have happened if Eirik and I hadn't come to the cabin – she would most likely have stayed underneath the snow through the winter. She might have been found in the spring, or not at all, and eventually she'd be nothing but a few bones, scattered across the hillsides by the wind, where wild animals roam, picking up what were once parts of her and putting them back down somewhere else.

He nods and looks stricken.

'I covered her well. She, uh, they'll remove her by tonight, I imagine. I'm going now; hopefully, I won't be long.'

'Just hurry, okay?' I say, though in spite of the pain I am in, I hope he takes a good long while.

71

Supernova

It is my hope that you'll come to understand why I've done what I've done with Carúpano. I just wanted to set you free. I want to set you free in more ways than just one, though, and this is where Eirik comes into it. The thing is, Kristina, I've failed. I've fucked up big time. I know you'll have been freaking out at the mention of your darling beloved husband, and at the suspicion of where this is heading. The perfect man – your golden guy in the middle of your golden world. You'd do anything to hold onto him; maybe because deep down, you know you can't – not really.

He's the type that does what he wants and takes what he can, and you know it. We're alike in that way, you and me – successful and beautiful and accomplished by most people's standards, but fundamentally always at the mercy of some man who loves himself more than he could ever love someone else. Maybe you should ask yourself how far he'd go for you and whether he really matches your devotion. You've said it to me before and it always felt like a sucker punch in the gut, so now I'll say it to you – do you think, perhaps, that you deserve better?

For what it's worth, I think you deserve everything.

But this wasn't about him, at least not to begin with. It was all about you. I got close to him because I wanted to get close to you, or as close as I could to actually being you. I laughed with your mother. I spent time with your best friend, and gained her trust so much that she finally felt able to release what she'd kept for herself for so long. You may not believe me when I say that with Eirik, my intentions were entirely innocent. I wanted to know if he deserved you. He doesn't.

You remind me of someone, he said that first night I approached him at the bar, wanting to gauge how easily he could be led astray. Easily, is your answer. The someone, of course, was you. The thing I didn't factor in, Kristina, is that he reminded me of someone, too. It has taken me a while to figure out who it was, and I'm sure you will use all your impressive psychology credentials to arrive at the same conclusion. This is my excuse; I don't have a better one. I just didn't see it coming, that I'd love him. Or that my attention would be wrenched from you to him. I didn't mean to create a situation that will no doubt bring you deep hurt. I believed him when he said that he'd never loved anyone like he loved me. He knew what to say to the fatherless little girl who lives inside of me, the girl who just wants to be taken care of. He made me feel taken care of. I believed him when he said he would leave you, and for a while, I saw myself stepping into your shoes, living your life, for real. I talked myself out of my persistent feelings of guilt by thinking that if that was truly how he felt about me, then you'd be better off without him. I suppose I felt that he and I deserved each other and that neither of us deserved you. Still, I felt bad, terrible, doing what I did, and I have no other excuse than that I love him, even now.

72

Kristina

In the same moment I read her last words, the MacBook shuts down. The fire has gone out inexplicably, and the logs are still intact, only flame-licked on one side. I am shaking so hard that my fingers fumble with the matches, lighting one after another, then dropping them to the floor where they extinguish. My fingertips are still raw and sore from last night's crawl through the snowdrifts to the cabin, but after several attempts I finally manage to relight the fire. In less than twenty-four hours my life has been left in ruins. I try to think but now it is as though my entire brain has gone blank, not just the parts I lost after Carúpano.

Eirik has betrayed me. He's come here with her before, how else would he have known how to silence the refrigerator or gotten past the barrier? They've all betrayed me: Elisabeth, my mother, everyone I love. And now, Leah is dead. Elisabeth is dead. Thank God.

I'm still alive and Eirik is still alive and Leah and Elisabeth are both dead. If I could find a way to let it all go, if I can lock all this away somewhere inside me, I can still have everything. My home and my work and my family and my calm, controlled mind. My husband. But do I still want him? *I just didn't see it coming, that I'd love him.* Leah didn't have the faintest concept of love. And just because she thought she loved him, it sure as hell doesn't mean he loved her. So he bought her a few drinks, he fucked her, maybe he came here with her for a faux-romantic weekend to fuck her some more, but Eirik loves me. That much I know. And I don't know any of the rest of it; it's all speculation, I don't ever have to know. I can live with blank patches.

I want to throw the MacBook into the leaping flames, destroying Leah's insane words. What I would give to never have come here, to never have read her words. To not have found her dead. She would just remain where she is until nothing would remain of her at all.

I hear a sound, footsteps approaching. Eirik appears in the doorway, his face red with exertion and the biting cold. In his right hand is a thick coil of blue rope, in his left the pickax. I try to smile at my husband, because I am terrified by the look in his eyes. I want him to look at me the way he usually does, with adoration and awe. *You're my crown jewel,* he always says. He loves me so deeply; he always says it and shows it in a million ways, but could it be that Leah was right, that he treats me like a queen, but a queen in a game of chess? Is his love about him and how it makes him look and feel, not about me? Could it be that she was right, that I deserve better? His eyes are empty of love now. They are distant and haunted, like he's been pursued all the way back up the hillside. I realize again that I'm afraid of him.

He watches me from the doorway with those cold eyes.

'Hey you,' I say, shrinking back into the sofa, making myself look vulnerable, which of course I am. He doesn't answer. 'Is something wrong? Did you manage to reach the car?'

Eirik nods. He places the pickax on the floor in the vestibule and takes a few steps toward me, leaving lumps of tightly packed snow from his shoes in his wake. He's still holding the rope and I recognize it vaguely as one he keeps in the boot, coiled inside the spare tire, in case of an emergency. *In case of an emergency.*

I swallow hard. 'What's happened?' I ask, careful to keep my voice soft and calm. It's like the Eirik I know and love isn't really here, that this man standing in front of me is a stranger, living a separate narrative playing out inside his head. I have to connect with him, to bring him back around to this moment with me. 'Eirik. Did you get reception on the phone?'

He gives a faint nod, a brief flick of the head, but it's as if the movement isn't in response to my question but rather in response to whatever is happening in his mind. Eirik stops a couple of steps away from where I'm lying on the sofa, my splintered and aching leg propped up high. He is clutching the coil of rope so tightly his knuckles have turned white. He stares at me and I'm shocked to see tears pooling in his eyes; in all these years, I've never seen Eirik cry.

'You haven't called anyone, have you?' I whisper.

'No.'

'Can you please talk to me and tell me what is happening for you in this moment?'

'I—' He begins to speak but interrupts himself. He stares at the floor and at the rope, sending tears flowing down his face. 'I didn't want to have to do this,' says Eirik.

'Do what, honey?'

'Get rid of you.'

73

Leah, two days before

He was the only one, out of all of the men, she'd brought to this cabin. The only one she'd wanted to. Inviting him here was the same as inviting him into the inner chambers of her heart, she knew that. She hadn't seen it coming, and what started as a way of getting closer to Kristina, or closer to being Kristina, perhaps, had turned into something else entirely. It had brought so much joy but also remorse and heartache.

But now, seeing him at the door, face cast in shadows and hair whipped up on the fierce wind chasing down the hillsides to the clearing, she feels none of the feelings that caught her by surprise. She feels fear. She should have known that he might have come for her here – he's the only one that could. Except...

We need to talk, he says.

No, she says.

You always say no.

There's nothing more to talk about.

He pushes past her into the tiny vestibule and in the faint glow from the oil lamps in the next room.

I'm sorry for Friday.

Sorry?

Yes.

You screamed at me. You threatened me to abort our baby.

Leah... I'm sorry.

Fuck you. You'll be pleased to know that there's no baby anymore. You'll have it your way.

Her face is deathly pale and her hair is stuck to her skull in greasy strings.

What... what have you done? And what happened to your face?

What have I done? She screams the words, and they burst from her empty insides with such force he actually takes a step back. *What have you done, you mean? Everyone is going to hear about this. I'll make sure they all know about the promises you made, the way you said you love me, how you lied to your wife night after night, how you got me pregnant and then threatened me to get rid of the baby we made, how you said you'd ruin my life if I didn't. No, wait, you said you'd hunt me down and fucking kill me like an animal if I didn't. Well, I bet you're pleased now. But let me be very clear with you – you're going down, you fucking asshole!*

Wait, wait, baby, listen to me, I came here because I was so worried about you. I wanted us to talk more, better, properly, I can't live with what I said to you the last time I saw you.

I was confused and upset and what happened should never have happened, Leah please listen to me, please, please.

But she's already outside, running fast down the hill. And Eirik's behind her.

74

Kristina

'Get up,' says Eirik. His eyes are wild, far away in the recesses of his own mind. I need to find out what he sees there, or I am never going to get out of here alive.

'I can't,' I whisper.

He comes over to me and yanks me hard by the arm. 'I said get up!' I move slowly, pulling myself up to an awkward standing position, placing all my weight on my right leg and holding on to the low table in front of me, avoiding his eyes.

'Eirik—'

'Shut up!'

Eirik pulls something from his pocket, some kind of little book, and flicks through it before throwing it onto the table in front of me. It's my diary, the orange leather-bound one that was in my Neverfull bag that Leah stole.

'You know, I meant what I said. I really didn't want to have to do this. Can you even begin to fucking imagine what the last few days have been like for me?'

'For *you*?' I scream it out loud, without thinking, and for a long moment, Eirik and I stand staring furiously at each other. I need to defuse the situation here or I'll end up dead like Leah. Dead like Elisabeth. 'Eirik, wait. Listen to me. We need to talk, not get all crazy with each other. A lot has happened here. But first, we need to focus on getting out of here. We need to get home.'

'Home!' Eirik begins to laugh incredulously. 'What, you think we're going to leave here and go home like nothing happened?'

'Eirik, please help me home. I'm in so much pain.'

'Soon you won't be.'

'What—'

'Write.' Eirik fishes a Montblanc pen from his jacket pocket and slams it onto the table in front of me.

'Write what?'

'A note.'

I can't stand up for a moment longer and sink back down onto the sofa, my leg hurting beyond anything I've ever felt before, wave after wave of crashing pain, my heart hollering in my chest. I can't stop the tears that begin to flow, and don't try to wipe them away; I just keep my eyes trained on my hands folded in my lap. I hear a huge crash and when I look up I realize Eirik has smashed a chair against the timber wall, splintering both the chair and the wall with the force. He lets out a wild cry and bursts into tears. I have never seen Eirik, or anyone for that matter, like this before. He's muttering to himself, his eyes roaming the room as if trying to find a cue to his next move.

'What the fuck?' he screams suddenly and scrambles past where I'm sitting. He climbs onto a chair and reaches for

Elisabeth's painting on the wall. 'What the fuck,' he says again, over and over. 'How—'

'Eirik,' I say, keeping my voice low, 'You and I have both been the victims of a very twisted individual. Leah Iverson—'

'Shut up!' he screams at the top of his lungs. 'I don't understand! I don't understand…'

'Listen to me,' I say. 'You haven't done anything wrong. You're in shock. We need to get out of here. Eirik, please. Think about the elections. Think about our home. Think about our baby. The baby we're going to have. You and me. When we get out of here. We just need to get out of here.' He falls silent and sinks down on the floor in front of me, crying quietly now. It's several minutes before he speaks again, and when he does, his voice is strangely controlled.

'I can't bear it any longer, I'll never get over what happened. Venezuela. Then Elisabeth committed suicide. And then my client, Leah Iverson, committed suicide, too, not even two months later. I love you, Eirik. Please find a way to move on without me,' says my husband in that strange, low voice.

'What—'

'Write it,' he hisses. 'Write what I just said. Along those lines. In your own words.' He picks the pen off the table again and throws it at me. 'I didn't want to have to do this, Kristina,' he whispers, burying his face in his hands. 'When you told me on Friday that she was your client, my world just fell to pieces. It had never occurred to me, not for a moment. But it was pretty obvious that you genuinely had no idea about what had happened, or about the pregnancy. It meant nothing, I swear on my life, it meant nothing at all, and I made it really fucking clear to her that I wanted her to get rid of it. I think she lived in some crazy fantasy world where she thought I'd leave you for her and we'd shack up together and play happy families. She threatened me and said she would tell you, and everyone else, the truth about me. Then she just disappeared. I assumed she'd come here, so I drove here but when I got here, the sleazy ex's car was parked next to hers so I went straight back home.'

'Wait, last Saturday? When I was at Camilla's? That's why you didn't come?'

Eirik nods. 'The week passed in a blur and I was consumed with work. Every goddamned minute of my days were filled until late in the evening and I had no chance to get back here, so I decided to just wait until she got back to Oslo to try to reason with her again, or pay her off or something. But then, on Friday, when you told me she was one of your clients, and that she'd begged you to come here so she could tell you the so-called truth, I realized I had to get rid of her. So I did.'

'The Saturday when I was at brunch.'

'I came up here again. She was a fucking mess. I only did what she would have done herself. She'd clearly even planned it. You said so.'

'So you came up here and found Leah alone, having lost her baby. And you shot her.'

He stares at me hard.

The enormity of what Eirik has just said dawns on me and my mouth must drop open, and it's as if my husband suddenly notices me again after being lost in his own moments of confession. 'Write it, I said. I can't bear it any—'

'No.'

'What do you mean, no? I said, fucking write it. You know, I still didn't think I'd have to do this, even after you came here and I came after you. She was dead by then, after all, and I didn't have to worry that she'd talk. It would get ruled a suicide for sure, especially after you told me about the note. So I told you she'd taken her shoe off and fired the weapon with her toe. That could have been that, Kristina. Leah's therapist testifying she was suicidal, the note, all of it. It wasn't until this morning when I came back inside and saw you with her laptop that I realized it was too late. You'd have to go. Look. On the side, there. Yeah, that little dent. I recognized it. I knew you were lying when you said the laptop was yours and when I saw how hysterical you were. I'd feared that she would write something to you, especially when you said she'd begged you to come here, but I assumed I'd shut her up in time.'

'She actually tried to email me what she wrote on Saturday, when I was still at home. But it never came through, only her email.'

'Wait. What? There is no phone reception here.'

'Where is her phone?'

'I took it with me. When I got to the main road, I messaged her mother. Then I threw the phone into one of the lakes I passed on my way to Bergen.'

'She must have tried to send it to me earlier and when you brought the phone from here it picked up reception and processed her outbox, sending it.' We stare at each other again, the shock of the past week hanging on the air between us.

'If only you hadn't read it. If only...'

'You know, what she wrote was all about me and her

and how she was obsessed with me. Whatever happened between you and her wasn't the focus of what she wrote.' I'm acutely aware of talking Eirik down here; there is no doubt in my mind that he is set on silencing me.

'She threatened to ruin my career, my marriage, every-thing. My whole life. I won't let her. It didn't mean a thing, she was just some girl. She reminded me of you when we were young, you know? That was all. She was a diversion. And she's fucking cost me everything. Now just do as you're told and write what I said.'

'What are you going to do? Get rid of me and tell everyone that you came up here to look for your wife and found me dead, having killed myself like Elisabeth and Leah?'

'Precisely. Now write it.' Eirik grabs my arm hard with one hand, and holds me by the back of the neck with crushing force with his other hand. It feels as though I am going to black out. I think fast. I can get out of this, I know I can. I pick up the pen.

I can't bear it any longer, I write. *I've failed as a friend and as a therapist. And as a wife. I love you, Eirik, more than life itself.* I push the little book over to my husband and as he reads the words, fresh tears gather in his eyes.

'Come,' he says.

'Where?'

'Outside.' He picks up the coil of blue rope from where he dropped it on the floor and then he stoops down and gently picks me up from the sofa. It's his gentleness that breaks my heart, he thinks he has no choice in this moment other than to kill the woman he loves. I need to give him a choice.

'It was me who killed Trine Rickards,' I say, straight into

his ear, as he carries me toward the door. 'I shot her. Point-blank. Like you shot Leah. We played Russian Roulette and it was me who pulled the trigger. I saw her go from everything – every beautiful, living, irreplaceable thing, to nothing at all. I didn't have a choice, Eirik. My mind blanked it out and Elisabeth told everyone that it was the man, Rodriguez, who just randomly shot her, but it wasn't, it was me. He's still doing time, for fuck's sake. And all those years, Elisabeth kept the truth quiet, trying to protect me and it killed her, really. No, actually, that's not true; it was basically Leah who killed her.'

'What are you talking about?'

'Leah. You and I are both Leah's victims, Eirik. She set you up, and me. None of this is your fault. None of it. You have to listen to me. She infiltrated my life, holding the twisted beliefs that she was somehow freeing me by telling me the so-called truth. But her truths were all lies. Can't you see? It's all Leah's fault. She went and found Elisabeth at Villa Vinternatt and convinced her that she should speak out about what happened to Trine, that it was me who shot her. Elisabeth then came to me, wanting to speak about Carúpano, saying she couldn't bear to carry it alone anymore. She left me no choice, Eirik. And it was all because of Leah. It's her fault.'

'What do you mean, she left you no choice?'

'I couldn't let Elisabeth use the most personal, painful thing that has ever happened to me, a terrible trauma that's ruined so many lives, as some kind of entertainment. And fucking stupid Leah got it all wrong. She thought that Elisabeth killed herself because she couldn't bear keeping Carúpano secret any longer and wanted to protect me from knowing the truth. But she *did* tell me, and that's why she died, not because she didn't. And she was going to tell everyone else, splashing it out for all to see in some lurid art house picture book. Think about it. It would have cost you the elections, Eirik. Imagine the headlines – Conservative Party's PM candidate's wife is a teenage murderer? And think about the poor Rickards; it would have killed them. She left me no choice.'

'No choice for what.'

'I got rid of her, Eirik.' He stares at me, sheer shock etched on his face. 'I killed her. For us. Just like you killed Leah for us.'

'Shut up, Kristina,' he says, kicking the cabin's door open, letting a gust of icy air inside. 'Shut up. I need to think. I don't... I don't believe you.' Eirik steps outside and begins to drag me toward the trench he's dug in the snow, up toward an inky black night sky throbbing with stars. I bite my lip to stop myself from screaming out loud from the pain in my leg; I don't want to antagonize him more than I have to.

I glance at the rifle cabinet on the wall in the hallway and notice that it is still open and empty. Where is the rifle? Last night when Eirik came back inside the cabin from inspecting Leah's body, he said he'd brought the weapon back with him and secured it in the cabinet. Smart – that would justify to the police why his fingerprints are on it. So where is the rifle? Is he planning on giving me the same ending as Leah – a shattered skull, a bared ice-blue toe on the trigger, a spray of blood in the snow?

'I killed her, Eirik,' I say, my voice trembling, then breaking as I speak the words out loud. 'I killed them both.'

'You're fucking with my head, Kristina. I know you are. You're trying to manipulate me, just like you always manipulate everyone, knowing full well that your calm demeanor falsely makes everyone trust you, but it doesn't work on me, not anymore—'

'I killed Elisabeth, Eirik,' I say again, louder this time, practically shouting the words, letting all the horror of that night loose into the night air. Her sweet face. The way she spoke about the future. She looked forward to it. The way she tried to fight me off, but couldn't – she didn't stand a chance. 'I fucking killed her,' I scream. 'I killed my best friend for us, and you need to listen to me, right now! I know why you did what you did. I know that you fucked Leah and I believe you when you say it meant nothing. But you and I, Eirik, we are so much more than that. So I don't give a flying fuck that you screwed her. She's dead, and can't hurt us now. We have a life together, a whole, beautiful life in Incognito Gata, and soon we'll have an even better one in the prime minister's residence. With our baby. Think about that, goddammit! Are you going to let all of this be for nothing? Think about it, Eirik. Even if you get away with it – a wife who kills herself in the middle of your electoral campaign? It's not going to look good. I'm telling you right now, I'm no better than you. I've done the same, if not worse. And I can keep my mouth shut if you can. We can get off this mountain together. We can go home. Eirik, Jesus Christ, no, stop it, what are you doing, don't, baby, please don't.'

I pause for breath for a brief moment, adrenaline coursing through my blood at the sight of my husband looping the blue acrylic rope around a tree branch at the edge of the clearing. I remember the vivid vision I had of Leah hanging, of her twisted and stiff body swinging slowly back and forth on the breeze, her neck at a strange angle, the milky white palms of her hands turned outwards. Perhaps it was myself I saw there all along, hanging beneath the branches.

Eirik moves slowly toward where I'm lying in a heap on the ground, gathering the other end of the rope into a noose, expertly tying strong, unbreakable knots. I'm running out of time. Is this really what the last few minutes of my life will be like? No. I won't allow it.

'Your mother would be so ashamed of you,' I say, using the last of my strength to keep my voice strong and unfaltering.

'Shut up,' he hisses, a look of surprise and pain washing over his face.

'She wouldn't believe that you could do this to me. That you'd be able to. She just wouldn't believe it. It's not too late, Eirik, it's not too late to make Juliane proud of you still. Think about it. You've spent your whole life trying to make her proud. Did you think I didn't know that about you? But it's not too late. It's up to—'

'Shut up, Kristina, Jesus Christ.'

'Juliane would have been the proudest mother on Earth to see you as prime minister. With me by your side. It's why you chose me, isn't it? Because I'm the kind of woman your mother would have chosen for you. If only she'd lived. But she lives on in you, and you're right to honor her in everything you do. If you do this to me, it will all be for nothing. All of it. Her life, and yours, and mine. All of our sacrifices. Think about the promise eleven-year-old Eirik made to himself that night, on her deathbed. You would make her proud. You promised. It was the last thing she ever heard...'

My desperate words are having the right effect; Eirik is sobbing openly now and has dropped the rope to the ground, but just then a gunshot tears through the night and my husband falls to the ground.

75

Elisabeth, August

'Look what I got you,' she says, pressing the bag into Elisabeth's fist. The words sound distorted and far away, blurred with all the alcohol. Elisabeth doesn't understand at first, but she recognizes the feel of the smack in the palm of her hand, the fine powder taking the shape of her hand as she grips it through the plastic.

'No,' she whispers.

'Yes,' whispers Kristina. 'It's okay.'

'No.'

'Let me help you.' Kristina takes the little plastic bag back, zips it open, sets about preparing the hit. The room is swimming and Elisabeth is face-down on the bed, trying to focus on the chair in the corner to regain control of herself and the situation. How does Kristina know how to do this? Elisabeth turns toward her, but the movement makes the room lurch, vodka-vomit splashing from her mouth and onto the bedsheet. She can't fully focus, but she registers Kristina's fluid movements as she holds the flame under the spoon and she hears the hiss of the smack as it crystallizes, then runs clear. It's as though all her senses are heightened; she can even hear the little sound as the heroin is sucked into the syringe – it sounds like a kiss.

'No,' she whispers again, but her tongue feels thick and foreign in her mouth and the word comes out distorted and faint. 'Please.'

But Kristina doesn't look at her or pause for a single moment. She flicks her fingernail against the syringe, dislodging air bubbles, Elisabeth can hear the tap tap tap. She picks Elisabeth's arm off the bed where it lies flung, immobile. Elisabeth tries to retract it, but finds she can't. Kristina looks for a vein, prodding her skin hard, angling the arm into the light from the hallway. When she doesn't find one, she tries the other arm. Elisabeth writhes in pain, but the movement causes more vomit to flow into her mouth, making her splutter and choke.

The other arm is examined, twisted toward the light, hard, but there isn't a single viable vein; they've all collapsed too many times, leaving the arm a strange overall shade of light blue, but with no discernible veins. Kristina swears under her breath. Elisabeth tries again to move and to speak, to fight, to do something, anything. But her limbs are dead and heavy, so heavy she can't even move her toes. Still, she can feel it when Kristina pulls her left shoe off, then the sock, and when she finds what she's looking for – that one, big, clear vein that travels straight from Elisabeth's foot to her heart. She can feel it when the syringe goes in, when the heroin rushes hotly through her blood, so much of it she's dead in less than a minute.

Kristina

My screams bounce across the clearing and return in echoes. I can't move or get away or defend myself; all I can do is wait for a volley of bullets to hit me. I hear the crunch of the gunman's shoes on the snow as he comes closer, but I'm face-down and can't muster the strength I'd need to roll over and face him. Eirik is whimpering and muttering to himself somewhere nearby. I feel about me in an attempt to touch him and comfort him and reassure him that I meant every word I said, I wasn't just saying it to save myself. *Hang in there*, I want to say, but no words will come.

I hear a crackling sound followed by several loud voices shouting. I try to turn my head to discern where they are coming from, but even the slightest movement brings another onslaught of terrible pain. *Five oh one*, says someone. Or am I imagining it? Could it be that I've already died, that these moments are just the remnants of a life already over? Crackle, crackle. *Five oh one, Dragonfire has a visual. Copy.*

There is a kind of chopping noise, as though someone were drilling holes in the earth.

'You fucking psycho,' I hear someone say close to my ear. I follow the sound with my eyes and look into the mouth of the rifle, and at the other end of it, Anton's icy, cool eyes. For a long while, he holds the weapon trained straight at my face and I make myself look him in the eye, daring him to pull the trigger, knowing he won't. Behind him, the nimble body of a black-and-white police helicopter comes into view, lowering itself into the clearing.

Epilogue

Anton, hours earlier

He feels a growing restlessness every day when he wakes up, gasping for air, feeling as though he is emerging from a dream in which someone was trying to drown him. Today is no different. It's already past midday and he can taste yesterday's booze in his mouth. The bed is empty next to him and he runs his hand across the cool sheets.

He's been waiting for many days now. He considers going back up there to Bekkebu, but after the last time, the day after he lost it completely and hit her, finally turning her lie about him into truth, he's not sure it's a good idea. When she opened the door to him she held her head high, letting the golden rays of the autumn sun settle on her deep violet skin, and he realized that his apologies just wouldn't cut it. Still, she let him in and they talked. He had the sensation of having driven down a dead-end road – that there really would be no more going back this time. *I'm sorry*, he kept saying. She kept nodding, but her eyes were miles away. *What are you doing here?* he asked, looking around the sweet, familiar cabin. *Writing*, she said. *Waiting*. She wouldn't say what for, or for whom. *I'll be back on Thursday*, she said. *I'm going to need you to be out of the apartment when I come.*

No.

Yes.

He doesn't like to think about what happened next. He can't fully remember, anyway, besides screaming at her so loud his voice broke. He's still hoarse now, several days later, that's how loudly he screamed at the woman in front of him. She doesn't get to do the leaving. It's not how it works between them. He leaves, she begs for him to return, he hates her for being so pathetic, but he misses her too, and he's learned to call those emotions love. So he returns to her and they have a few weeks of relative peace after whichever drama came before. They do this again and again. Until now.

She didn't come back on Thursday like she said she would. Anton didn't leave her apartment like she asked him to, because he doesn't have anywhere to go. He doesn't know that after he left Leah at Bekkebu, she felt liquid and unsettled, as if Anton's voice were still hollering inside her head, so she decided to go home. Only she couldn't, because Eirik Moss had slashed the tires of her car while Anton was at the cabin. He doesn't know that she slipped on a wet root looping from the earth on her way back up to the cabin, or that she fell hard to the ground and while she was able to get back up and return to the cabin, the impact caused a small rupture in the developing placenta. He doesn't know that she began to bleed that evening.

Anton doesn't know any of this. It's been a week and he

is growing increasingly restless. Maybe he really was right about there being someone else; maybe they weren't just empty accusations to undermine and humiliate her.

He's sitting on Leah's sofa, looking out into the living room at her possessions, wishing for her presence. He wants to stay here and to make a life with her. He can do better, be a better man for Leah, he knows he's capable of it. He tries to call her yet again, but like every other time he's tried, it goes straight to voicemail. He goes into the bathroom and splashes cold water on his face. He looks at himself in the mirror and wishes it was Leah's warm, hazel eyes that were looking back at him. He opens the bathroom cabinet and rummages around for a painkiller; a vicious headache sits at the base of his skull, like a claw. He finally finds some in an old washbag at the back of the cupboard and in addition to the paracetamol, there's an elongated white object at the bottom. A pregnancy test. Anton's heart leaps in his chest and he holds it up to the light; it reveals two clear, strong lines.

It's his natural instinct to smash something, to wield destruction on physical objects in response to his feelings; whatever they are, he can't tell. A baby. Leah is carrying his baby. Anton bursts from the bathroom into the apartment's corridor. It feels as though his mind is on fire. He stands there for a long while as if paralyzed. Then he tears some clothes from his single shelf in Leah's closet and puts them on quickly. He glances around the apartment one last time, shellshocked, before grabbing his car key and rushing through the door.

Five months later

Dagsposten, article by Selma Eriksen.

There was a record turnout for the *Supernova* vernissage at Villa Vinternatt last night. Tragic novelist, Leah Iverson's unfinished work was displayed alongside paintings and illustrations by Elisabeth Eliassen, a previous resident of Villa Vinternatt. The event was the latest development in the Iverson Eliassen case, which has received worldwide attention since last November. The artist and the novelist were murdered a couple of months apart in a case that has shocked the nation and indeed, the world. The onetime strongest contender for the Conservative Party's highest appointment, Eirik Moss, and his wife, Dr Kristina Moss, once a highly respected Doctor of Psychology, were convicted of the crimes. The couple have been dubbed the 'sociopathic socialites' and both husband and wife are facing imminent trial for the first-degree murders of Iverson and Eliassen.

But last night wasn't about Mr and Dr Moss; last

night was very much a celebration of the remarkable achievements of their victims. *Supernova* is, 'an evocative and visceral account of the descent into madness', according to *Aftenposten*. *Publisher's Weekly* calls it, 'a multi-layered psychological study, chilling to the bone'. 'Terrifying and well-crafted,' says *Stockholmsposten*. 'The work of a writer in her most brutal and uncompromising prime' – *Deutsche Zeitung*.

Ms Eliassen was met with similar praise for her haunting depictions of trauma and its effects on the human psyche. It is safe to say that this undefined work, though most likely not intended for publication, written in the style of autofiction, like Iverson's previous *Nobody* (2018), is already causing major waves both internationally and in Norway, no doubt exacerbated by the extraordinary circumstances of its author's and illustrator's shocking killings, which have shaken the very foundations of Norwegian high society. *Dagsposten* will be running an in-depth headline review of *Supernova* for Saturday's special literary supplement magazine.

Acknowledgements

*C*abin Fever was written during the pandemic and provided a refuge from everything going on in the world; a therapeutic pursuit about friendship, betrayal, and therapy itself. I already miss its universe and the escape it provided. This novel would not, could not, exist without the work, support and guidance of so many wonderful people.

A very big thank you is due to my agent, Laura Longrigg – I enjoy working with you so much and am so grateful for your sound advice and support over the years. Thank you also to the whole team at MBA Literary Agents, and especially to Tim Webb and Andrea Michell. Louisa Pritchard, I know how enthusiastically you champion my work in the foreign territories and appreciate it so much.

To my editors at Head of Zeus – Madeleine O'Shea and Laura Palmer – your insights and expert knowledge on all things books have hugely benefitted *Cabin Fever*. I love our often insane and creepy chats about plots and timelines and baddies and odd Norwegian customs. Thank you both for being a true joy to work with. Thank you also to the whole team at Head of Zeus, working with you is always a pleasure. A big thank you is also due to Louis Greenberg, for your pitch-perfect insights into *Cabin Fever*. Also, you managed to make me laugh out loud repeatedly during the rather stressful final stages of edits – so thank you.

I'd like to thank my writing group – I just can't wait for our next retreat together. Thank you to Tricia Wastvedt; as always you are such a gift in my life, both personal and professional. A very big thank you is due to Kristina Takashina, for longevity, loyalty, love and laughter. You helped me so much in creating Dr. Kristina Moss in this book. Martin Philips also helped me so much in understanding the therapeutic process and the psychotherapist's role, thank you so much. Rhonda Guttulsrod – I don't know how I got so lucky! You (and your family) are truly family to me (and my family), and I am so very grateful for you. Thank you, a million times over, for everything.

Thank you to Trine Bretteville, who kindly lent her name to one of the tragic protagonists in this novel. I absolutely adore you – thank you for all the years and maybe especially this past year. Our 8 A.M phone calls never fail to make me laugh and I can't wait for our next Paris adventure. Thank you to Elisabeth Hersoug, who lent her name to another tragic protagonist in this book; I appreciate our friendship so much. A special thank you to Olivia Foster who contributed to the preservation of (some kind of) sanity with our fantastic 'coronawinus' sessions over the past year and whose presence in my life is much appreciated. Thank you also to my lovely ladies in Wimbledon – I can't wait to paint the town red and the air Chanel with you guys soon.

Thank you to Fevziye Kaya Sørebø, for all the good times, I so wish there would be more.

To all my other friends – I am very fortunate to be surrounded by such awesome people, so thank you.

To Lisa L – thank you for holding the mirror with the steadiest of hands. I promise I'm not as creepy as the events in this book!

As with every novel, the music is hugely important to me in the writing process. For *Cabin Fever*, I was in excellent company with Lana Del Rey, Birdy, Eminem and Ane Brun, so thank you for the music.

A final, and very big thank you to my family, for putting up with me and allowing me this life as a writer. Thank you to my mother, Marianne, for always instilling in me that this would be possible. Thank you to my grandmother, Karianne – I know how much you would have loved to hold my books in your hands. Thank you to Chris and Judy. Thank you to Oscar, Anastasia and Louison for choosing me as your Maman. Thank you to Laura, for believing, for always fighting my corner, and for everything you are to me.

Enjoyed *Cabin Fever*?
Discover your next read
from Alex Dahl.

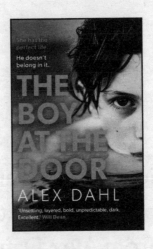

Everyone has secrets.
Even those who seem to be perfect...

On a rainy October evening, Cecilia Wilborg – loving
wife, devoted mother, tennis club regular – is waiting
for her kids to finish their swimming lesson. It's
been a long day. She can almost taste the crisp, cold
glass of Chablis she'll pour for herself once the
girls are tucked up in bed.

But what Cecilia doesn't know, is that this is the last
time life will feel normal. Tonight she'll be asked to
drop a little boy home, a simple favour that will
threaten to expose her deepest, darkest secret...

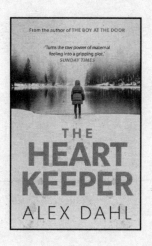

From the author of THE BOY AT THE DOOR

'Turns the raw power of maternal
feeling into a gripping plot.'
SUNDAY TIMES

THE
HEART
KEEPER

ALEX DAHL

What would you do to get your daughter back?

Three months ago Alison's world fell apart when
her five-year-old daughter drowned at the local lake.
Lost in grief, her husband and friends
are unable to reach her.

Across town, Iselin's life is about to change. Her
seven-year-old daughter has survived a life-saving
operation. After years of treading water, they can
now start thinking about the future.

These two mothers have never met. But their
daughters will bring them together. And the
consequences will be devastating...

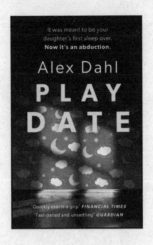

It was meant to be your daughter's first sleepover
Now it's an abduction.

Lucia Blix went home from school for a playdate
with her new friend Josie. Later that evening,
her mother Elisa dropped her overnight things
round and shared a glass of wine with Josie's mother.
Then she kissed her little girl goodnight and drove home.

That was the last time she saw her daughter.
The next morning, the house was empty.
No furniture, no family, no Lucia.

Who has taken her, and why?